S0-BWL-491

Heroes of Folk Tale and Legend

Heroes of Folk Tale and Legend

by Vladimír Hulpach
Emanuel Frynta
Václav Cibula

Illustrated by
Miloslav Troup

Translated by
George Theiner

PAUL HAMLYN
LONDON · NEW YORK · SYDNEY · TORONTO

COLLEGE OF THE SEQUOIAS
LIBRARY

Designed and produced by ARTIA
Published 1970 by

THE HAMLYN PUBLISHING GROUP LIMITED
London · New York · Sydney · Toronto

Hamlyn House,
Feltham, Middlesex, England

Graphic design by Jiří Rathouský
© Copyright ARTIA 1970
Printed in Czechoslovakia by Svoboda, Prague
S 2411
SBN 601072081

CONTENTS

NOW LET THE LUTE SING, SING OF THE GOLDEN AGE,
AND LISTEN TO THE STORY-TELLER...

Hear his tales of perilous voyage and high adventure,
of kings and knights, and the many wars they waged,
of chivalrous men who rode under a banner,
of selfless men who sought no gain.
Also other deeds of nobility and valour are set down —
strange prophesies and plots, jealousy and rage.

Wherever adventure was to be found the minstrel was at hand.

He wandered down the centuries,
over the boundless sea, through kingdoms far and wide,
riding out with hunters, watching battles rage;
he saw cities under siege, saw cities razed and charred,
saw many different faces on his journey's every stage.
As he wandered round Europe,
meeting knight and lady, peasant, fool, and sage . . .
As he himself grows older, his mind and body scarred,
Then memories of past glory his grief assuage:

NOW LET THE LUTE SING, SING OF THE GOLDEN AGE,
AND LISTEN TO THE STORY-TELLER...

ENGLISH AND IRISH LEGENDS

The mountains of Armorica shall erupt and Armorica itself shall be crowned with Brutus' diadem. Kambria shall be filled with joy and the Cornish oaks shall be flourish. The island shall be called by the name of Brutus and the title given to it by the foreigners shall be done away with.

❋

Beowulf

There are many songs of ancient times that tell us of the Royal House of Scyld, the kings of Denmark.

It was King Hrothgar of the Scylds, brave in war and merciful and just in times of peace, who with God's help built the magnificent palace of Heorot. Men came from near and far, on horseback and by boat, to admire the fine building and to feast together in the banqueting hall.

The glory of the palace of Heorot soon spread throughout the land and to all the neighbouring nations, where King Hrothgar was already known for his magnanimity and wisdom.

This magnificence was not to remain undisturbed. One day, the banqueting hall, inlaid with rare wood and decorated with antlers, was darkened by the shadow of horror and woe. It was not that a foreign army had come to pillage and kill — death in another form appeared at dusk from the nearby lake.

It was at the very end of the day, when silence had settled on the banqueting hall. The talk had died down and the music of the harp and the song of the bards, telling of the creation of the world, had ceased. The only sound was the breathing of the sleeping men.

Then the huge monster Grendel rose up out of the depths of the lake and, carried on the wings of darkness, swept into Hrothgar's palace. His glowing eyes picked out thirty sleeping warriors for his helpless victims. And no sooner had the monster sunk his claws into the first, than the scent of blood spurred him on to further slaughter. Like some fiend out of hell, Grendel killed and rent one man after the other. As long as there was a vestige of life left in the great hall, he continued to glut himself with blood and with the death cries of his victims. Then, picking up the thirty corpses like some ghastly bunch of flowers, he carried them off to his lair in the lake. When morning came, only a line of scarlet tracks remained to bear witness to his invasion.

Overnight, King Hrothgar's happy land had changed into a vale of sorrow. With heavy heart the king attempted to console his faithful subjects. Full of anxiety, he waited for what was to come.

He was right to be afraid — the following night the horror was repeated. No one was able to challenge Grendel, who slaughtered as and when he chose. And it was of no avail to try and trap the monster by day, for the lake would not yield up its terrible secrets.

Night after night, month after month, winter after winter, the palace of Heorot decayed, having become the dwelling place of death. In vain did the desperate king hope that his golden treasure might assuage the monster's greed — Grendel did not so much as touch any of the precious objects.

For a full twelve years the monster wrought havoc, his many adversaries helpless against his diabolical power. The bards sang of nothing but sorrow. As time went by their songs spread the dreadful news farther and farther abroad.

In the twelfth year it reached as far as the land of the Geats, where it was heard by Beowulf, nephew of Hygelac, King of the Geats.

Beowulf was young, stalwart and brave, and his noble heart was moved by the song of the bard. He lost no time, chose fourteen strong and well-born warriors, had a fast boat built and made full preparations for his journey.

Soon the armour, shields and swords of the fifteen warriors could be seen glittering on board the new ship, and then Beowulf gave the order to sail. Like an impatient bird, the boat left the land and plunged into the churning sea. It skimmed over the grey water, not stopping until sunrise of the next day. Then, at last, the billowing sails drooped and the keel scraped on the sea bed. The warriors cast anchor below the glistening cliffs, for they had arrived in Denmark.

They were giving thanks to heaven for their safe passage when a voice called to them from above:

"Who are you, and why have you come here in full armour?"

Beowulf turned and saw a man on horseback riding down the hill towards them. It was one of King Hrothgar's warriors who was guarding the coast. As the horseman stopped, Beowulf answered him:

"We are Geats from the land of King Hygelac. We have come to find out if the tales we hear from the bards are true, and, if they are, to offer you our help. These men," said Beowulf, pointing to his followers, "will not be daunted by any foe, and I, myself, am the son of the famous chieftain Ecgtheow, whose long life was full of immortal feats of valour."

"Let us hope that you will have the chance to follow your words by deeds," replied the man on horseback. "My men will look after your ship while I take you to the palace of Heorot."

Shortly afterwards, with their boat safely moored by the shore, the Geats set out for Hrothgar's palace, with the coast-guard leading the way on horseback. When at last they arrived at the palace gates, the man bade them farewell:

"This is your destination. I must now return to my post by the sea. God be with you!"

And with these words he turned his horse round and galloped away.

Beowulf and his company made their way to King Hrothgar's chambers. Before their eyes had had time to accustom themselves to the rich splendour, Beowulf found himself in front of the Danish king, and he bowed low in accordance with courtly custom.

Hrothgar's face, grown old and lined with the heavy cares of recent years, lit up with a smile.

"Welcome, son of the gallant Ecgtheow, and welcome to your faithful friends. It is no easy task you have set yourselves, and although the strength of your arms exceeds that of thirty ordinary men, I must warn you — many brave warriors have spent a night at Heorot, yet not one of them lived to see the sunrise. Grendel broke their lances like so many blades of grass; he killed them off like flies."

"I salute you, King Hrothgar," replied Beowulf. "If death is waiting for me here, then such is my fate. But I shall not give my life cheaply — I shall fight Grendel while there is still a single drop of blood left in my body, and I shall fight him without sword and shield, for against him they would be of no avail."

Beowulf's words were greeted by murmurs of approval from all the Danes present. A great feast was held in the banqueting hall, which shone with glittering armour and with the beauty of the ladies of the court. When Queen Wealhtheow herself appeared, her robes adorned with gold and precious stones, and offered Beowulf the goblet, he declared:

"Our ship will either return home with heroes who deserve to be toasted by the queen, or it will remain anchored by Danish shores as the barrow of friends who met an honourable death fighting on your behalf."

The evening shadows lengthened and the banqueting hall became quiet; King Hrothgar shook hands with Beowulf, as the Danes took leave of their guests and retired to safer quarters.

❄

Beowulf told his fourteen friends to try to sleep. They therefore lay down on their mats and were soon breathing regularly. Only their leader, having laid aside his shield and weapons, kept a vigilant watch in the dark.

He had not long to wait; a whistling noise like an oncoming storm suddenly swept round the slim towers of Heorot.

The next moment Beowulf heard the creaking of wrought-iron bars and the rumble of falling masonry.

His enemy was approaching.

The monstrous Grendel appeared, slimy with mud, and with fiery, bulging eyes. He was thirsty for human blood. Little did he guess what awaited him that night.

He immediately pounced on the nearest sleeper, killing him with a single blow of his terrible claws. Then he sank his wolf's fangs into the man's flesh and eagerly drank the warm blood.

Grendel's claws sought a second victim. But, instead of seizing a helpless man in his fierce grip, Grendel himself was gripped by an iron hand, and a cruel pain shot right through the monster's body. He was opposed by Beowulf, whose strength was greater than that of thirty ordinary warriors.

In vain, the monster tried to free himself. He realised that he was soon to die, and he tried to flee, but Beowulf would not let him go. He broke the monster's talons, and Grendel writhed and groaned so ferociously that the palace shook to its foundations.

The tumult of the struggle in the banqueting hall grew louder all the time. Stone walls trembled and the noise spread throughout Denmark, filling people's hearts with terror.

The remaining Geats were now on their feet. They struggled to help their leader, but neither their swords nor their lances could penetrate the monster's heart.

Beowulf fought valiantly. Grendel, bleeding profusely, made one more attempt to escape. Howling with pain as one of his enormous arms fell, severed, to the floor, the dying monster stumbled out of the palace and away towards the lake. Beowulf did not pursue him.

In the morning, King Hrothgar's men came crowding into the banqueting hall to look in amazement at the monstrous arm which for so many years had threatened them with destruction. They then set out together, following the bloodstained tracks. They did not, however, witness the monster's death. Only the blood-reddened surface of the lake showed where the monster had come to rest.

The tidings of Beowulf's deed sped through the land like a joyful bird in flight. Chieftains from near and far began to arrive at the palace of

Heorot before the sun had reached its zenith, to join together in praise of the Geats.

King Hrothgar, holding aloft the monster's arm, gave thanks to the hero:

"I shall never be able to express my gratitude to you, even if I were to shower you with all my treasures. Perhaps I can only show you how grateful I am by saying that you are as a son to me, and that I shall be a good father to you."

"It was God's will that we should triumph," Beowulf replied. "I only wish that the monster had died here, in my hands. Who knows what may still be hiding in the depths of that lake."

They all returned to the banqueting hall, which was soon as busy as a bee-hive. Mead ran freely and gay laughter sounded with the songs of the bards and the music of the harp. King Hrothgar gave to Beowulf and his friends many rich gifts: a gold-embroidered banner, suits of armour, a fine sword, and eight of his best horses with exquisite saddles. The queen, with her court attendants, took part in the revelry and the queen added a ring, a shirt of mail, and a golden collar to Beowulf's gifts.

It was late at night when the guests began to disperse. Beowulf and his followers did not remain in the hall, which was again guarded by the Danes, as in former years.

As the celebrations in the palace of Heorot were drawing to a close, the lamentations of a witch rang out in the monster's lair at the bottom of the lake — for Grendel had not lived there alone, but with his mother. It was to her that he had brought his plunder and it was there that he had come to die.

As Grendel had always despised and slaughtered human beings, so now his mother loathed them and thirsted to revenge her son. Never before had she ventured from the lake, but now her boldness grew out of anger and despair.

Like a vampire she flew to Heorot and swept into the banqueting hall. The Danes were up in arms at once. Protected by their shields, they advanced slowly towards the witch. Realising too late that she lacked

her son's prodigious strength, she turned to flee. She seized Grendel's severed arm and, picking up one of the Danish warriors, she slaughtered him and fled from the palace with his body.

The warrior who was killed was Hrothgar's most devoted counsellor, Aeschere, and when the king heard the terrible news his grief was unbearable.

"I must ask your help once more," he implored Beowulf the next morning. "God knows that it is the last time. Aeschere's death is a heavy blow indeed."

"I shall gladly help you, King Hrothgar. Let us not delay but saddle our horses immediately. I shall not rest until I have sought out and destroyed this witch."

18 ❋ The warriors, led by King Hrothgar, mounted their horses and galloped along the trail left by the witch as she dragged her lifeless victim away. The spoor led along bridle-paths, through forests, and across moors, ending finally by a crag overlooking the lake. Here, in defiance of her pursuers, the witch had left the severed head of Aeschere.

The angry sound of war trumpets rang out over the lake. Strange creatures, like monstrously shaped worms and serpents, writhed on the surface of the waters.

Beowulf saw in this a sign that this was where he would find his enemy. Without the slightest hesitation, he plunged into the lake.

Deeper and deeper he sank, until at last he felt firm ground under his feet. Before he could look about, the witch was upon him, intending to rend him apart. But her talons slipped harmlessly off Beowulf's armour and the hero went slowly forward, forcing her towards her underwater lair, although he was attacked on every side by strange monsters.

On reaching the lair Beowulf stopped in amazement — no water was there. A fire burning in the centre of the floor illuminated the entire place. In the bright light Beowulf saw the witch as she lunged at him once more. He drew his sword and dealt her a frightful blow, but the steel blade did her no harm. The witch sprang forward, brandishing a huge dagger, and toppled Beowulf over on the floor.

Only Beowulf's shirt of chainmail prevented his opponent from making good her revenge. With a mighty effort he shook her off and sprang to his feet. He spied a sword hanging on the wall, the like of which he had never seen before. He seized the large and heavy weapon and, with the strength of thirty men in his arms, he swung it down upon the witch, who fell dead at his feet.

At that instant the sun appeared overhead, its rays resting on the dead body of Grendel, and though the monster lay there unmoving, Beowulf could not restrain a shudder; even in death Grendel was capable of chilling the heart of anyone who beheld him. The hero raised his sword for a last blow, severing Grendel's head as a token of his victory before he set out on his return journey to the shore.

Beowulf was looking forward to the joyful surprise he would give to King Hrothgar, but when he emerged from the lake he found that the king and his followers had gone; only the faithful Geats were waiting for him. His friends came running to him with thankful cries, over-joyed to see him alive.

"We waited hour after hour for your return," they explained. "When the lake clouded over with blood King Hrothgar thought you must have been killed. He went back to Heorot with his people, but we did not give up hope."

Beowulf, having acquitted himself gloriously in his fight with the mon-sters at the palace of Heorot, grew homesick for his own native land. He took leave of King Hrothgar, who gratefully bestowed twelve more magnificent gifts on the hero. The warriors, thus rewarded, triumphantly set sail for Geatland.

Beowulf became the hero of many songs composed by the bards and when his uncle, King Hygelac, died, Beowulf was made king of all the Geats — over whom he ruled wisely and in peace for fifty years.

THE PALACE OF THE QUICKEN TREES

There was a time when Denmark, or as it was then called, Lochlann, was ruled by the mighty King Colga. Colga was very powerful, but he was troubled by his failure to conquer one island across the sea, whose inhabitants refused to accept him as their ruler.

He called his leading advisors to a war council, and said to them:

"You all know that people call me King of the Islands, yet not far to the west there lies an island which does not recognise my sovereignty."

Seeing their puzzled glances, the king went on:

"I am speaking of Ireland, a land of green hills, where our forces have suffered many defeats. The time has come for a final battle. Prepare the boats, for we must attack without delay."

Before long, Colga's boats sailed along the Irish shores, driven by a cold wind. Cormac, the King of Ireland, received an early warning of the enemy's approach, and before the first boat had landed he sent fleet-footed runners to Allen, the home of Finn, who was leader of the brave warriors, the Fens.

Finn prepared an unexpected welcome for the raiders. No sooner had they set foot on shore than they were attacked by the Fens.

In the ensuing battle the Danes slowly but surely gained ground. Then Oscar, son of Ossian and grandson of Finn, seeing the danger, fought his way towards Colga's banner. King Colga watched the bloody path hacked out by Oscar in the Danish ranks, and he accepted his challenge. Both armies stood by with bated breath as they watched the two men duel: the shields of the two adversaries were split asunder, their heavy helmets cracked, and still the two men circled one another like a couple of hawks. Both bled from many gashes and wounds, but the decisive mortal blow was to be struck by Oscar, felling Colga.

The battle was not over, though. The Danes preferred to die than quit the field, and so the fighting continued until only a single Dane had been left alive. Finn was loath to kill this mere boy, who was Midac, the youngest son of King Colga.

It was the custom to hold no malice against a defeated foe and Finn looked after and raised Midac in the midst of the greatest of Ireland's warriors, the famous Fens. The boy shared all their secrets.

The young prince, however, had not forgotten the bitterness of his father's defeat and, the older he grew, the greater was the hatred he secretly felt for the Irish. He carefully hid his own feelings and memorised every word he heard at the war councils of the Fens, resolving to use his knowledge when the time came.

Conan the Bald noticed Midac's behaviour, and at one great council meeting held in the absence of young Midac, Conan declared:

❋ "I fear that the Fens are threatened by a grave danger. We are cherishing a snake in our bosom, here at Allen. Young Midac sits with us, listening to all our secrets and plans, but never uttering a word of advice on his own behalf. Oscar killed his father in battle. I fear that since then Midac has thought of nothing but how to revenge himself on us!"

Finn knew that Conan had a venomous tongue and was never known to say a good word for anybody, but this time he took Conan's advice. He called Midac to him and said:

"You have been a long time in my house, and it is our custom that when a boy reaches manhood, he lives on his own property. Since you are a prince of noble birth, you can choose two fiefs: there will you build your houses, and there will your descendants live in time to come."

Midac seemed to have been waiting for these very words, for he replied at once:

"Then let me have the fief of Kenri in Shannon and another that lies on the northern side of the river."

Midac had good reasons for demanding this particular territory. The country by the Shannon was among the richest in Ireland, and in the wide mouth of the river there were countless little islands and inlets where enemy ships could land unnoticed.

Finn gave Midac several herds of cattle and many servants, and the Danish prince soon became one of the richest men in Ireland. None of the Fens were ever invited to his estates, nor did he visit Allen, though he still remained a member of the brotherhood.

It was not until fourteen years later that Finn met Midac again.

Finn and the Fens were out hunting one day, and so engrossed were they in the chase that they failed to notice that they had reached Knockfierna Hill, which was on the border of Midac's domain. There they stopped. As they sat in a circle, they saw coming towards them a tall warrior, whose heavy armour and sword and two lances showed that he was of Danish origin — as did his broad shield, his helmet, and his satin robe.

"Who are you?" asked Finn when they had exchanged greetings with the stranger. Before the other could reply, Conan the Bald interrupted:

"Why, it is none other than Midac, whom you looked after in your own home. Fourteen years he has been master here and he has never once invited his old comrades to visit him, nor has he himself ever come to Allen."

To this, Midac — for it was really he — replied:

"I alone am not to blame, for you have not remembered me either. But let bygones be bygones. I now invite you all to my Palace of the Quicken Trees, which lies on the other side of this hill. I have another, the Palace of the Island, but that is too far away for us to visit today."

Finn gladly accepted the invitation, but he left five men on the hill-top, including his two sons, Ossian and Ficna, as Conan's warnings aroused his suspicions of Midac.

The Palace of the Quicken Trees was aptly named. It towered above a rocky precipice, with only a single narrow path leading down from it to a river ford. The palace was completely surrounded by brambles and trees.

A splendid sight awaited the visitors inside the palace. A large fire was burning welcomingly in the banqueting hall, filling the entire room with an unrecognisable but delicious scent. The walls were inlaid with many woods, and soft rugs and mats were strewn about the floor.

The Fens entered by a wide doorway and sat down round the fire, looking about the banqueting hall with amazement, for a king would have been proud of such magnificence.

Just then Midac came in. Without a word he looked gravely at every single warrior, leaving as suddenly as he had appeared. An embarrassed silence fell.

"This is very strange. Perhaps Midac's people have prepared a feast in the Palace of the Island by mistake," said Finn.

"Stranger still that the fire, which gave off such a sweet scent, is now gushing forth soot and black smoke," pointed out one of the Fens.

❄ "And look!" exclaimed another. "All those beautiful mats and rugs have vanished. We are now sitting on the bare, cold floor!"

A third man noticed an even stranger thing:

"There were seven wide doorways in this hall when we came in, but now I see only a single closed door."

"Let us not stay," advised Conan, leaning on his lance to raise himself to his feet. His face went deathly pale; no matter how he exerted himself, he could not pull himself up from the ground.

Panic now seized the Fens. None were able to move an inch. Finn tried to calm them by saying:

"I shall ask my wisdom tooth, which alone can reveal the cause of these strange happenings." And he put his thumb in his mouth.

After a moment he gave a groan.

"For a full fourteen years Midac has been plotting our downfall. He can now succeed. Sinsar, King of the World, leads a large army of the enemy, which is camped by the Palace of the Island. With him are three kings from Torrent Island. They brought the magic soil, which holds us captive, from their island, and only a drop of their own blood falling on to the soil can break the terrible spell!"

Finn's explanation brought no comfort to his men, some of whom indeed gave way to despair and began to lament aloud. Their leader spoke to them once more:

"You behave like cowardly women! If we cannot avoid our fate, let us meet it by singing Dord-Fian, as is the custom of heroes."

Ossian had been waiting a long time on Knockfierna Hill for some news from the Palace of the Quicken Trees. And when no messenger came he sent his brother, Ficna, and Innsa, the son of Swen Selga, to investigate.

The two men rode up to the palace and they heard voices singing the sad strains of Dord-Fian. Looking at one another in surprise, they were about to enter when they heard Finn call out:

"Who is it out there?"

"It is Ficna, Father, and I have Innsa with me."

"Don't come in, or you will be imprisoned here as we are!" Finn warned them. He quickly explained what had happened. "If you wish to save our lives, hurry to the ford. There, a single man can withstand a whole army. I fear that our enemy is already approaching."

It was so. Looking across the river, Innsa saw enemy warriors on the opposite shore. Just then one of the vassals of Sinsar decided to bring the head of Finn to his liege.

The group of warriors entered the water but, as Finn had said, only one man at a time could cross the ford and Innsa was already on guard.

Selga's son fought valiantly. With blow after blow he felled his adversaries, until the river grew red with blood. His youthful strength was finally spent, and when the last and strongest of the enemy faced him, Innsa could no longer resist, and fell.

26 ✳ Ficna then appeared on the bank, eager to avenge his friend. Again the sounds of battle drowned the murmur of the river, and another body collapsed into the waters. This time it was the son of Finn who came out of the duel victorious.

In the meantime Midac had learned what had happened at the ford. Beside himself with rage, he set out with his men from the Palace of the Island.

"Hey, Ficna!" he called across the river. "Stand aside and make way for me!"

"That's easily done," replied Finn's son, laughing. "All your knights have to do is defeat me in battle!"

Ficna had good reason to laugh, for he knew his own strength and fought like a wolf among a flock of sheep. At last he was face to face with Midac himself.

They fought furiously, the clatter of their arms ringing out far in the still air.

Ossian by this time had become fearful about the fate of his brother and Innsa, and he sent his last two warriors, Dermat and Fatha, to the Palace of the Quicken Trees, to find out what had happened there.

No sooner had they started off than they heard the sounds of a distant battle.

"It's Ficna!" exclaimed Dermat. "I recognise his war cry." The two warriors ran towards the ford as fast as they could.

Reaching the crest of the slope above the river they saw both combatants as they did battle in the moonlight. Ficna had been wounded and was now merely warding off Midac's blows with his shield. Seeing that they could not reach the ford in time to save Ficna, Dermat took his lance, aimed it and threw.

The steel head penetrated Midac's body, and he, knowing that he was about to die, put all his strength into his last blow. He killed Ficna and both fell dead into the river.

With a heavy heart Dermat left Fatha on guard at the ford and set off for the Palace of the Quicken Trees, to break the sad news to Finn.

"Whoever you are," cried Finn, from within the palace, when Dermat arrived, "do not enter! What was the outcome of the fighting by the ford?"

"I am Dermat," the newcomer replied, "and I have just avenged the death of your son Ficna, whom Midac has killed."

There was a short, sad silence inside the palace.

Then Finn spoke again.

"Accept my blessing on your victory. But one more battle awaits you. The three kings of Torrent will come charging down to the ford, and it is only their blood that can release us from this trap."

Dermat then heard Conan's voice from within.

"What good will it do us to be set free if, in the meantime, we all perish of hunger. Go, Dermat, to the Palace of the Island and bring us food and drink!"

Dermat promised to do so, fearing Conan's wicked tongue more than the enemy.

Under the cloak of darkness he hid in a dark corridor of the palace and waited for his opportunity. Before long a servant came by, carrying a horn filled with wine. Dermat slew the servant with a single blow of his sword, taking care not to spill the wine as he did so. Then he entered the noisy banqueting hall, picked up a dish of the choicest foods, and hurried back to the Palace of the Quicken Trees.

Conan was impatiently waiting for him.

"How am I to give you the food?" Dermat asked him. "You know as well as I do that I cannot enter."

"Do you see that small window? Just push the food through that and it will fall right at my feet," Conan advised him.

"And what am I to do with the wine?"

"Climb up on the roof and make a hole in it with your lance. Then you can pour the wine right into my mouth."

Again Dermat did as Conan told him, and when he heard appreciative murmurs from below, he left the palace and returned to the ford.

Fatha had gone to sleep and was lost to the world. He did not wake even

when the entire enemy host, led by the three kings of Torrent, assembled on the other bank.

He slept on while Dermat, standing there like some mighty rock, threw back wave after wave of attackers. At last, Dermat slew the three kings of Torrent — and, with a laugh, he cut off their heads. Hurrying back to the Palace of the Quicken Trees, he hastened to set his comrades free.

The wide doors of the banqueting hall flew open before him. As soon as he had anointed the ground under the Fens with drops of the blood of the kings of Torrent, his friends got joyfully to their feet.

"You have saved us, Dermat," Finn told him, "but we are too weak to face the enemy immediately. You and Fatha must hold the ford yourselves, until dawn."

The night passed slowly. More and more of the enemy came surging down to the river. Then Sinsar, King of the World, sent his own son, Borba, into the battle. Dermat and Fatha stood their ground, and when the first light of dawn touched the horizon the dead body of Borba joined the countless others already lying in the river.

The revived Fens came storming out of the Palace of the Quicken Trees, to engage with the army of King Sinsar, while others hurried to join Ossian.

The last battle broke out in all its fury. Heroes fell on both sides; lances whistled through the air, bloodied swords gleamed like fire.

Oscar fought his way to Sinsar, who greeted him with angry laughter, motioning to the others to cease fighting. Like a beast of prey the king came warily forward, wishing to avenge his son by killing Finn's youngest relative. His dreadful blows fell heavily on his opponent's shield. Oscar turned as if to flee, his back to Sinsar, but just when all watching the terrible duel fully expected him to be felled by Sinsar's sword, Oscar whirled round. With a movement like lightning his own weapon severed the head of the king.

The battle was over; the battle was won. The remaining enemy warriors fled in chaos and boarded their ships. The Fens rallied and, tired but victorious, marched under their banners back to Allen.

BEAUTIFUL DEIRDRE AND THE SONS OF USNA

Ireland, the Emerald Isle, had defeated all her enemies. The clamour of war gave way to the sound of the lute, poets wrote songs in praise of the victors and bards sang of happy times.

It was in the reign of King Conchobar that a feast was given by Fedlimid, one of the finest court poets, in honour of the sovereign and his retinue. During the revels Fedlimid received the joyful news that his wife had given birth to a beautiful daughter.

His joy was not to last for long. As all the other guests came forward with their congratulations, Cathbad rose from his seat.

"The girl's name is Deirdre," he said, his countenance grave, "which means a threat . . . a threat to all, for her beauty will provoke hatred among us and that same beauty will lead to strife and bloodshed, however innocent of evil the girl may be."

The prophet's words were followed by a profound silence; he was a man who knew how to read the future from the constellations of stars and the appearance of the sky. He was highly respected by some and greatly feared by others, and only the king dared to interrupt him.

"There is still time to prevent your prophecy from being fulfilled. I shall see to it myself that Deirdre is brought up in a secret place and when she comes of age she will become my wife."

King Conchobar's plan was carried out. Deirdre spent her childhood in isolation, with only her faithful old nurse Levarcham for company. As Deirdre grew older, the more beautiful she became.

One winter's day the girl witnessed a curious scene. The white snow on the ground had just been stained with the blood of a freshly killed heifer, when a pitch-black raven swooped down and began to swallow the blood-stained snow. The girl was fascinated by the sight.

"Just imagine, Levarcham," she said dreamily. "Imagine a man with a complexion as white as freshly fallen snow, cheeks as red as blood, and hair as black as a raven's wing."

"I know of just such a one," her old nurse admitted unthinkingly.

"Oh, but where, where shall I find him?"

Levarcham remembered Cathbad's prophecy and the task entrusted to her by the king. She prevaricated until she saw that Deirdre would not forget the matter. She then told her the truth.

"The man's name is Naisi. He and his two brothers, Ainnli and Ardan, are among the noblest knights of King Conchobar's group of followers, the Red Wing."

"I must see him!" whispered Deirdre.

"You must not, or we shall both suffer the king's wrath," protested her old nurse.

But she could not oppose her beloved charge for long.

One day she secretly brought Naisi to Deirdre and, seeing that the two young people had truly fallen in love with each other, she advised them wisely:

"Flee from Ireland if you wish to stay alive. King Conchobar is sure to slay you both when he discovers that you have met and fallen in love!"

Knowing that Levarcham spoke the truth, the lovers did not delay their departure. That night Naisi told his brothers of his plans and, gathering together thrice fifty warriors, thrice fifty women, servants, and all their dogs, they set off from the Irish shores and made for Scotland.

While Naisi with his beloved Deirdre and their followers lived in humble cottages on the Scottish coast, frequently gazing across the waters to where they knew their home to be, King Conchobar held many gay feasts at his royal seat at Emain Macha.

In the course of one of these festivities, when the merriment was at its height, the king said to his knights:

"You can see that there is no palace in the world to equal mine. The

only people who care to spurn my hospitality are the three sons of 33
Usna."

"No, they do not, great king," replied the knights. "They would gladly
return to Ulster, and we should be pleased to see them back, for they
did much credit to the Red Wing."

"Let them come back, then," said the king. "Let them again take their
places at my table and I swear that as long as they obey my orders,
their estates will be returned to them and no one shall harm a hair of
their heads."

Thus spoke the king, but in his heart smouldered a concealed hatred.
When the fast was over, Conchobar called to Fergus MacRoy and said:

"You know the sons of Usna best. Go to them and bear the good news
that they may return to Ireland. Remember one thing, though — when
on your return journey you land on Irish soil by the house of Barach,
let Naisi not delay there but make him hurry to my palace. I mean to
give him a ceremonial welcome."

Fergus saw through the king's subterfuge and mistrusted him. He set
sail for the Scottish coast, trusting no one but his two sons, Illan the
Handsome and Buinni the Red-haired.

In the meantime King Conchobar sent for Barach, whose house was by
the coast.

"Naisi and his people, accompanied by Fergus, are going to disembark
near your house," the king told him. "The sons of Usna will be in
a hurry to reach my palace, but you must make Fergus stay behind at
all costs!"

There was much rejoicing in the settlement of Naisi and his people
when Fergus appeared, and their joy knew no bounds when they heard
the message from King Conchobar.

Only Deirdre was sad. That night she had had a strange dream. She saw
three birds come flying over from the palace of Emain Macha, each
one of them with a drop of honey on its beak. When the birds returned,
however, their beaks were red with blood.

The news from Fergus had been like honey to the exiled Irish.

❋ But nobody knew what the intentions of the king really were.

Deirdre did not keep her doubts to herself but revealed them to all. Naisi himself discounted them, and Fergus reassured his friends:

"I vouch for the king's word, and even if all Ireland turns against you, I shall defend your lives as long as I can hold a sword."

Deirdre said no more, but instead of being happy at the prospect of returning home she watched the preparations for the journey with a deep anxiety. When the prows of their ships turned for home and cut through the waves, her tearful eyes watched the receding coast of Scotland.

"As though they meant to caress the gentle slopes of the
green hills, as though they meant to pierce the waterfalls
of Kil-Cuan, as though they meant to say goodbye to the sun
over Glen Ettiv, as though they meant once again to follow
the cuckoo's call above Glenda-Roy."

No sooner had they landed on Irish soil than Barach came hurrying to greet them.

"Welcome, Fergus," he cried. "When I learned of your mission I decided that I had to invite you to my house on your return. Come, the tables have been laid."

Fergus grew red with embarrassment — custom forbade him to refuse a friendly invitation, but he wished to keep his promise and accompany the sons of Usna to the royal palace. Naisi saw the predicament and said:

"Stay here, Fergus. We know the way to Emain Macha and you can follow us there later."

Fergus hesitated, but then he accepted Barach's invitation, leaving his two sons, Illan and Buinni, with Naisi and his people.

The group travelled quickly, recognising familiar places and meeting many old friends. Only Deirdre slackened her pace. Once she even lay down and slept.

"Wake up, my queen," Naisi roused her, laughing.

"I have had another bad dream," she said. "I dreamt that we were

TROUP

36 ✻ attacked by King Conchobar and that Buinni had betrayed us. Illan was killed in the fighting."

"You must not believe such dreams," Naisi consoled her. "Nothing of the sort can possibly happen."

They continued their march until they were less than an hour distant from Emain Macha. Deirdre then warned them for the last time.

"I dreamt that the king had prepared a welcome for us in the house of his knights, the Red Wing, and not in the palace, as he had promised. If this is so, we are betrayed and we are doomed."

Her words were drowned in a torrent of laughter.

"The Red Wing is our own home, too — why should we not enter it?" said Buinni.

It was as Deirdre had predicted; King Conchobar had prepared a feast in the Red Wing. At first the returning exiles were frightened, but the tables richly laden with food and drink quelled their suspicions, and the exiles were soon feasting and singing merrily.

Only the three sons of Usna drank sparingly. They were waiting to see what the king would do.

King Conchobar was restless and he sent for the old nurse, Levarcham.

"Go at once to the Red Wing and see if Deirdre is still as beautiful as she used to be," he instructed.

Levarcham obeyed. When she and Deirdre embraced each other the nurse nodded gravely and said:

"Be on your guard, all of you. King Conchobar is up to no good. Emain Macha is full of strange warriors."

The nurse returned to the royal palace and told the king that Deirdre had lost her former beauty. This satisfied King Conchobar, and he might perhaps have given up his wicked plans, had he not been approached by Trendorn, an old enemy of the sons of Usna.

"Levarcham lied to you, my lord," he said. "They say that Deirdre is more beautiful than ever. I shall find out for you myself."

Under the cover of darkness Trendorn crept up to the Red Wing, climbed to a small window under the eaves, and looked inside.

Deirdre was playing chess with Naisi. She became aware that someone was watching her and, receiving a look of hatred from the intruder, she blanched. Naisi spun round to look and hurled a chessman at the face in the window.

Trendorn gasped and fell to the ground. Picking himself up, he hurried to the king.

"Levarcham deceived you, my lord," he said, covering his face. "Deirdre is indeed more beautiful than ever. I lost an eye just looking at her."

Conchobar was seized by a paroxysm of jealousy and rage.

"Arm yourselves!" he ordered his men. They stealthily advanced towards the Red Wing with drawn swords, but the stout oak walls, and the well-guarded doors and windows resisted the onslaught. Inside, Naisi and Deirdre continued playing chess.

When the attackers failed to gain entry to the Red Wing, the king ordered that the building should be set on fire. Armfuls of dry wood were stacked up and lit, and before long the building was enveloped in a veil of pungent smoke.

"I shall try to put the fire out," Buinni volunteered.

He ran out and kicked aside the burning wood, but he failed to come back. He had not been killed by the enemy; the eldest son of Fergus had gone over to the side of King Conchobar.

Deirdre's dream had begun to come true. Flames darted up afresh, hungrily licking the wooden walls of the house.

"I shall make amends for Buinni's treachery," cried Illan as, sword in hand, he charged at the enemy. He fought most valiantly, dealing blows to right and left, but the odds against him were too heavy. He succeeded in removing the pile of burning wood once more and, before the veil of death blotted out his vision, he threw his arms and armour to his fellow-warriors inside the Red Wing, like a true hero.

During the night King Conchobar's men were reinforced by fresh mercenaries. They met with fierce opposition from Ardan, Usna's youngest son, who, with his men, foiled every attempt at setting fire to the Red Wing. Then Ainnli took over the command from Ardan, and at daybreak Naisi took the field. He fought bravely, not giving a single inch of ground. He was desperately hoping that Fergus would come and force the perfidious king to make peace with them. However, no help came, and when the fighting died down a little, the three brothers agreed to withdraw from the Red Wing and to lead Deirdre to safety under cover of their shields. But before they could carry out their plan, King Conchobar intervened. The king had been watching the battle from a distance and seeing that three hundred of his mercenaries had already been killed, he made a decision and had Cathbad brought before him.

"I see that the sons of Usna are truly valiant," he said. "It is not fitting that we should fight with them. Go and tell them to lay down their arms and come to us in peace. I give my royal word that they will not come to any harm."

Trusting the word of the king, Cathbad hastened to the battlefield.

"Peace!" he called out above the clamour. "Peace! Throw away your arms; the king wants to make peace!"

Swords and lances fell to the ground, and the sons of Usna made their way to King Conchobar with no weapons in their hands.

"Seize them and tie them up!" cried the king, his countenance distorted with a bitter frenzy. When his henchmen had done his bidding, the king stood over his prisoners and cried triumphantly:

"At last you are in my hands. As you have seen fit to oppose me, I shall have you beheaded this instant."

No one came forward to carry out the bloody deed, until at last a foreigner, called Maini of the Rough Hand, offered to do so.

Naisi offered him his huge sword for the execution, so that the brothers could all die by one blow and none should have to watch the death of the others. Then the sons of Usna leaned their heads together and the terrible blade swished through the air.

Lamenting loudly and tearing her golden hair, Deirdre knelt by the lifeless bodies.

"Oh, why have you left me? You fought in battle like the three royal hawks from Slieve Cullin; you were gentle, faithful and inseparable —

Ainnli, Ardan and Naisi. You I picked for my husband, Naisi, and I cannot live when you are dead. Dig a grave for four bodies. Only next to the sons of Usna can I hope to sleep in peace."

The beautiful Deirdre fell dead on the green grass next to Naisi. They buried her with the three brothers, carving all their names on the tombstone for eternal remembrance.

HOW ARTHUR BECAME KING

When the ships of foreign invaders landed on the shores of Britain, when armed men marched through the forests and the thunder of hooves, the clash of swords and lances was heard in the meadows, there lived a strange and wise old man by the name of Merlin.

People said that he was strange because he could see into the future, perform magic spells and could even change his appearance at will. He was known to be wise because as a boy he had earned himself the position of the king's chief counsellor.

It was said that he was the son of a demon, but that it had been God's will that Merlin retain his magic abilities and only his evil power had been exorcised by a priest.

Merlin caused King Uther Pendragon to fall in love with the beautiful Igraine. The king defeated her husband, the Duke of Tintagel, in battle, and the duchess was made a queen.

It was then that the king's wise counsellor made his only request for some reward for his long services. He asked for the unchristened son of Uther Pendragon and Igraine.

The king guessed that the trusted Merlin had some special plan concerning the boy's future, and so he gladly agreed to the counsellor's request. Merlin took the child and wrapped it in a gold-embroidered cloak; and the king was never to see his son again.

Shortly afterwards he fell gravely ill. The efforts of his doctors and the tears of his queen could not restore the king. And, to make matters worse, the Northerners invaded the land like a scourge, fast advancing towards London.

Merlin came to the ailing king and said:

"My lord, you must take the field yourself if you wish to halt the enemy. Only your own presence can give fresh heart to your men."

Ill as he was, Uther Pendragon gave orders that he was to be carried to the field of battle. There, outside St Albans, his warriors killed many Northerners and set the rest to flight.

All of London celebrated the victory, but the king was failing fast. Seeing that he did not have long to live, Merlin reminded the king of his son.

"My lord, is your son to succeed you on the throne?" he asked. Whereupon Uther Pendragon spoke his last:

"He has my blessing . . . may he wear the crown and reign in honour . . . let him pray for the salvation of my soul . . ."

The king closed his eyes, his head sank back on the pillow. Igraine's sobs were the only sound in the hall as the barons stepped forward to pay homage to their dead sovereign.

Unrest again grew in Britain. The throne was temporarily vacant, and

❋ many a noble and many a knight-errant sought to occupy it and to place the crown on his own head.

The wise Merlin kept silent all this time, but when the fighting and the pillaging had lasted fifteen years and a large number of castles had been razed to the ground, he heeded the voice of the barons and visited the Archbishop of Canterbury.

The Archbishop was a man of profound faith and, wishing to follow Merlin's advice, he summoned all the noble dukes, barons, and simple knights to a meeting in London that coming Christmas.

At dawn on Christmas Day there was a great crowd outside London's largest church. Nobles came from far and near to celebrate Holy Mass, and to pray together in peace for the new king who was to be chosen by divine will.

When the congregation left the church, they saw how the choice was to be made known. Outside in the square there had appeared a large rectangular stone on which stood a steel anvil. And buried up to the hilt in the anvil was a sword, and carved in letters of gold upon the stone was an inscription:

WHOEVER SUCCEEDS IN WITHDRAWING THE SWORD
IS THE RIGHTFUL KING OF ALL ENGLAND

One after the other, all the noblemen tested their strength, but to no avail. When they had all tried and all failed, the Archbishop knew that the chosen one had not yet arrived. He therefore had it proclaimed that there would be a tournament in the New Year, open even to those who had no desire to possess the royal crown.

Among those who arrived to take part in the tournament were Sir Hector and his son Kay, together with the youthful Arthur.

It was to be Kay's first tournament, but as he was about to ride out on to the tilting-ground he found that he had mislaid his sword. He asked Arthur to go and find him another weapon without delay.

Arthur willingly obeyed his brother, for he wished him success in the

tournament, but no matter how hard he tried, he could not find a suitable sword. Then outside the church he saw just what he wanted — the
beautiful, shining sword buried in the anvil. He made sure that no one
was watching and then quite effortlessly pulled the sword out of its
strange scabbard.

He happily handed the sword to his brother, Kay, who at once called out
to his father, Sir Hector:

"I have the sword from the anvil, therefore I am the King of England!"

"Did you withdraw it from the anvil?" was all Sir Hector asked.

"No, it was brought to me by Arthur," replied Kay. "It must belong to
me, though, for it was I who needed it."

"We must make sure," said Sir Hector, and all three went back to the
church. They halted in front of the mysterious anvil, and Sir Hector
ordered his elder son:

"Strike the anvil and confirm your right by your deed."

Kay struck at the anvil, but the sword only recoiled from the anvil.

"And now it is your turn," said Sir Hector to Arthur.

The youth lifted the huge sword in both hands, the blade described
a glittering arc and was embedded in the steel as if it were a knife
slicing into butter. Sir Hector and Kay at once knelt in front of Arthur.

"Why are you, Father, and you, my brother, bowing before me?" asked
Arthur, greatly astonished.

"Now I know that you are a king, not only by birth, but also by right,"
explained Sir Hector. "You are not my son, nor Kay's brother. Shortly
after you were born you were brought to us by the wise Merlin, who
asked me to bring you up. I had you christened Arthur, but, in fact, you
are the son of the brave king Uther Pendragon and his queen Igraine."

Saying this, the noble Hector rose to his feet and led the young king to
the Archbishop, whom he told of what had taken place.

Many of the noblemen present still refused to believe that Arthur was
their rightful ruler. Three more times he pulled the sword from the
anvil and finally, at Whitsun, he convinced them that he should be
crowned.

His coronation was a truly splendid occasion. First of all the Archbishop consecrated the king's sword on the altar, then the most valiant among the warriors knighted him. Thereupon Arthur took the oath, promising the nobles and the people that he would be a good and just ruler for all the days of his life. He made Kay his Lord Chamberlain and recalled Merlin as his counsellor.

He heard many suits concerning the wrongs and injustices perpetrated since the death of his father, King Uther Pendragon, and to the joy of the victims he at once put them right.

Leaving London, Arthur and his retinue of knights went to the castle of Camelot, there to hold a great feast.

Many noble guests came to Camelot, including six kings, who presented themselves with a large and well-armed company of men — not to pay their homage to the new king, but rather to overthrow him by force.

Arthur took Merlin's advice and with his knights he withdrew to the castle tower. He waited fourteen days and only then, when the vigilance of the besiegers had slackened, did he strike.

Arthur's knights, though greatly outnumbered, fell upon the unsuspecting enemy camp. Sir Kay, Sir Brastias and Sir Ulfius showed their mettle that day, while King Arthur himself wielded his sword in an incredible manner. The enemy was quickly set to flight by the valiant attack.

Arthur did not pursue the defeated foe, but Merlin knew that it would be no easy task to subdue the six powerful kings. He therefore urged Arthur to seek aid against such heavy odds from the brother kings Ban and Bors, who lived across the sea.

Merlin's proposal was enthusiastically accepted, and Sir Ulfius and Sir Brastias set out at once on a long journey with a secret message for the two kings.

The two knights travelled over sea and land to the kingdoms of Benwick and Gaul, governed by Ban and Bors respectively, and returned with ten thousand armed men from the two kingdoms to reinforce King Arthur's forces. Merlin led this army by secret paths to the forest of Bedegrain, where they pitched camp and prepared for battle.

The six enemy kings had not remained idle in the meantime. They had won five more kings to their side, all of whom were well versed in knightly accomplishments: King Lot, King Urience, King Nentres, King Caradoc, and others, who swore to lead some fifty thousand mounted warriors into the field against Arthur.

❋ A great battle was to be fought. King Arthur brought his own twenty thousand men to the forest of Bedegrain and his sentries captured an enemy advance guard, learning where the Northerners were encamped. At the hour of midnight the silence was rent by the trumpets of war.

Like a whirlwind Arthur's knights came charging forward; like a storm the horsemen of King Ban and King Bors galloped to join them. Their enemies, in great confusion, pulled the tents down on top of themselves, ran about frenziedly trying to find their horses, and were hard put to form their ranks. During the night's battle the enemy lost ten thousand men, but by the time the morning mist cloaked the battlefield they had turned the scales in their favour.

Seeing that the fortunes of war were turning against them, Merlin led ten thousand warriors, with the kings Ban and Bors at their head, to a place of concealment.

The mists rose, and with them rose the courage of the eleven kings. But it was Arthur's knights, Sir Ulfius and Sir Brastias, who took the initiative. In the following battle riders charged at one another with their swords drawn. Ulfius' horse fell under him, Sir Kay wounded King Lot with his lance. And King Arthur, taking the field like a mighty lion, smote an enemy rider and brought his steed to the dismounted Sir Ulfius.

During the fighting Sir Kay saw his father, Sir Hector, defending himself, on foot, against heavy odds. The son hastily helped his father to a horse. Sir Brastias came to the assistance of Sir Lucas against fourteen of the enemy, his blows causing limbs to fly from their bodies like so many withered branches from a tree.

The battle seemed endless. At one moment King Arthur flew into such a rage that he slew twenty knights and attacked the wounded King Lot. Then, with the eleven kings dividing their ranks in an effort to encircle Arthur's army, Ban and Bors came out of their hiding-place.

Their banners fluttering in the air and the war-cries of the two kings struck terror into the hearts of the surprised enemy, who again re-formed, fighting staunchly until the end of the day, so that no decision

was reached by nightfall. Only the numbers of the dead increased on
both sides. They would perhaps have drowned each other in blood had
not an angry Merlin suddenly appeared in the midst of the battlefield, mounted on a tall black horse.

"Has death not daunted your spirits?" he cried, turning to King Arthur.
"See, it commands the field, for the dead far outnumber the living.
I say to you that if you continue, the fortunes of war will desert your
party. The eleven Northern kings will not take the field again. Their
kingdoms have been attacked from the sea by the Saracens, who are
plundering their lands and killing their subjects."

The great battle thus ended. The enemy fled the field and King Arthur
left all the spoils to his friends, kings Ban and Bors, rewarding his own
knights himself.

King Arthur and his knights returned to Camelot, but the peace follow-
ing the great battle was but a brief one. Tidings were received that King
Rience of North Wales had taken arms against King Leodegraunce of
Cameliard.

This news greatly angered Arthur, for Leodegraunce was an old friend
of Uther Pendragon, whereas the Welsh king had always been his
enemy. Kings Ban and Bors were rallied and King Arthur and his
comrades rode out to battle once more.

During their journey, when he and Merlin were passing a certain lake,
Arthur discovered that he had lost his magnificent sword.

"That is easily remedied, my lord," said Merlin softly. "Look over there,
at the water."

King Arthur turned his head to look. To his great astonishment the
surface of the lake was suddenly disturbed and in the centre of the
ripples a slender arm appeared, as fair as white alabaster and holding
aloft a sword.

"Row across and take that weapon," his counsellor said to Arthur. "It
is yours."

As soon as Arthur leaned over the side of the rowing-boat and grasped
the sword, the white arm disappeared. He then saw a beautiful maiden

walking across the lake as though she were on firm ground. The maiden bowed to him and then vanished once more into the waters.

Much amazed, King Arthur rowed back to the shore, where Merlin explained to him the strange sight he had witnessed.

"My lord, you have seen the Lady of the Lake, who rules these waters.

The sword she has given you is called Excalibur, and it will bring you many victories."

"It is truly splendid," said the king, examining the gold blade and the diamond-studded hilt.

"Yes, but the scabbard is of greater value than ten such swords," his counsellor told him. "As long as you have it on you, you will not lose a drop of blood in battle. If you lose it, you will lose your life. Never forget that, my lord," Merlin added warningly.

The wise old man prophesied correctly. After six days of travel they reached the kingdom of Cameliard and joined battle with the forces of King Rience. King Arthur used his new sword to such effect that wherever his banner with the red dragon appeared, the enemy turned tail and fled.

Before long only lifeless bodies were left in the field. King Rience and his surviving men fled from the scene of battle in chaos, glad to have been able to save their lives.

His friends and enemies were not the only ones to admire Arthur's deeds of valour on the battlefield — Guenevere, King Leodegraunce's daughter, had watched the fighting from a castle window, and as the battle proceeded she became conscious of a strange excitement at the sight of the young king.

When the battle came to an end she hastened to Arthur's side, accompanying him to his quarters, and then treating him to choice food and rich wines.

King Arthur could not take his eyes off Guenevere. She was the fairest maiden he had ever beheld. They grew fonder of each other every hour, and when the time came to part, Arthur said to the wise Merlin:

"Guenevere is the fairest bride fate can give me, and my heart tells me to make her my queen. Do you approve my choice?"

"The dictates of a man's heart are surely the best choice," said Merlin. "I could hardly hope to find a better wife for you, my lord, even though the distant future does not appear as settled as this present day and may not be as happy."

❋ King Arthur asked Guenevere's father for her hand in marriage, and King Leodegraunce gladly assented, for he respected no knight in the world more than his old friend's son.

One and all rejoiced at their joint victory and at the forthcoming royal wedding. The only sadness Arthur and his friends felt as they rode home was at the parting from kings Ban and Bors, who had to return to their own kingdoms, which had suffered from their long absence.

The wedding celebrations were quickly arranged. King Arthur sent Merlin at the head of a large train of courtiers to his future father-in-law, and while the wise counsellor was away, Camelot prepared gaily for the happy days ahead.

Merlin returned in haste, with a hundred brave knights whom King Leodegraunce had sent with the bride, faithfully to serve her and their new lord. The old king sent countless other treasures as well, including the most valuable gift of all — the Round Table. Merlin told Arthur:

"Upon this table, my lord, depends your power and your glory. Already the bravest and most faithful of knights under Uther Pendragon have sat round it, in token of their loyalty and in remembrance of the Last Supper.

"A hundred and fifty chairs belong to the table, none superior in rank nor age to the others, just as the knights who shall take their places here will be more than brothers. They too shall be equals.

"A hundred knights have already been sent by King Leodegraunce, and I shall now find the remaining fifty in your kingdom."

Before the wedding was celebrated in the church of St Stephen, Merlin had chosen the fifty knights. These men with the rest of the faithful company took their place at the Round Table, after celebrating Mass. And then the wedding feast was begun.

SIR GAWAIN AND THE GREEN KNIGHT

King Arthur and Guenevere had a splendid wedding. After the ceremony,
the king, according to custom, knighted the bravest of his young followers. Merlin advised the king whom to choose, his powers of divination
revealing who most deserved that honour.

Among the newly-knighted nobles was Sir Gawain, son of King Lot of
the Orkneys. King Lot had been married to the sister of King Arthur,
but he had been killed in the fierce battle in Wales when he had sided
with the eleven kings.

COLLEGE OF THE SEQUOIAS
LIBRARY

The knights all sat down at the Round Table, each having his own consecrated place. The name of each knight suddenly appeared in letters of gold on each of the chairs, only two of which remained empty. About one of these chairs Merlin said: "This is the Siege Perilous and it is intended for the holiest knight of the Round Table. It will be many years before he comes to occupy it. None of you must sit there, or the Siege Perilous will bring about our death."

The wedding feast lasted all through Christmas until the New Year, which they all wished to celebrate together at Camelot. The knights told their remarkable tales, minstrels sang the most beautiful songs, and Queen Guenevere with her court ladies graced the company like so many lovely roses in a garden of fine trees.

In the midst of the revelry King Arthur could not help thinking that he preferred to live through these adventures rather than listen to others speaking of them. He did not suspect how soon his wish was to be granted. Just then the door of the hall flew open and an unexpected and unusual guest came riding in.

Dressed all in green armour with gold spurs and mounted on a green horse with a beautifully embossed saddle, the visitor was without doubt the largest knight on earth. He was given a friendly welcome, even though his thick beard and the huge axe he gripped in his hand were an awesome sight.

The strange guest did not reply to their greetings. He merely asked:

"Who is the master here?"

King Arthur rose from his chair.

"Welcome among us, unknown knight. Join in our merrymaking, if you come in peace."

"I come in peace, unless any of you has the courage to measure his strength against mine," the guest replied.

There was a deep silence.

"What, is this the famous court of King Arthur?" cried the Green Knight derisively. "It seems to me that I'm looking at a flock of frightened children who only pretend to be brave."

King Arthur became very angry at this and exclaimed:

"I myself shall fight with you, to show you that we are not afraid of your big words!"

Sir Gawain, King Arthur's nephew, then rose and said:

"It is not only the honour of the throne that is at stake, my lord, but also the honour of all the knights of the Round Table. Permit me, therefore, to test my prowess in combat with our guest, so that I may show myself deserving of the distinction you have recently accorded me."

Turning to the Green Knight, Sir Gawain asked: "What are the conditions of our duel?"

The Green Knight smiled.

"The conditions are simple. First you will take your sword and smite my bare neck, and I shall do likewise to you a year from this day."

The company of the Round Table murmured with astonishment — no one had ever heard of such a duel before.

King Arthur then handed Sir Gawain his own sword, Excalibur.

"Hold it firmly," he said.

The Green Knight lifted his long hair off his neck and Sir Gawain hit the bared spot with such force that the head was cut right off.

However, his strange adversary did not fall. Picking his head up in his hands he mounted his green horse, saying before he left the banqueting hall:

"Do not forget. I shall expect you in the Green Chapel exactly a year from today. It is a long journey, but you will find your way. See that you keep your pledge."

The Green Knight then disappeared. Sir Gawain and the king, his uncle, looked at each other in amazement and then the festivities were resumed with much talking and laughter.

The winds of winter died down, bird song was again heard in the woods as the birds built their nests, and the meadows displayed rich carpets of flowers. The knights held tournaments and King Arthur led his men on many victorious expeditions.

At Whitsun a youth arrived at King Arthur's court, a youth so handsome that his beauty impressed everyone who saw him. Instead of asking to be accepted as a knight of the Round Table he merely requested employment as a kitchen-boy. Arthur put him in the charge of his Lord Chamberlain, Sir Kay, who, finding that the boy would not tell his real name, gave him the mocking nickname of "Lovelyhand".

The summer passed and a chill wind again blew over the land, tumbling the coloured leaves from the trees. The grass turned grey and there was much rain and fog.

Sir Gawain had not forgotten his pledge. On All Saints' Day, King Arthur gave a feast in his honour. Then Sir Gawain took leave of his friends, put on his armour, had his horse, Gringolet, saddled, took his sword and his shield — which was decorated with a picture of the Virgin Mary — and set out on his journey in search of the Green Knight.

Sir Gawain was greatly pitied and many doubted that he would return from his dangerous mission alive.

In vain he rode through the kingdom, asking everyone he met where the Green Chapel was to be found. He journeyed on until he reached North Wales, where he forded many rivers, climbed many rocky mountain-slopes, and crossed many barren plains. He fought and killed wild beasts, and he suffered from the growing cold.

Christmas Day found him in a deep oak forest. He rode on and on, certain that he would never meet a human being again, but when he at last came out in a clearing he saw in front of him a large castle on the crest of a hill.

A path took him to the main gate, and when he called out the gate-keeper at once lowered the drawbridge for him to enter.

The lord of the castle welcomed him warmly, and when he learned that Sir Gawain was one of the knights of the Round Table he could not do enough for him. His wife, whose beauty equalled that of Queen Guenevere, also lavished every attention on the guest, as did all the noblemen and ladies who had gathered at the castle to celebrate Christmas together.

Christmas passed quickly in a spirit of good-fellowship, and the time

came for Sir Gawain to continue his journey. He explained to his host that
he wished to reach the Green Chapel by the New Year, and he was told:
"The Green Chapel is only two miles away; you need not hurry."
And, to the joy of everyone at the castle, Sir Gawain stayed on for a few
extra days.

On the last evening of the year but one, the lord of the castle said to the
knight, during a long and friendly conversation:

"Tomorrow I shall hold a big hunt. You had better stay behind and rest,
to be fit and strong for your journey. I promise that the finest game
I shall kill will be yours, if you for your part promise that everything
you receive during the day will be mine."

Though his host's request seemed very strange to Sir Gawain, he readily
agreed to it, and they both went to their own rooms.

It was still dark the following morning when the castle courtyard was
filled with the clatter of armour, the excited voices of the hunters, and
the neighing of impatient horses. When the dogs were released, their
furious barking was drowned only by the three loud fanfares sounded
by the hunting-horns to announce the beginning of the chase.

With a great cry the hunters entered the murky forest, driving the
frightened game from the frosty undergrowth. A leaping doe was felled
by a feathered arrow; the pack surged on, following a fresh spoor.
A pale sun came out to look down on the thrilling scene below as the
hunt continued through copse and dale, over brook and gully, the
horsemen urging their mounts to greater effort, the noise of the chase
pounding excitingly in their heads.

Sir Gawain slept soundly. He was awakened by the sound of his door
opening, and he looked up when he heard someone sitting down by his
bed. He saw the smiling face of the beautiful lady of the castle.

"Why, you would sleep away Judgement Day itself, Sir Gawain," the
lady said. "It is broad daylight outside. They have all left long ago,
leaving us behind. You will have to look after me, dear knight."

So surprised was Sir Gawain that he could scarcely think of what to say
in reply.

"As a knight of the Round Table I am at the service of all, beautiful
  lady," he said at last.

"Will you really be my knight?" she asked.

"I shall consider it the greatest honour."

"You must confirm your pledge, then," his visitor told him, and before

Sir Gawain had recovered from his surprise she kissed him and departed.

Sir Gawain got up quickly, dressed and went to Mass. All that morning he entertained the lady of the castle as best he knew how. When they were left alone together again, his hostess kissed him a second time.

"For the way you're looking after me, chivalrous knight," she said.

After a short afternoon the moon came out. The people in the castle all retired to their rooms and Sir Gawain settled down to await the return of his host from the chase.

Instead of the lord of the castle, it was his wife who first appeared in the doorway. She embraced Sir Gawain and asked:

"Would you rather serve another lady?"

"No," replied Sir Gawain, his heart beginning to pound uncomfortably, "not even Queen Guenevere herself. And were you not married already, I should ask you to become my wife."

Whereupon the lady kissed him a third time.

"I too should wish nothing better," she said, untying her lace belt, which she handed to the knight. "I want you to have this as a secret keepsake, so you shall never forget me."

Sir Gawain hesitated to accept the gift, but the lady told him that it would keep him safe from even the most deadly blow, and he thought of the task that awaited him on the morrow and gladly took the offered belt.

The huntsmen eventually returned — the sound of horses' hooves was heard in the courtyard, and the horns were blown to mark the end of the hunt. The lord of the castle, still flushed from the chase, came up to greet his guest and had his bag brought up to them.

"This," he said, pointing to a stag, "I shot early in the morning."

Sir Gawain stepped forward and kissed his host.

"And this is what I received on your behalf," he explained.

The lord of the castle seemed nonplussed at this, but he instructed his servants to bring a second trophy — the head of a large boar.

"I killed him just after noon. It was no easy kill, believe me."

❊ Again sir Gawain responded with a kiss.

Finally a fox's skin appeared on the table — the lord of the castle being this time rewarded with three kisses in succession. In vain he asked Sir Gawain how he came by such gifts. Sir Gawain did not reply, nor did he say anything about the belt he had been given by the lord's wife . . .

A snowstorm was raging outside next morning when Sir Gawain prepared to set out in search of the Green Knight. Round his waist he tied the lace belt he had received; he had his armour put on and placed his helmet on his head.

Then the servants saddled the faithful Gringolet and Sir Gawain took leave of his kind host, his beautiful wife, and the entire court. They were all sorry that he had to go out in such terrible weather, and the lord of the castle sent a guide lest Sir Gawain lose his way.

The road to the Green Chapel led through wild, barren country. When they reached a small valley, his guide told him:

"Here I must leave you, sir, for it is not safe to tarry in these parts. The Green Knight will kill anyone who dares trespass here. The chapel is not far away. Just keep straight on till you reach the stream. You cannot lose your way then."

Saying this, Sir Gawain's guide turned his horse round and rode away, leaving the knight alone. Sir Gawain went on and very soon he came to the stream the guide had mentioned. The water bubbled merrily, but then its sound was suddenly lost in a loud roar. It seemed to the startled knight that the rocks were crumbling and toppling down into the valley. Following this awe-inspiring noise a huge figure in green armour appeared at the mouth of a cave opposite Sir Gawain. It was his adversary, the Green Knight.

"I see that you have kept your word," said a voice like an icy wind.

"The knights of the Round Table always keep their pledges," Sir Gawain replied. "Come, let us not delay," he added, baring his neck, and glancing at the gleaming axe which the Green Knight held in his right hand.

The Green Knight came forward and raised his terrible weapon. Sir
Gawain trembled in spite of himself.

"What, are you shivering with fear?" cried the Green Knight. "I stood
my ground firmly when it was your turn to strike."

"Try it now!" exclaimed Sir Gawain, inclining his head once again. This
time he did not move a muscle. The axe whistled in the air and struck
the knight at the nape of his neck. His blood coloured the snow red, but
incredible though it seemed, the wound was not at all deep. Sir Gawain
saw that his adversary was getting ready for another blow.

"Oh no!" he cried, drawing his sword. "It was agreed between us that we should each strike just one single blow."

"That is true, sir, we did so agree a year ago. But you yourself failed to keep your word only the other day."

Realisation came suddenly to Sir Gawain.

"Yes, the other day," went on the Green Knight, "did you not promise to give me everything you received at my castle?"

Sir Gawain blushed, untied the lace belt, and said, "You are right, but let me explain that I kept this gift a secret from you at the request of your wife, who insisted that I should take it."

"She deceived you, sir, for everything that passed between you took place with my knowledge," explained the Green Knight, laughing. "Keep your lace belt, and let it be a warning to you against the wiles of women, for many an excellent king and warrior, such as Solomon, Samson and David, have been defeated by them."

Sir Gawain, discomfited, accepted the Green Knight's advice, but he refused an invitation to visit the castle once more. Sir Gawain regretted that he did not even know the other's name, and as if he were able to read his thoughts, the Green Knight said:

"I am Bernlac de Hautdesert, and I was taught all the magic I know by a certain fairy, who was taught by Merlin. I wished to test the courage of Arthur's knights. And you did well by answering my challenge."

These were the parting words of the Green Knight, and Sir Gawain mounted his horse and made his way back to Camelot, there to recount his adventures to his friends of the Round Table.

KILWICH AND OLWEN

The days at King Arthur's court flowed by like water in a quiet stream, until another strange adventure befell one or another of the knights. One Whitsun, Lovelyhand was knighted when it was discovered that he was Gareth, the younger brother of Sir Gawain. In the course of his travels Sir Gareth visited many lands, defeating three terrible foes during his journey: the Black Knight, the Red Knight, and the Blue Knight. At the end of his struggles he gained the magic ring, by which means he could change the colour of his armour and his horse, much to the bewilderment of friends and foes alike.

The knights of the Round Table did not, however, always ride out in search of adventure themselves; as the years passed their fame spread far and wide, so that others often came to ask for help.

One day a young and handsome knight arrived at Camelot with a request. His spirited horse made the turf fly with his hooves, a pair of greyhounds with ruby-coloured collars kept circling round their master like sea swallows, and the knight's two steel-topped silver lances glittered threateningly, as did his sword with its golden hilt. The war horn at his side was made of real ivory.

"What is your wish?" asked King Arthur, as soon as he had recovered from the surprise they had all felt at the young knight's unexpected appearance in the banqueting hall.

"I have a great request to make, my lord," replied the stranger.

"You may ask for anything you like, except my sword Excalibur, my ship Prydwen, and my wife, Queen Guenevere."

"First cut my hair as a sign of kinship according to custom," said the knight, and when King Arthur had done so, the knight continued:

"I am Kilwich, son of Kilydd, and my mother, Goleudid, is the daughter of Prince Anlawd."

"You are then my cousin and I shall gladly fulfil your request," said King Arthur.

"I am searching for Olwen, the daughter of Yspadaden Penkawr, for she is fated to become my wife. But I have been unable to find her."

"I have never heard of that maiden," replied Arthur, "but we shall set out at once and find her."

To accompany them on their journey King Arthur picked Sir Kay, for he was very strong and could go nine days without sleep, as well as being able to hold his breath — even under water — for the same length of time. Kyndelig he chose as their guide, for he never lost his way; he also took with him Gurhyr Gwalstatt, who knew every existing language; Meneu, who enchanted everyone he met; and also Sir Gawain, who always got to the bottom of every adventure, as well as the faithful Sir Bedivere.

They set out together and travelled a long time until, in the distance,
they saw a mighty castle.

In front of the castle a shepherd dressed in furs was grazing a herd, and
the knights asked him:

"Whose are that castle and the sheep you're looking after?"

"Why, don't you know?" said the man in reply. "They belong to
Yspadaden Penkawr. And who might you be?"

"We are the knights of the Round Table and we're looking for Yspadaden's daughter, Olwen."

"An ill fate awaits you then, but come to my cottage; perhaps my wife
will be able to advise you."

In the shepherd's cottage they learned the awful truth. Yspadaden
Penkawr had killed twenty-three of the shepherd's sons, the only one
to have stayed alive, Goreu, having been hidden by his mother in a
stone coffer.

"It is a sin to hide such a strong fellow," said Sir Kay. "Let him come
with us. I swear that no one shall harm a hair of his head unless they
kill me first."

They asked about Olwen, and Kilwich was overjoyed to learn that the
girl came to the cottage every Saturday. He had by this time almost
given up hope of ever finding her.

Olwen then arrived. She was wearing a red silk dress, her white throat
set off by a gold necklace with emeralds and rubies, her hair fairer than
flax, her cheeks redder than roses, her eyes as sparkling as those of
a falcon.

She entered the room and sat down next to Kilwich, as though she had
known him a long time.

"I know why you have come," she said. "I also know that upon the
advice of your mother Goleudid you have long loved me, although you
never set eyes on me until today. If you really mean to marry me, go
at once to my father and promise to fulfil all his wishes, however difficult they may seem. You will not achieve your desire otherwise."
And, saying this, Olwen left them.

She did not know that Arthur's knights followed her, nor that they overpowered nine guards and killed nine watch-dogs in order to enter the palace.

Then Kilwich presented himself to Yspadaden Penkawr.

"You want my daughter for your wife?" the terrible old man asked him, and went on, not waiting for a reply: "You must first carry out several tasks that I shall give you.

"I expect you have seen the ploughed field below the castle, which is lying fallow. A long time ago I had nine bushels of flax sown there. Go and pick the seeds, sow them elsewhere and harvest the flax, from which Olwen's wedding veil will be woven. That is your first task."

"I shall fulfil it," replied Kilwich.

"Do not rejoice too soon. If you succeed in this task, you must then go and find Mabon, my forester, who was lost when only three days old. Then you must catch the two cubs of the she-wolf Ghast Rhymni and, in order to prevent them from escaping, bring them to me on a lead made from the beard of Dillus Warwawc, the robber. Finally I want you to bring me the sword of the giant, Gwernach.

"Only if you fulfil all my wishes will Olwen be your wife."

King Arthur set his knights to the tasks Kilwich had been given by Yspadaden Penkawr.

Sir Kay was the first to set out. He travelled for a long time before reaching what is, perhaps, the largest castle in the world — that of the giant Gwernach.

"I know how to polish swords to perfection!" Sir Kay called out to the guard at the gate. "Announce me to your master."

Before long Sir Kay was sitting in the giant's hall, and Gwernach marvelled at the visitor's skill as the blade of his sword was polished until it glittered with a blue light. The giant returned the sword to his scabbard, well satisfied with Sir Kay's efforts. But the knight frowned and said:

"That scabbard now only mars the beauty of your sword. Let me polish it for you as well."

Suspecting nothing, the giant handed him his weapon once more. Sir
Kay turned his back and, pretending to examine the scabbard, he drew
the sword and struck Gwernach with such force that the giant fell like
a mighty tree under the woodman's axe.

Sir Kay securely tied the sword of Gwernach to his saddle and rode
swiftly back to King Arthur.

Gurhyr Gwalstatt also travelled far, since it fell to him to find the lost
Mabon. In vain did he ask the people he met if they had seen the lost
forester. As he could also speak the languages of animals he decided to
question them. First he asked the Blackbird of Cilgwri:

"Do you happen to know anything about Mabon, son of Modron, who
was lost when only three days old?"

"I have never heard of him," replied the bird. "Go and ask the stag —
his memory goes further back than mine."

But not even the Stag of Redynvre was able to help the knight. He sent
him to the eagle.

"Yes, I remember hearing the name once," said the Eagle of Gwern Abwy.
"If I'm not mistaken, it was the Salmon of Llyn Llyw who mentioned
it, but that is all I can remember now."

And so the knight called on the salmon.

"Yes, I can tell you where Mabon is to be found. I have swum past the
walls of Gloucester prison several times, listening to him moaning in
his cell. You can only free him by force of arms."

Sir Kay and Sir Bedivere were carried by the Salmon of Llyn Llyw to
the prison and they set Mabon free, while King Arthur and his men
were scaling the city walls of Gloucester, to draw off the fight when
the escape was discovered. Their mission was successfully completed
and the knights, with Mabon, rode away in safety.

Gurhyr Gwalstatt was returning by himself and on his way he came to
a large ant-hill around which the grass was burning. The flames were
already starting to torment the unfortunate ants, and the knight therefore dismounted quickly and put the fire out with the flat of his
sword before it spread too far.

❋ "Thank you for saving our lives," cried the ants. "We will gladly repay you for your good deed . . . just name your wish and it will be fulfilled."

Gurhyr recalled another of Kilwich's tasks, and said:

"Will you, then, bring me the nine bushels of flax-seed which Yspadaden Penkawr once had sown in the field in front of his castle."

The ants quickly did his bidding, and before the day was out the last of them, who happened to be lame, had brought his flax-seed to make up the full nine bushels Gurhyr Gwalstatt needed.

In the meantime King Arthur had learned where the she-wolf Ghast Rhymni had hidden her cubs and he set out in his ship Prydwen to catch them. He knew that he could only hope to bring them home if he made a lead from the beard of the robber Dillus Warwawc, and so he sent the strong Sir Kay and Sir Bedivere to shave it off.

The knights could not kill Warwawc, for the strands of beard would not hold together if they did. They waited until the robber fell asleep and then quickly cut off his beard. Having made the lead, they followed King Arthur to the lair of the wolf and helped him to capture the cubs.

And so, with the aid of the knights of the Round Table, Kilwich fulfilled all the tasks Yspadaden Penkawr had set him. Accompanied by his friends he rode to the castle to claim Olwen.

That day proved to be the last for Yspadaden Penkawr — for Goreu, the shepherd's son, avenged the death of his twenty-three brothers by justly slaying Penkawr with a single blow of his sword.

SIR LANCELOT AND THE HOLY GRAIL

Many brave knights sat at the Round Table and they had many adventures and endured many trials in honour of the king. One of them excelled above all others in the strength of his arms, his chivalry and his riding prowess. His name was Sir Lancelot.

Sir Lancelot was the son of Arthur's faithful friend and ally, King

Ban, and he had many adventures before he ever arrived at Camelot. Shortly after the birth of Lancelot, King Claudas invaded Ban's kingdom with a large army, which plundered and pillaged Benwick, finally forcing King Ban to find refuge at Trèbes Castle, where the enemy laid siege.

King Ban's couriers escaped from the surrounded castle to seek help in other lands, but King Arthur was busy fighting the Saxons and Ban's brother, King Bors, lay on his deathbed.

Finally, King Ban, accompanied by his wife and baby son, left the fortified castle, leaving his Lord Chamberlain in command. The king was hoping to raise other allies abroad.

Halting their desperate flight by a beautiful lake, the king turned to take a last look at the castle. To his great dismay the building was aflame. The treacherous Lord Chamberlain had surrendered without a fight and the enemy had set fire to the castle and surrounding land.

The sight broke the king's tired heart and he lay down to die. Queen Helen put little Lancelot down in the grass, and vainly attempted to restore her husband to life.

Her husband's death was only the first of her misfortunes; when she had recovered enough from her grief to tend to her baby, she discovered that it was no longer beside her in the grass.

The Lady of the Lake had taken the baby and was walking across the water, little Lancelot in her arms. She never returned him to his mother.

Lancelot became known as Lancelot of the Lake, and he was brought up by the Lake Queen, Vivian, to become the greatest of all knights.

When Lancelot reached his eighteenth year the Lady of the Lake sent him to the court of King Arthur, where the young knight quickly gained a highly esteemed favour — that of the beautiful Queen Guenevere.

When he was knighted, Guenevere brought him a sword covered with her train to show that she had chosen him as her own champion. And Sir Lancelot was full of great admiration for the queen and undertook all his future exploits on her behalf.

Ancient manuscripts tell how he defeated the terrible Sir Tarquin, who held twenty-four knights of the Round Table in captivity; how he borrowed some armour from Sir Kay, who had grown old and had lost his youthful strength, and how Lancelot had worn this armour when he challenged and killed the two giants who owned the castle of Tintagel. In that same armour Sir Lancelot later defeated four of King Arthur's knights, including the famous Sir Gawain.

But Sir Lancelot had an even more remarkable adventure than any of these. It was at Corbenic Castle, where he wielded his sword to slay the dragon which was plaguing King Pelleas and his daughter Elaine.

Queen Guenevere was not the only lady to admire this knight, for the maiden Elaine also took a great liking to the kind and handsome Lancelot. And since he too became fond of her, their mutual love brought them a son, whom they called Galahad.

It was at Corbenic Castle that Sir Lancelot was to see the most wonderful sight of his life.

One day, as he sat with King Pelleas, a beautiful maiden entered the room, carrying a golden goblet covered with a white veil. The room was immediately flooded with a scent more beautiful than that of any other in the world, and the tables covered themselves of their own accord with a variety of choice dishes and wines. King Pelleas and all the courtiers knelt in pious devotion, and clasped their hands together.

As soon as he had recovered from his surprise, Sir Lancelot gasped: "What miracle was that?"

"That is the most precious thing in the world — the Holy Grail or Goblet, out of which Our Lord drank at the Last Supper. Inside it were several drops of the blood of our holiest martyr when the goblet was brought to this country by Joseph of Arimathea.

"It has been prophesied that because of our sins the Holy Grail will be taken from us, and until the time that one of King Arthur's knights sets eyes on the precious goblet again, the Round Table will cease to exist."

Sir Lancelot was struck speechless by this prophecy. He left Corbenic Castle in haste, hoping to discover the secret whereabouts of the Holy Grail. But though he travelled far he was unable to find any clue.

Only the wise Merlin could have helped him, for he had the gift of clairvoyance and would know who was to be initiated into the secret.

But the king's counsellor was nowhere to be found. It was as if the earth had swallowed him. His disappearance was a mystery to one and all. King Arthur himself was very puzzled by it.

Merlin had at that time taken a liking to the Lady of the Lake, on whose account he left Camelot; all his great wisdom did not prevent him from succumbing to her feminine wiles. And Vivian, in her turn, only wished to learn all his magic secrets, for which reason she allowed him to accompany her wherever she went.

Once she found that the old man had taught her all he knew, she took him to a deserted spot in the Forest of Broceliand. There she sat down with him under a hawthorn bush and waited for Merlin to fall asleep.

The old man suspected nothing and closed his eyes in tranquil sleep. Vivian got up softly and with her veil she drew nine magic circles round the sleeping Merlin, who was now imprisoned on that spot and could not leave the place unless Vivian wished him to do so. But she did not tell anyone of Merlin's whereabouts, nor did she lift the magic spell she had cast upon him.

That was why Arthur's knights spent many long years vainly searching for Merlin, and why Lancelot could not penetrate the secret of the Holy Grail.

However, Merlin did manage to give them some final advice.

When Sir Gawain came to the Forest of Broceliand and arrived at the invisible wall of the magic circles, he heard a familiar voice:

"Make haste to Camelot! The Holy Grail is leaving us, and it is time to send out an expedition in search of it. Those of you who will recover the Grail are now ready for your task."

The voice died down beyond the invisible wall, and it was then that

Sir Gawain realised whose voice it was. He lost no time in returning to Camelot, calling together all the knights of the Round Table as he went, so that they should set out on their expedition without delay.

At the castle they were preparing to celebrate Whitsun, and when Sir Gawain entered the Hall of the Round Table he found there many familiar faces — there was Sir Kay, Sir Gareth, Sir Hector, Lancelot's brother Sir Bors, as well as some new intrepid warriors such as Sir Percival, who sat right next to the Siege Perilous, which was still empty and covered with a veil.

Sir Gawain had not had time to look round properly when a hermit entered the hall, accompanied by a young knight in red armour.

To the amazement of all, the hermit led the youth straight to the Siege Perilous, and the knight sat down on it without the slightest hesitation. No harm befell him as a result. Therefore King Arthur rose and, in the profound silence that followed, removed the white veil from the chair. No sooner had he done this than an inscription appeared on the high back:

THIS IS THE SEAT OF THE HOLY KNIGHT, SIR GALAHAD.

It was then that Sir Gawain noticed how like Sir Lancelot the young man's features were, though he was more delicate, almost girlish, in appearance. He also saw how affectionately Sir Lancelot was smiling at the newcomer.

Queen Guenevere also wished to see the knight who had been fated to occupy the Siege Perilous, and so King Arthur decided that after the feast a great tournament was to be held on the wide meadow outside Camelot.

The riders who were to participate lowered the visors of their helmets, took up their shields and their lances, dug the spurs into their horses' flanks, and rode out into the tilting-yards. The Queen watched the jousting from one of the castle windows, and a magnificent spectacle unfolded itself in front of the spectators. Before long only the three best knights were left in the saddle, none of them being able to unseat the others — Galahad, Lancelot of the Lake, and Sir Percival.

The tournament over, everyone went to vespers in the church, before they entered the hall for supper. There was, however, to be yet another miracle that day. A sudden clap of thunder reverberated through the castle, and as the sound grew louder it was accompanied by a blinding flash of light in whose brilliance they could see the Holy Grail floating in the air, covered with a piece of snow-white velvet. As on that former occasion when Sir Lancelot was staying with King Pelleas at Corbenic Castle, a heady scent of spice filled the air and the tables appeared laden with the most delicious foods and drinks imaginable.

When the moment had passed, Sir Gawain rose from his seat at the Round Table to tell his friends of Merlin's message and to tell them of his own decision.

"The time has come for us to set out in search of the Holy Grail, for it remains a secret to us. Here and now I swear that I shall travel abroad for a year and a day to find the Grail."

One after the other the knights rose to their feet, a hundred and fifty of them all told, and took the same oath as Sir Gawain.

King Arthur and his court were much distressed at this, for they feared that they would never again see their comrades at their places by the Round Table. The country people in the village below Camelot lamented too when they saw the knights pass by and Queen Guenevere despaired at having to part with her champion, Sir Lancelot, as he departed with the others on their long journey.

The knights of the Round Table each agreed to go in a different direction, but some of them were destined to meet again during their travels.

On the fourth day Sir Galahad reached the White Abbey, where he was given an ancient shield with a red cross painted on it in the name of Him who had died on the cross.

Shortly afterwards, he encountered Sir Lancelot and Sir Percival, who

did not recognise him and rode forward to attack. Only when he had unseated both of them did Galahad reveal his identity, but before they could join him he had ridden off again.

Shortly after this incident Galahad came to Sir Percival's aid when he discovered the knight surrounded by a band of twenty armed men. But for Galahad's valiant efforts, Sir Percival would certainly not have escaped from the ambush alive.

Meanwhile Sir Gawain wandered for many days without achieving anything or meeting anybody, until he came across Sir Hector. Together they went to a certain hermit, who told them that they would not find the Grail, no matter where they journeyed.

Sir Bors later visited this same hermit, and when the knight had made his confession to him, the holy man said:

"Put on a red robe as a token of your mission and prepare to fast from now until the time you shall once more see the Holy Grail."

Overjoyed, Sir Bors did as the hermit had told him.

Sir Lancelot had travelled alone, and one moonlit night he found himself approaching a large castle. He had no difficulty in entering by a gate in the rear walls and he walked right through the castle, until he reached a chamber where the doors opened slowly in front of him. At that moment he heard a mysterious voice warning him:

"Flee, Lancelot, it is not your destiny to find the Holy Grail."

It felt as if a flame had shot through his face and Lancelot fell, fainting, to the floor. He lay a long time as one dead, and when he at last recovered, he found that he was at Corbenic Castle. King Pelleas often came to sit by his bedside, but Lancelot asked in vain to see the beautiful Elaine; finally he learned that she was dead. King Pelleas advised Lancelot to give up his expedition in search of the Holy Grail and he was finally persuaded to return to Camelot.

Lancelot of the Lake was not destined to see the Holy Grail at Corbenic Castle, but his son Galahad, Sir Percival and Sir Bors did see it there and they were overwhelmed by its holy presence. All three knights had a vision in which the Lord ordered them to follow the

Holy Grail to the city of Sarras, where they were to serve Him faithfully.

The knights made haste to the coast where they found waiting for them a white ship. On board was a silver table, on top of which stood the holy goblet.

They spent many days and nights at sea, giving thanks to the Lord, and when they landed near the city of Sarras they soon discovered what miracles the Holy Grail could accomplish. It had the power of healing the sick and the lame, and the fame of the three knights who looked after this holy relic was spread far and wide. The youngest of them, Galahad, was made king of the holy city. His mind, however, was not on earthly things and he found much favour in the eyes of the Lord, who finally summoned his soul to heaven.

There was mourning in Sarras following Galahad's death. Sir Percival, much saddened, became a monk and spent a year searching for peace as a hermit in the wilderness. Then he, too, resigned his soul to God.

Sir Bors, having outlived his two companions, did not wish to remain alone in that distant land and he made preparations to board a ship and return home.

The people of Camelot were overjoyed when Sir Bors appeared one day at the castle gates. The tale of his adventures, and those of Sir Lancelot and the other comrades who had joined the quest for the Holy Grail, astounded the court, and King Arthur wisely sent for a chronicler so that the glorious tales could be recorded and preserved for the benefit of prosperity.

Everyone who had returned alive and well from the expedition in search of the Holy Grail rejoiced when they heard that it had been found and safely preserved in the holy city. None were more pleased than King Arthur and Queen Guenevere.

But peace and tranquillity were not to last long at Camelot. Some of the knights began to envy the favours Sir Lancelot received from Queen Guenevere, and they even began to slander their queen and the knight. The queen, hoping to appease the knights by showing that she held them all in high esteem, decided to give a banquet in London, to which she invited all the knights of the Round Table.

But it seemed that all her good intentions were to be of no avail.

During the banquet Sir Patrice ate a poisoned apple which had been placed on the table by Sir Pinel, who had intended Sir Gawain to eat it. As it was the queen's banquet, she was suspected of perpetrating the treacherous act. Sir Mador of Port, Sir Patrice's cousin, was the most outspoken in demanding revenge.

"An eye for an eye!" he cried, and as no one present felt certain of the queen's innocence, no one spoke up on her behalf.

King Arthur had to pass judgement on the matter, and was forced to decide that Guenevere was to be burned at the stake unless a knight could be found who would be willing to defend her honour in combat with the wrathful Sir Mador.

Sir Lancelot, who was best fitted to undertake the task, was not at the court, and no one knew where he had gone.

The queen waited for many anxious days, and she had almost given up all hope of being championed when Sir Bors de Ganis came forward to fight for her honour.

"I shall gladly take up my lance on the queen's behalf," he told King

Arthur, adding: "But only if no better knight than I comes forward."
Sir Bors was thinking of Lancelot of the Lake, for he knew where to find him and meant to give Sir Lancelot news of the impending duel.

On the day of the duel the entire court, headed by King Arthur and the queen, went to the tournament field in front of Westminster.

Sir Mador was waiting and he cantered impatiently round on his horse, calling out mockingly to his adversary:

"Come and fight, or if you are afraid, give the queen up to the flames!"

At these words Sir Bors took up his position and lowered the visor of his helmet. He was ready for the charge when a knight mounted on a white horse and carrying an unknown coat-of-arms appeared from a nearby wood. He approached as quickly as a storm and, to the astonishment of all present, attacked Sir Mador before Sir Bors could move. The unknown knight was a valiant combatant, and Sir Mador was soon helpless on his back, asking his vanquisher for mercy. The victor obliged Sir Mador to retract his accusations against the queen.

Guenevere stepped forward to thank her saviour. The knight removed his helmet, revealing that he was none other than Sir Lancelot, who had returned to protect her honour and her life.

Shortly after this combat another wicked knight threatened the queen's honour. He was Sir Meliagraunce, who during the May festivities took Guenevere, with ten members of her bodyguard, prisoner. He intended to hold them in his castle, in order to make the queen his wife. But Sir Lancelot came to know of this, and he delivered the queen by killing the treacherous knight.

Although he tried to avert the approaching misfortune and the disintegration of the Round Table, Sir Lancelot was not able to prevent the events that followed.

The final disaster was caused by King Arthur's own nephews, the brothers of Sir Gawain, Sir Agravain and Sir Mordred. These two knights publicly sullied the reputations of Sir Lancelot and Queen Guenevere, accusing them of devoting more attention to each other than to their respective duties.

These two jealous knights, accompanied by a gang of armed men, surprised Sir Lancelot and Queen Guenevere in her chamber. Sir Lancelot, though unarmed, faced them bravely. He killed the first man to attack him and, taking the fallen sword, Lancelot then outfenced and killed all the others, except Mordred, who managed to escape.

Sir Lancelot called together all his faithful friends. Many of them were knights of the Round Table, including Sir Bors and Sir Hector de Maris, and they all waited to see what King Arthur would do.

The traitor Mordred could have given the king a true report but, instead of admitting that he and his people had set upon Sir Lancelot, he claimed that Sir Lancelot had attacked them, using the death of his companions as proof of his shameful lie, and he demanded the queen's life in forfeit.

Arthur allowed himself to believe Mordred's story and, ignoring the advice of Sir Gawain, who urged him to forgive Lancelot in respect of his friendship and his valour, the king angrily decided that Guenevere should be burned at the stake.

Sir Lancelot, hearing about this, prepared for battle. The queen had already been tied to the stake when Sir Lancelot and his companions swooped down and began to fight like lions in her defence.

No one could withstand Sir Lancelot and his sword, and in his wrath he did not care where his blows fell. In a terrible anger he killed Gawain's brothers, Gareth and Gaheris. Sir Kay and many more of the knights of the Round Table also fell in the battle. Having driven Arthur's army off the field, Lancelot lifted Guenevere on to his horse and took her with him to his castle, Joyous Gard.

The king assembled a large army, supported by Sir Gawain, who had vowed to avenge the death of his two brothers. It was proclaimed that Sir Lancelot had kidnapped the queen, and a full-scale war now broke out.

The army at Joyous Gard had made their preparations, and when the castle was besieged by Arthur's troops, they resisted so well that neither side was able to gain a victory.

The fighting continued without any decision being reached, and the news of the fratricidal struggle spread throughout the Christian world, until it reached the Pope himself.

The Pope knew that such a war could benefit no one, and he sent King Arthur a sealed Bill in which he requested that peace be made with Sir Lancelot, whom he in turn commanded to restore Queen Guenevere to her sovereign.

All would, perhaps, have been well, for both sides had acquitted themselves honourably and many knights now regretted having taken part in this wrongful war in which the finest noblemen had lost their lives; all might have been well, but for the inexorable hatred in Sir Gawain's heart.

No sooner had Lancelot peacefully left England to return to his kingdom of Benwick, accompanied by several knights of the Round Table, than Sir Gawain attempted to persuade King Arthur to follow across the sea, in order to punish Lancelot in his own country.

Arthur's army left England from Southampton, and the first night of the voyage, as the wind rocked his ship, the king had a strange dream.

He saw a huge bear fighting a dragon in the air, and the dragon kept attacking his adversary until he finally struck him to the ground.

At first King Arthur thought that as he had a dragon on his banner the dream was a good omen for the ensuing battle.

However, when they landed at the port of Barfleur, they learned that the country was being ravaged by a terrible giant, who had just carried off the young niece of Duke Hoel, the ruler of the surrounding countryside.

Thinking that this would be a good opportunity to find out whether he was still strong enough to fight, the aging king set off for the Mount of St Michael, where the giant lived. He went alone, telling no one of his intention.

Arthur found the giant sitting by the fire, his face smeared with the blood of some cattle he had just devoured. Catching sight of the intruder, the giant picked up his huge cudgel and gave King Arthur a terrible blow. Though he staggered under it, Arthur did not fall.

Drawing his sword, he smote the giant several times and killed him. But he was too late to save the duke's niece, for she lay lifeless at the giant's feet.

King Arthur had proved his strength but he did not look forward to starting this new campaign against Sir Lancelot. The king encircled the city of Benwick, but at the cost of many lives. Sir Gawain was so severely wounded in three combats with Sir Lancelot that he almost died. Sir Gawain made no secret of his hatred, but three times his adversary had withheld the death blow, refraining out of old friendship.

Many more knights might have been killed if the struggle had continued, but one day a messenger burst into Arthur's tent, bringing fearful news.

"My lord, while you and your army are kept busy here, your nephew Mordred has usurped your crown in England. He has produced false documents to prove that you are dead, and many nobles believe his ruse. Only a handful of the most faithful are fighting to defend the queen in the tower. They are holding the usurper at bay, and, God willing, they may continue to hold out until you yourself return."

"Alas!" cried King Arthur, covering his face. "The brotherhood of the Round Table exists no more."

But then his mood of despair changed to one of rightful anger.

"This time the wretch Mordred shall pay dearly for his treachery!" he exclaimed, realising, too late, who had been the real instigator of all the strife.

Arthur's warships returned to Richborough, and a bloody battle followed on the shore — Mordred's ranks sweeping down with reinforcements of pagan Huns, who had come to help him.

Yard by yard the king's men gained ground. Using his military experience to good advantage, Arthur sent his foot soldiers into the fray while his knights on horseback penetrated deep into the enemy rear.

In the end Mordred was forced to flee, but not before many excellent knights had fallen in the field, including the bravest knight of all, Sir Gawain.

King Arthur knelt by his side to look for the last time into his eyes that
were already clouded by death. It was then that his friend of the Round
Table spoke his last:
"I am dying, my lord, and I deserve to die. The wounds justly inflicted

on me by Sir Lancelot at Benwick have opened again . . . may he forgive me, for it was I who in my anger set you against him."

"He *will* forgive you . . ." said the king with conviction.

"Give him this paper," asked Sir Gawain, handing Arthur a scroll of parchment. "It contains my final request, sealed with blood. And my plea for help . . . let Sir Lancelot pray on my grave . . . for the love of God . . ." he whispered before his head sagged, lifeless, into the king's arms.

With a sad heart Arthur led his army in pursuit of Mordred. The pretender had withdrawn to the city of Winchester, but those stout walls could not protect him for long, and he was forced to flee once more.

The decisive battle was imminent, and when the king's troops reached Cornwall, they found Mordred waiting for them by the Camblam river with sixty thousand rebels to support him.

The two opposing armies clashed in a fearful and merciless battle. Hundreds and thousands fell on both sides, and when the long day ended and the sun was about to set, Mordred was left quite alone beside a mountain of bodies of the dead and wounded.

King Arthur ignored the warnings of his only two followers still alive, the faithful Sir Bedivere and his cup-bearer Lucan, and he rushed forward with his lance poised to kill the evil-doer.

Perhaps it was because his mind was so clouded by terrible anger but King Arthur forgot to draw his sword Excalibur — and Mordred, though he had been run through by the king's lance, was able to lift his own sword and mortally wound Arthur before he himself fell and died.

The gruesome battle over, Sir Bedivere carried the king away from the battlefield and prayed to God that the king might live a little longer.

His prayer was answered, but Arthur's first words filled his heart with a great sorrow.

"I beg you to do me a last favour," whispered the wounded king. "Take my sword Excalibur and throw it in the lake."

Sir Bedivere still hoped that Arthur might recover, and so he hid the beautiful sword under a tree.

But King Arthur saw that Sir Bedivere had deceived him and sent him once more to the lakeside. Again his faithful companion could not bring himself to throw the splendid weapon away. This time Arthur grew angry, and Sir Bedivere therefore took the sword out of its hiding-place, wound the belt round its hilt and threw Excalibur far into the lake.

No sooner had he done so than a white arm holding the sword emerged from the water. The arm waved the sword thrice in the air, and, like a phantom, vanished below the surface.

Sir Bedivere sped back to King Arthur and told him what he had seen. The king listened and said:

"I see it is time. Carry me in your arms and hurry to the shore, lest I be late."

When Sir Bedivere and King Arthur reached the shore they saw a boat carrying three sad queens dressed in black. They were Morgan le Fay, the Lady of the Lake, and the Queen of Northgalis.

"Where have you been so long, brother?" asked the first reproachfully, helping Sir Bedivere lay King Arthur's body in the boat.

The boat quickly drew away from the shore. Sir Bedivere heard the soft splash of the oars and the piteous weeping of the three women. Calling out to the king he could just hear Arthur's last words coming across the waters in reply:

"I am leaving for the happy isle of Avalon, where my wounds shall be healed forever . . ."

After the death of Arthur, Sir Lancelot forgave all who had sinned against him, and shortly afterwards he died at Joyous Gard, wearing a monk's habit. Queen Guenevere was left to live out her days in a convent.

As these tales are handed down from generation to generation, so the Round Table continues to live on in people's minds, and with it King Arthur — REX QUONDAM, REX QUE FUTURUS.

FRENCH
LEGENDS

Olivier stands on a hill; from the top he looks out at the Spanish kingdom and sees a large force of Saracens. Says Olivier: "There is a multitude of the heathen and, it seems, only a handful of us, the French. Friend Roland, sound your horn: Charles will hear us and order his army to return." "I should first have to lose my reason," replies Roland, "for I should thus surely lose my fame in sweet France. No, instead I shall deal so many blows with my sword that blood will cover it right up to its golden hilt. And all the other Frenchmen will also fight with great enthusiasm. The wretched heathen were ill-advised to march into the gorge: I swear to you that they are all condemned to death."

THE SONG OF ROLAND

For seven years King Charles had fought in Spain against the Saracens. He had conquered the entire land except for the town of Zaragoza which Marsil, the King of the Saracens, defended from within its walls. He knew he could never defeat Charles on the battlefield and the Saracen therefore resorted to trickery, offering the king a large reward if he would agree to end the war and return to France.

King Charles sent one of his knights, Ganelon, to discuss the proposal with Marsil. But the knight was persuaded to betray his sovereign. Ganelon was to advise King Charles to leave a rearguard behind in a gorge, to cover the French army's withdrawal. The most gallant warriors, including the king's nephew Roland, were to be the ones to stay. The Saracens were then to ambush the rearguard and kill every single man. With his bravest knights dead, King Charles would never dare to renew hostilities.

The traitor Ganelon did as the enemy king suggested, receiving as a reward seven hundred camels laden with gold and silver.

King Charles had begun his journey back to France and the rearguard, including twelve of his best and most loyal knights, as well as Roland and his good friend Olivier, were left protecting the gorge when suddenly they saw a large enemy force approaching, and Olivier urged Roland three times to sound his horn, Oliphant, to summon back the French army. But Roland refused, disdaining to show fear in the face of the Saracens. Three times he denied Olivier's request, preparing for battle with these words:

"The king has left twenty thousand men here and not one coward among them. No sacrifice is too great for our homeland; we must be prepared to bear the evil with the good, shed our blood and, if need be, lay down our lives. Take up your lances as I shall take up my trusty sword Durandal. And if I should die, I want anyone who picks up my sword to be able to say: 'Here is a hero's sword!'"

Roland was brave and Olivier was wise. Both were heroes who, on horseback and with their swords in their hands, knew no fear no matter how fierce the battle. The enemy was drawing near; they could hear the thunder of horses' hooves and the clatter of arms, and then the Saracens appeared in view at the other end of the valley.

"Look," said Olivier, "just look, Roland, how many there are! And how quickly they draw near, while Charles is too far away to help us. If only you had blown your horn, Oliphant — had you done so, the king would have come back and we should be free of danger now. Look up ahead there, towards the Spanish passes, for which our army is making; we will never reach them, for we will not live to see this night. We are looking at those riders for the last time."

Turpin, the priest, came riding towards them up the hillside, spurring on his horse and shouting:

"The king sent us here and it is up to us to show bravery on his behalf. We cannot avoid this battle but, if we are to die, let us die like heroes and true warriors!"

The battle started. The adversaries rode out into the fray, in pairs; the gilding and the emeralds on the ornamented shields were broken off by wooden shafts; swords split armour, and splinters flew off the lances.

Meanwhile, far away from the battle, the king's army watched as a fierce storm broke out over France. Peals of thunder rang out, rain and sleet poured down from the sky as the gale gathered force, one lightning flash following immediately after another; there was not a house in the land whose walls did not crack under the mighty gusts of wind and the fearful downpour. It was noon, but there was darkness everywhere as in the middle of the night, only the lightning relieved the terrible blackness.

Without exception everyone was terrified and there were many who said: "This is the end of the world, Judgement Day is here!" No one knew that the elements were mourning the death of many young heroes.

The battle raged on. Roland attacked one adversary after another, warding off their blows. His friend Olivier, and Turpin the priest also, struck the enemy on every side. The Saracens fell from their horses and those who did not succeed in escaping could expect no mercy. Roland, Olivier and Turpin urged their men to further feats of valour, with tears rolling down their cheeks as they saw their army's determination not to retreat a single step, even though they were greatly outnumbered. It was a cruel and bloody engagement. Seeing the terrible carnage, Roland called out to Olivier:

"So many heroes now lie on the ground. Truly, we have reason to mourn for our homeland. She has lost many brave men this day, all because of base treachery!"

Roland then wanted to sound his horn, not to ask for help but rather for a just revenge. This time it was Olivier who disagreed: "When I suggested it, you scorned to do so. If Charles had been able to return to us, we need not have suffered such losses. But he is not responsible for what has happened!"

"Why are you so angry?" asked Roland.

"This is your fault, Roland," Olivier replied. "Bravery and folly are two different things — and discretion counts for more than pride. Oliphant will not help us now, for even if the king did come to our aid, he would arrive too late. Your courage, Roland, has brought about our destruction. Never again shall we be asked to help our country in her hour of need. Today will see the end of our old friendship; we shall say goodbye to each other before nightfall, and it will be a sad and cruel parting."

Turpin heard them arguing and, digging his golden spurs into his horse's flanks, he rode up and admonished them:

"Sir Roland, and you, Sir Olivier, I beseech you, do not waste time in argument! Indeed Oliphant will not help us now. But, though it be too late, sound it nevertheless, so the king may come back and avenge us. It is unthinkable that our foes should return home victorious. Our comrades will ride down from the passes and, finding us here in the grass, they will take our bodies away on mules and prevent the wolves and boars from scavenging. Let Charles see how foully Ganelon has betrayed him!"

"You have spoken well," said Roland, putting Oliphant to his lips and blowing with all his might.

The echo carried the sound of the horn a good thirty miles, over mountain and valley; King Charles heard it and knew at once that his rearguard had been ambushed. The French quickly turned their horses round; only Ganelon tried to persuade the king not to go back. Charles then realised that they had a traitor in their midst, and he had Ganelon ride ignominiously on a mule, while he made all haste back to the defile.

High were the mountains, dark and steep; deep were the valleys and wild the mountain streams. The trumpets sounded at the front and in the rear of the French army, answering Roland's horn. The king spurred on his horse, his riders no longer concealed their tears as they lamented and cursed the enemy. But neither laments nor curses could help. It was too late to assist the heroes — the army could not arrive in time to save them.

The king's long white beard streamed out like a banner as he rode. They all galloped as fast as they could, and there was not a single man who did not regret that they were not at Roland's side, helping him hold back the foe.

In the meantime only sixty of the faithful rearguard were left, and King Charles would never find better warriors than these. Roland looked round at the nearby slopes and hilltops — his dead companions lay everywhere. "I have never known heroes greater than you!" he lamented. "You have served your homeland well, and you have fought nobly for your king. Oh, beautiful land in the North, what a terrible loss you have suffered today! These heroes have died on my account, and I can do nothing now to save them!"

Again he plunged into the thick of battle, Durandal in his hand. Like hunted prey before a pack of hounds, the enemy fled to escape his blows. Olivier fell, still grasping his sword Hauteclaire, and Turpin, too, lay dead. But now the king's army was approaching. Hearing it, the Saracens all shot their arrows at Roland before turning to flee. Roland's shield shattered, his horse fell under him, and Roland himself wandered like a lost soul over the battlefield, looking for the bodies of his best friends, whom one by one he laid on the ground. He found Olivier last of all and placed him next to Turpin on top of a broken shield. His own strength was ebbing fast by this time, but he was still determined to die like a hero. He set out on foot after the retreating enemy, intending to fight again, but he had to stop

91

under a large tree in a clearing, unable to go on. He could not let his sword fall into the hands of the enemy, and so he tried to destroy it, striking the rock with Durandal until the sparks flew from the stone. The steel was left undamaged, however, and looking at his sword Roland lamented:

"Oh, Durandal, bright, glittering Durandal, how long is it since you were presented to me by King Charles! Together we have fought in many lands for the honour and glory of our country, in Provence and in Aquitania, in Flanders and in Bavaria, in Saxony and in Scotland. Despair fills my heart at the thought of the disgrace that would come to us if the enemy were to possess you."

Again and again he smote the rock with Durandal, but all in vain: the sword was unscathed. Roland was exhausted. Staggering to a lonely pine, he fell face forward on the earth, his hands buried in the pine needles that covered the ground. He put his sword and Oliphant under his body, lying there with his face towards the enemy so that everyone would see that he had not fallen while trying to escape but had died a victor.

It was there that King Charles discovered him. A warning horn was sounded, and the army spread out to look for the dead on the hillsides and in the gullies, so that all the bodies could be buried with honours. The king had Roland, Olivier and Turpin washed with wine and anointed with sweet-smelling ointments and wrapped in precious silks and covered with deerskins. Then each was placed on a waggon to be taken home, to France.

The army was preparing to set out on its way back to the frontier passes when two messengers appeared and rode quickly up to Charles to tell him that the Saracen emperor was leading another huge army towards them. It was as if a mighty flood were threatening to engulf them. Emperor Baligant's army included men whose names were well known from past campaigns — some of them were covered with bristles like pigs, their heads resting on their shoulders, apparently without necks; others had skin so thick that they needed neither helmets nor armour. They came from many distant lands, some from Jericho, some from Africa, others from Turkey and from Persia and some from the home of the Huns. Their trumpets sounded shrilly; the hooves of their horses raised great clouds of dust. They came surging across the broad plain, their banners fluttering, helmets shining, and metal ringing upon metal. But King Charles was undaunted and the desire to avenge the death of Roland gave him renewed strength. Plates fell from cuirasses; sparks were struck from armour; precious stones were hewn from intricate breast-plates struck to the ground. A knight, weakened by the blow of a sword, rode by, holding on to his horse's mane; a hero stood defending himself with a broken shaft. The son of the Saracen emperor had fallen, as well as the emperor's brother, yet the emperor himself still urged his riders forward. But then, when the battle was at its height, the emperor's banner was struck down, and the dragon insignia was trampled in the grass. The Saracens then gave way to panic, abandoning the field in hundreds. With curses on his lips, Emperor Baligant tried to stop them and make them fight, but he did not succeed. Charles pursued the Saracens back to Zaragoza, where he stormed the gates, and took the city.

Later the king returned to France and had the traitor tried.

"Judge him and give your verdict," he told his counsellors and judges. "Ganelon went to Spain with me and caused the death of twenty thousand of our finest warriors. He betrayed Roland, my nephew, and the wise Olivier, as well as the brave Turpin, with the most faithful of our friends. And all for gold and riches!"

Ganelon was tried and justly condemned; on a meadow below the city he was quartered by four horses, and thus was brought to an end the sad story of the faithful Roland.

HOW BERTHA BECAME QUEEN

The French King Pipin was a man of great courage, and he had been from his earliest youth. As a little boy he lived in his father's palace, in the garden of which there was a lion in a wooden cage. One day the wild beast smashed the bars of its cage and escaped. Even the bravest courtiers ran away and climbed trees for safety. Only Pipin showed no fear and when the lion attacked two helpless children, he defended them with his sword and drove the beast away.

Pipin was eventually crowned King of France. It was not thought fit for a king to rule alone, and so all his counsellors recommended that he marry as soon as possible, saying the country needed a queen as well as a king. For a long time Pipin was unable to choose a queen, until a minstrel told him of the beautiful Bertha, daughter of the King of Hungary. She was a wise young woman and kind, her only defect being somewhat large feet. The king thought it over and called his most intimate advisors to ask their opinion. They agreed that if Bertha were really so wise and good and beautiful, such a slight physical defect was of no consequence. Bertha should be invited to Paris.

Pipin had thirty horses laden with gold and silver; twelve messengers were dressed in the finest clothes and, taking with them their best weapons, painted shields and golden swords, as well as helmets studded with precious stones, they set out for Hungary. Bertha at first refused to go to Paris, but her parents reassured her. "Do not cry," they said. "However much you may regret leaving home, sweet France will give you rich compensation, for there is no more beautiful land anywhere in the world. And we shall think of you very often."

And so the girl set out for France. After several days the procession stopped in Mainz, where they called on the duke. He was astonished at the sight of Bertha, for he had a daughter by the name of Aliste, who resembled her so much that they might have been twin sisters. Bertha was overjoyed at having a new friend, and she asked the duke's daughter to accompany her to Paris as her lady-in-waiting. Aliste accepted gladly and prepared to leave with her new mistress. On reaching Paris the young Bertha was so tired after her long journey that she asked Aliste to appear before the king in her place. Aliste willingly put on the princess' best clothes and went to the royal chamber for the reception. She enjoyed being at the king's side so much that she wanted to remain there forever, and so Aliste bribed two servants to take Bertha far out of Paris and kill her. The servants bound Bertha and secretly left the palace with her, riding away to a large forest. There they untied their prisoner and were about to kill her, but her beauty made them relent and they could not harm her. Leaving her unprotected in the forest, they hurried back to Paris.

Bertha, all alone, wept bitterly, not knowing where to turn. On every side she was surrounded by thick undergrowth, ferns grew as high as her waist, and the eyes of wild beasts glowed in the bracken and in the swamps. Bertha did not dare to leave the little clearing in which the two men had left her. She called for help, but no one heard her and so no one answered.

Night fell and it grew dark. A wind blew, bending the trees so that the boughs creaked eerily, and owls hooted in the rustling leaves. Towards midnight a storm broke, and poor Bertha could find no shelter against the cold rain. Wolves howled in the darkness, getting nearer and nearer until they encircled the clearing. Bertha started running, though she knew not where; her bare feet were scratched by thorns; she stumbled through some marshy land and finally sank exhausted in the wet grass.

Then the wind died down and it stopped raining. The moon came out above the trees and Bertha, waking from a short, fretful sleep, saw the light and thought it was dawn.

"What am I to do?" she asked herself. "I'm so cold and hungry. Who will give me food and let me warm myself by a fire?" She thought of home and started crying again. "Oh, Mother," she lamented softly, afraid that the wolves might hear her if she spoke out loud, "and you, Father, how long ago it seems since you kissed me and stroked my cheek! We shall never meet again now. But, if I stay alive in this desolate place, I'll not put you to shame. I shall tell no one that I am the daughter of the King and Queen of Hungary, that I am Pipin's wife and the Queen of France."

As she sat sorrowing, the wind rose again, and it began to rain once more. Bertha hid in a thicket, her teeth chattering and her whole body trembling with the cold as she waited for the dawn. With the first morning light she left her hiding-place and wandered through the forest, sinking up to her knees in the marshes, pushing her way through thorny thickets and stumbling over the rotting trunks of fallen trees.

After some time she found a narrow path that led through the fir trees. It was an animal track by its appearance, for it had grown over with grass in places and in others it vanished from sight in the undergrowth. While her strength lasted Bertha followed the path as best she could; then, half-dead with cold and fatigue, she heard a dog bark somewhere ahead. Making a last effort she stumbled into a small clearing where she saw a humble cottage built of wood and earth. She got as far as the door and fell there, exhausted, unable even to knock.

Simon, the charcoal-burner, who lived in the cottage, found her there. He picked the girl up in his arms — she was as light as a feather — and carried her into his cottage, where his wife Constance laid her on some furs for warmth. The couple were so moved by the girl's beauty that tears sprang to their eyes, and they felt a great pity for her, seeing how woebegone and utterly spent she was.

When Bertha opened her eyes, they gave her something to eat and drink, and treated her as kindly as if they were her own father and mother. Bertha soon recovered and she rested in their cottage; when they discovered that she was all alone and had no one to turn to, they begged her to stay with them.

Bertha quickly made friends with Simon's two daughters, and the whole family loved her as if she were one of them. They gave her all the keys to the cottage, and looked after her when she happened to be ill. Bertha deserved all their devotion, for she was modest and good to everyone, and everyone loved her in return.

The years went by and Bertha lived happily in the charcoal-burner's cottage in the forest, but she never forgot Paris, and she often thought of her parents in Hungary. "Oh, Mother," she would sigh, when she was sure no one could hear her, "if only you knew how shamefully I was betrayed by my wicked lady-in-waiting!"

The Queen of Hungary had not forgotten her daughter and from time to time she would send a message to her in Paris. Aliste always replied with the utmost care, so as not to give herself away.

Nine and a half years had passed when the Queen of Hungary, who missed her daughter very much, decided that it was time for Bertha to pay a visit to her parents. She sent a message to her inviting her home, but the untruthful Aliste replied that she was ill and could not possibly undertake such a long journey. The queen grew most anxious.

"I shall go to Paris myself," she decided, refusing to listen to her husband's warnings about the discomforts of the journey. "If Bertha could endure the travelling, so can I," the queen declared. She asked for two hundred knights to be sent with her.

On her arrival in Paris the old queen went to the royal palace and demanded to be taken to Bertha. The guards told her that the queen was ill and not to be disturbed. The anxious mother, however, pushed them aside and went in search of her daughter. It was dark in the queen's chamber; the heavy curtains did not admit a single ray of light, and it was difficult to find the bed. The Hungarian queen groped her way forward and then sat on the edge of the bed, the tears running down her face as she embraced Aliste. She caressed her and whispered motherly endearments, but suddenly she was startled to discover that the sick young queen had small feet, like those of a child. The old queen rose, crossed over to the window, and swept aside the draperies. The

room filled with sunlight. The Queen of Hungary tore the blankets 🌿 99
away from the bed, looked at Aliste, and cried: "This is not my
daughter, Bertha!"

Aliste had no choice but to confess her evil deed to the king. Pipin
had both the treacherous servants brought to him and they went down
on their knees and begged his forgiveness, telling him that they had
not killed Bertha, as Aliste had intended, but only abandonded her in
the woods.

The king dismissed Aliste in disgrace, punished the two servants, and
accompanied by his knights rode out in search of his queen. They came
to the forest in which, ten years earlier, the two men had left the unfortunate Bertha. Although the woods were searched thoroughly, no
trace of her was found, and the king doubted if she could have survived
the many hazards she must have encountered.

Pipin's heart contracted with pain as the conviction grew in him that
he would never find his Bertha. Just then, as he rode out into a small
clearing, he saw a lovely girl carrying a pail of water from the well
to a nearby cottage. He spurred his horse, intending to ask whether
she knew anything about Bertha — but the girl, seeing him approach,
ran towards the charcoal-burner's house. As she ran before him, the
king noticed that she wore extraordinarily large clogs, and he rode
faster, catching up with her in front of the cottage.

The girl turned round to face him and Pipin, looking down at her from
the saddle, said:

"Tell me who you are. Answer me. I am the King of France."

Hearing this, Bertha stretched out her arms towards him, saying:

"Do not harm me, for I am Bertha, wife of Pipin and daughter of the
King and Queen of Hungary."

"I am Pipin!" cried the king, lifting her up and taking her to her mother
in his arms. The two women cried with joy as they fell into each other's
arms and embraced.

"Had you failed to find her," the Queen of Hungary said to Pipin,
"I swear I should have cut your head off with my own two hands!"

They rode back to the charcoal-burner's cottage, to tell Simon and his wife who Bertha really was. The poor man was deeply moved to learn that the girl he had rescued and sheltered in his home for ten years was the Queen of France. Simon was invited to Paris, where he was knighted by the king, and Pipin himself designed the charcoal-burner's coat-of-arms: a large golden flower in a blue field.

Celebrations were held, not only in Paris but throughout the whole land. All Frenchmen rejoiced, and the Parisians cheered Bertha so loudly that they could be heard four miles beyond the city gates. The Queen of Hungary stayed on as her daughter's guest for many days and, when she finally left, the most important French knights rode out with her on the first lap of the journey.

King Pipin and Queen Bertha lived happily together for a great many years. And shortly after their happy union, a son was born to them who was to become a great and famous king of France and one of her most renowned warriors.

WILLIAM SHORTNOSE

King Louis was renowned for his generosity, he frequently distributed gifts for faithful services, giving one noble a fine estate with ploughland and woods, another a splendid castle, a town, or perhaps a fort. All his noblemen received some gift from him, but there was one he forgot, and that the most loyal of all — William of Orange, or Marquis Shortnose, as he was called. William did not mean to be cheated of his rights, however, and he rode to Paris and asked for an audience.

"Sire," he said to the king, "I have served you well and often, not over a glass of wine or at the dinner-table, but with my fist and my sword! Not with songs, but in battle, when my country needed me!"

"Sir William," replied King Louis, "do have a little patience. Winter will soon be over and summer will put an end to your discontent. One of my faithful subjects is grievously sick. I doubt if he'll last much longer. When he dies I shall give you all his land, his castle, and, if you wish, his wife into the bargain."

William listened to his sovereign, scarcely able to contain his rage, his face growing redder and redder.

"It is a poor consolation to wait for another's misfortune!" he cried. "The road to happiness does not lead over the grief of others, and those who would seek it there have many a deep valley and craggy mountain to cross. I am a poor knight and do not even have fodder for my horse. I have served you for long, in good times and bad, and what have I received in return? What has been my reward? Just enough food and drink to keep me from starvation, no more! What have I gained for faithful service? Nothing but my sword wounds. My lance has unseated many an enemy on your behalf, and you do not give me so much as a piece of pointed iron to repair it! I say to you in the hearing of all: There is no justice in France!"

"Come, Sir William," said Louis, not daring to raise his head and look the enraged knight in the eye, "there are sixty others among my faithful friends who have not yet received any gift from me. For the time being I cannot even promise them anything."

"What, are there to be sixty rewarded before me?" cried William of Orange. "Which of them has done more for you than I? And if they think they are braver than I, let them mount their horses and ride out with me through the city gates to the meadow by the river! They can charge at me one after the other and I shall lay every single one out on the grass; you too may join them if you wish, my liege."

The king bent his head lower still and replied:

"Sir William, I see that you are angry. It is too true that the greater one's deeds, the scantier the reward. You have helped me and fought on my behalf as no one else has. I freely admit it. Come, step closer. I shall give you a worthy gift. Take the lands of the Duke of Fulk. You will then become the lord of three thousand horsemen."

"No, that I shall not do," said William, "for it would not be just. The good duke has left two small children, and they alone have a right to their father's castle, no one else! I cannot turn them out of their home."

"Sir William," said the king, "if you will not have Fulk Castle, then take the estates of Aubry of Burgundy. And marry his widow; she's a good and virtuous woman who never tasted a sip of wine. You will be the lord of a fine castle with three thousand knights to do your bidding."

"No," said William, "for the duke died and left behind a son by the name of Robert; he is yet so small that he cannot dress himself, but he will grow up and become a man — let him then have charge of his

 103
own castle and the command of his knights."

"Sir William," said the king once more, "listen to me. If you're wise and yet refuse what I have just been offering you, will you accept a quarter of France with the towns and castles, knights and commoners that go with it, as well as a quarter of my royal treasure and my stables. You cannot refuse such a generous gift."

"No!" exclaimed William. "No, no, no! You have no right to dismember France like that, though you are her king. Not for all the gold in the world would I accept such a gift. I don't want people to say that I've won the kingdom for my king only to take a quarter of it away from him again. I don't want them to sing malicious songs about Marquis Shortnose who snatched the last morsel of food from his sovereign's mouth and left him nothing but water."

"Sir William," said the king, quite at a loss, "if you refuse to take this gift, I really don't know what else to offer you. You tell me what you would like to have for your loyal service."

"My lord," replied William, "am I to beg and demean myself? Give me the town of Nîmes, that is held by the enemy. There being no other knight capable of driving out the Saracens and restoring Nîmes to our king and country, I shall go and conquer it for you. That is the only kind of gift that has any value. A gift I must first win back, not for myself, but for you and our homeland!"

The king agreed, giving William his royal glove as a token that he was setting out to fight on the king's behalf. William gathered together the younger sons of many needy knights and nobles, as well as some country squires; they had neither jewel-studded helmets nor gold-embroidered banners, nor even suits of glittering armour; some brought donkeys and mules instead of fleet-footed horses, and so equipped they took the road to Nîmes. They marched across the plains and along forest paths through the hills, in shade and blazing sunshine, past castles, villages and cities, singing and calling out to one another. In an olive grove outside Nîmes they met a man leading four oxen. The animals drew a wooden cart carrying a large barrel of salt, and on top of the barrel sat three tousled children, who laughed loudly and shouted at the soldiers.

William ordered the man to stop and the soldiers gathered round to find out where he had come from. The man said he came from Nîmes, where he was allowed to come and go whenever he chose, since he was poor and carried no arms. They questioned him about the strength of the Saracen army in the town and about its fortifications, and the man told them everthing they wished to know. William then called his friends to him and, pointing to the cart with its large wooden wheels, he said:

"Now listen to what I say. If one had a thousand such barrels, a knight could be concealed in each one; these could then be loaded upon carts and taken into the town. At a given signal the warriors would all come out of hiding and easily defeat the enemy."

William's men agreed to try this strategy, and said: "There are countless carts and similar vehicles, large and small, in this region. Let us try and put this plan into effect."

William turned his army round, and they marched back to the nearest village. There they pitched camp, and scoured the countryside for cattle, bulls as well as cows and oxen, carts and barrels of every size and description — large salt barrels, small wine barrels and even very small olive barrels. When they had collected enough of them, they loaded them on to the carts, and one man armed with a sword climbed into each barrel. The barrels that were left over were filled with wooden lances and shields, and signs were painted on the lids to show what was inside.

William Shortnose dressed himself as a merchant and, riding a lean, decrepit horse, set out at the head of the procession. He wore a pair of spurs more than thirty years old on his tough leather boots, and a pair of blue breeches held up by a leather belt in which he thrust a knife in a sheath. His hat was old and battered — they could not find a better one in any of the villages.

The sentries saw the procession coming from afar, and a report soon spread through the town of the approach of a merchant with a large supply of goods, so that people hurried out on to the town walls to look at the riches that were to be offered for sale. The caravan halted by the city gates, and the sentries called out to William:

"What is it you're carrying, merchant?"

"I bring you cloth," replied William, "brown and blue, green and scarlet. We also have helmets and breast-plates, reinforced shirts of mail, swords and shields and lances; you can take your pick. And I have saffron and mercury, alum and pepper, hides and furs. Let us stay in your town until tomorrow noon, for we would like to rest and to sell as many of our wares as we can."

"The gates stand open," said the sentries. "You may enter the town. We have need of your goods."

The caravan moved on, the oxen pulling their carts inside the town walls. The wooden wheels rattled on the cobbles, windows were thrown open and inquisitive heads appeared to look at the merchant. Crowds of people ran out into the streets and accompanied the carts as they drove to the palace. In the courtyard William dismounted; he jumped down on the green marble stairs and asked the guards whether he could have permission to sell his wares in Nîmes.

They took him to King Otranto, who at once began to question him:

"Where have you come from, worthy merchant?"

"From England, my lord," replied William, bowing low before the Saracen ruler.

"And where have you gained such fine merchandise?"

"That I will gladly tell you, my lord," said William obligingly. "I have travelled in many lands and over many seas, buying and selling in France and Lombardy, in Calabria, Germany and Tuscany, in Normandy and in Spain, in England and Scotland. I am at home in all these countries, nor am I a stranger in the palaces of Venice."

"Ah, no wonder," said the king with a sigh. "You are even richer than I."

William went on describing his voyages, and the king listened. But suddenly he interrupted:

"Tell me, merchant, how did you come by that scar on your nose? It must have been a nasty blow. William, Marquis of Orange, who is an advisor of the French king, Louis, has a nose such as yours; if I had him here before me instead of you, he would fare ill at my hands, for he is helping the King of France, my chief enemy. Without William's aid, Louis would have lost both his crown and his glory long ago."

"My lord," said William quickly, "allow me to tell you how I came by this scar. It is no secret; when still a little boy I was playing with my friends one day, and one of them injured me thus with a knife."

The king rose to his feet and, inspecting William with a frown, stepped up to him and said, in a voice tinged with suspicion:

"If you have all these splendid wares, merchant, why is it you're dressed so strangely? Why do your sons have such huge shoes, and coats full of holes? Surely the sons of a great merchant do not act as drovers and cartmen."

He stepped closer and, grasping William's white beard, shook it vigorously so that a piece of it remained clutched in his fist.

William stepped back and cried:

"All right, I'll tell you why my men have old leather shoes and coats full of holes, why I myself am wearing blue breeches, a battered hat, and a pair of spurs more than thirty years old: I am William, Marquis Shortnose, and I let no man who insults me go unpunished!"

Running out of the royal audience chamber he put his horn to his lips and blew it three times in succession, the sound carrying through the palace and into the streets of the town.

The warriors hidden inside the barrels heard it, drew their swords, and leapt out of their hiding-places, shouting the royal battle-cry.

The town's defenders were taken completely by surprise. They had not time to saddle their horses, much less to put on their armour. William therefore took Nîmes without bloodshed. His people occupied the watchtowers and entered the palace, its halls and cellars, where they

found sufficient wine and cheese, as well as other provisions, to last them six years under siege.

They took command of the fortifications, opened the city gates, and blew their horns. This was a signal for the remaining knights and riders, who had remained concealed in a wood outside the town, to come and join them. They rejoiced at their easy victory, and there was much drinking and singing. When the villagers came for their animals, their carts and barrels, William returned everything and richly rewarded them for their assistance. William then sent a fast courier to Paris to give the king the joyful news that Nîmes had fallen. Louis was extremely pleased, and there was much rejoicing at his court as well as throughout the entire land.

And William of Orange, Marquis Shortnose, was able to keep his just reward for the long and faithful service he had given to King Louis.

R
ENAUD OF MONTAUBAN
AND HIS BROTHERS

During the reign of King Charles of France all the French nobles, famous
warriors and faithful knights who had fought to defend their country
were invited to the court one year to celebrate Easter with their sovereign. They all came in answer to his invitation, except one: Boves of
Egremont. This infuriated King Charles, whose displeasure fell upon
the whole house, including the rebellious lord's brother, Aymon, and
his four sons: the eldest, Renaud, Alard, Guiscard, and the youngest,
Richard. Instead of presenting them with knights' golden spurs, the
king drove them from his palace. The four brothers were only able to
save their lives by fleeing on Bayard, Renaud's faithful steed.

110 For seven years they hid in the Forest of Arden. They grew thin, un-
kempt and sallow, their clothes were rags and they wore their rusty
shirts of mail next to their skins — this chilled them rather than kept
them warm, but it gave some protection against the icy wind. In the
rainy autumn season and during the winter snowstorms and gales they
sheltered, each under a different tree, with their shields on their shoulders. The branches of the fir trees were their only shelter when they
slept, and the weakest of the four brothers was kept warm by Bayard's
comforting breath. The brothers wandered aimlessly about the woods
in the endless days of winter; their only wish was to prevent themselves
from being cold, but the frost sparkled, dazzling them, the cutting wind
made all their limbs tremble, their rusty armour was like a shell of ice,
and the last remnants of their hope and courage dwindled slowly.

One day in the spring, when the last traces of snow had melted in the
forest and the sky was blue and cloudless, Renaud addressed his three
brothers:

"My heart grows heavy when I see what a terrible plight you are in; your
misery, not my own, makes me suffer. We have suffered many torments
in the Forest of Arden, and we cannot go on living like this, not knowing
what is to become of us tomorrow or the day after. The king's men are
sure to catch us sooner or later, if we stay here. We must do something
to overcome our misfortune."

They decided to journey southwards and when they set out they were
joined by their cousin Malgis, who knew a great deal of magic. The five
of them reached a desolate part of the country, where they built the
Castle of Montauban.

King Charles learned of this, and led a large expedition to the South,
to try to punish the brothers once more; for he could not bear to think
that they had dared to defy him by refusing to bow before his mighty
power. But Montauban was secure against any enemy, and neither
force nor cunning brought Charles victory. The four brothers and their
cousin Malgis asked for nothing more than justice and the redressing
of old wrongs, but the king was merciless and would not make peace

with them before he had meted out some punishment. Many times they were hard pressed by the king's men, but cousin Malgis always came to the rescue with his magic tricks, or faithful Bayard carried them to safety on his back.

When things were at their worst, Malgis secretly made his way into the enemy camp and gave the king some magic wine to drink. The magic potion caused Charles to be carried in his sleep to Montauban. And as he lay, still sleeping peacefully in one of the castle chambers, the four brothers discussed what they were to do with him.

"Now, my brothers," said Renaud, "we have the king at our mercy and we must decide how we are to treat him. He has brought us untold suffering; we had nowhere to lay our heads and knew much hunger and want through his injustice. And how he hates us! All this because we demanded our rights and refused to bow before him when he was unjust."

The youngest of the four brothers, Richard, said: "Let us deal with him as he would have dealt with us. An eye for an eye — what could be more just?"

Renaud considered this, and seeing him hesitate, Richard cried: "Why this indecision, Renaud? If you do not wish to punish Charles, I'll do it myself; heaven knows I have reason enough!"

Renaud looked at his brother with a stern expression and said: "We all have good reason to be revenged on the king, brother. But we must try to arrange a reconciliation. Charles' counsellors are on our side and they are trying to persuade him to stop waging this war against us. Should we kill the king now, all France will condemn our deed, and those who were our friends will become our sworn enemies. The king must be made to see that he has done us wrong."

They spent a long time talking and arguing, and they were unable to come to any agreement on their course of action.

In the meantime the candle in the neighbouring chamber burned low, the sun came out, and King Charles awoke. Looking round in some perplexity, he realised that he was in a strange bedroom. He got up and, crossing to the window, looked down at the courtyard and the countryside. One glance was enough to tell him that he was at Montauban, the castle belonging to Renaud and his brothers. It occurred to him that this must be Malgis' doing, and he ran frantically about the room, tearing his hair and swearing revenge against Malgis.

The brothers in the next room heard the king moving about and Richard, hearing the curses against Malgis, burst into the bedchamber.

"Is it so," he exclaimed angrily, "that even now you're threatening us, promising us the direst punishment! Had it not been for Renaud, you'd be shorter by a head already, take my word for it! You are our prisoner, and you know very well that prisoners often come to a bad end."

Richard's brothers ran in after him, and Renaud tried to calm him.

"Be silent, brother, not another word! It was our intention to speak differently to the king, without any threats and violence."

Renaud then turned to the king and said: "Sire, the war has gone on much too long, and we have suffered a great deal. Many brave men have died in battle. We are prepared to do anything you say — anything, that is, except giving up our demands for justice. I offer you my castle, Montauban, and everything I possess; I'm willing to depart from France forever, leaving all behind; only let us put an end to this senseless slaughter. Let there be peace between us at last!"

Charles heard him out, his eyes narrowed, his teeth clenched. When Renaud had finished, he raised his hand and said:

"Conciliation is unthinkable unless you hand Malgis over to me for punishment. His life is forfeit; he must be burned and his ashes thrown to the winds so that no trace remains to show that he ever lived!"

"Your Majesty," replied Renaud unhappily, "how can I do as you suggest? Malgis has proved so staunch a friend in adversity, helping us over and over again when we were all but lost. Do not ask us to hand him over to you, for that is something we can never do. However much we may desire reconciliation and peace, we cannot buy these with our honour, Sire."

"Then it is futile to discuss the matter further," said the king curtly. "Malgis has offended his sovereign, ridiculing him by dint of his magic tricks, and such treachery cannot be forgiven. If you refuse to hand him over to me, I shall raze Montauban to the ground and bring every one of you to heel. That I swear."

Renaud hung his head, for he realised that it was useless to argue. "Sire," he said, "you are our king and supreme lord, and we request no more than mere justice. Go, the gates are open."

"What's that you say, brother?" cried Richard, unwilling to believe his ears. "Charles is proud; he offers us nothing but further privation and war. Never has he shown the slightest good will, and from his lips we have heard only threats and still more threats. You wished to be reconciled with him; yet, if you release him now, you'll gain further bloodshed and death, nothing else! Just think how he has dealt with us — remember the Forest of Arden! Let me take him out of the castle and give him his just deserts, as I would the meanest thief!"

At this Charles clenched his fists, and Renaud exclaimed wrathfully: "Be quiet, brother, say no more! The king is our guest and is free to leave Montauban whenever he pleases."

He went out and gave orders for a horse to be saddled, and men helped Charles to mount. The king rode slowly to the gates and then, digging his golden spurs into the horse's flanks, galloped away from the stronghold of his enemies.

When he reached his camp, all his followers came out to greet him, and they asked: "Tell us, Sire, is there to be peace at last?"

"There will be no peace," the king replied, "until the sons of Aymon surrender that accursed scoundrel and sorcerer, Malgis, to me. Now listen to my command: this day we'll lay siege to Montauban. If the brothers refuse to yield, we shall scale the walls and storm the gates; and should they beat us back, we'll simply starve them out, not withdrawing from Montauban until we have brought our campaign to a successful conclusion. Then we can think of peace, but not before!"

And so the catapults again hurled large rocks and stones at Montauban, again they beat a tattoo on the walls and cobbles, damaging roofs, houses and towers. The days passed, and weeks, and months. Not a grain of corn was left in the castle, and the only remaining horse was

Bayard, Renaud's thoroughbred. The defenders of Montauban could not bring themselves to kill him; whenever they entered his stable and heard him neigh, their courage evaporated and their hands dropped helplessly to their sides. Renaud's friends did not know what to do, for the shortage of food was becoming really acute now. In the end Alard suggested that they bleed the horse and drink his blood. This helped to assuage their hunger for a full two weeks, at the end of which time Bayard grew so weak and lean that he could scarcely stand. He waited by his empty trough, his head down between his front legs, and he only gave a faint whinny whenever any of the brothers came to see him.

When their plight was at its worst, an old man came to Renaud, a former gardener who lived at the castle. Now he too was emaciated, dragging himself along with difficulty.

"My lord," he said to Renaud, "forgive an old man's faulty memory. This morning I suddenly remembered that we dug a long underground passage when the castle was being built. It starts in the cellars and leads right through the rocks and out into some distant woods. If it has not been filled, we ought to be able to escape that way."

Renaud was overjoyed to hear this, and he called his brothers together. They brought Bayard out of his stable and, gathering all the defenders of Montauban round them, entered the dark subterranean passage. They managed to escape and travelled a long distance to Dortmund, where they were recived with great honours by the lord of the castle. King Charles found Montauban quite empty when at last he entered it; his rage increased still further, and he and his army set out at once in pursuit of the fugitives.

Discovering their new sanctuary, he besieged the castle, allowing no one to enter or leave. Then he held a council of war, and he asked his counsellors: "What are we to do with Renaud and his brothers?"

"Sire," said the eldest counsellor, an aged knight with a long white beard, "permit me to give you good advice: make your peace with them."

When he had finished speaking, the king's nephew, Roland, said:

"My lord, if you do not make your peace with Renaud, I shall leave your service. You have wronged the brothers, and if they now seek reconciliation, you must not refuse."

"I shall go with Roland," cried Turpin, and Olivier spoke in the same vein. Their attitude angered Charles so much that he was left almost speechless. He still wished to get his own way, unwilling to come to terms with Renaud, whatever the consequences.

Roland looked from one of the king's knights to another and said: "Many are the occasions on which Renaud offered us his friendship, yet we refused every time. And still Charles would continue the feud that should never have started." Turning angrily to the pale king, he went on: "Enough of this injustice, my lord. I am leaving. What about you, Ogier? Will you come with me?"

"Yes, I'm coming with you," replied the Danish knight Ogier, "and all my people too. Renaud will receive us with open arms."

"And I," said Olivier, stepping up to Roland's side, "I, too, am coming. This we should have done long ago."

Now others followed suit, until King Charles was left all alone. He mused for a long time, and then sent for his advisors once more.

"You wanted reconciliation, and you shall have it. But I loathe Renaud so bitterly that I never wish to see him again. Go and convey my conditions to him: he is to leave France for a time and relinquish Bayard to me, nothing more. Which of you will go and give him my message?"

"I, Sire," said his eldest counsellor, "I shall go to Renaud and acquaint him with your will."

And so it came to pass. Renaud listened to the king's terms, embraced the old knight, and went to the stable for Bayard. Tears ran down his face as he led the horse out, for he was loth to part with him. The old counsellor took the horse's reins and walked slowly back with him to Charles' camp. The four brothers gazed after the knight and the horse from the battlements and wept silent tears.

The awful war thus came to an end.

Renaud laid aside his sword and armour and, taking leave of his brothers, left Dortmund, with Malgis. His brothers accompanied them as far as the city gates, embracing Renaud again and again before they too departed to return to Montauban to repair the ravages of war. King Charles also struck camp and marched towards Liege.

When his army arrived at the Mose river, he called a halt and ordered his knights to bring Bayard to him. Renaud's horse reared up on his hind legs and would not let anyone saddle him; he struck out ferociously with his hooves, his mane flowing in the wind. At last they brought him to the king, who had a mill wheel tied to the horse's neck, and they gave instructions for him to be thrown in the river. So they led the horse to the middle of the bridge and cast him over the parapet. Bayard fell into the surging waters.

"I've sworn revenge on you," cried the king, "and now I've accomplished it. Now at last I can sleep in peace."

The king's followers turned away, not wishing to witness Bayard's end, but then Charles cried out in amazement and they all looked.

Bayard had gone under, but then he had broken the mill wheel in two with his hooves, had risen to the surface again and, his head held above the water, had swum over to the opposite shore. There he climbed out of the river, stood still for a moment, a fine, strong stallion. Then he neighed, reared up, and broke into a trot, disappearing from sight in the thickets growing at the edge of the wood.

Bayard thus saved himself. He made his way to the Forest of Arden, where he had found shelter with Renaud and his brothers many years ago, and legend has it that he roams the woods to this day.

Renaud and his cousin Malgis travelled in many lands and had many adventures. Day followed day, week followed week, and month followed month. At last they decided it was safe to return home once more; Malgis went back to his native Dordonne and Renaud to Montauban. News of his coming preceded him and reached his brothers Alard, Guiscard, and Richard, who rode out to meet him. Overjoyed, they embraced Renaud lovingly, and together all four made their way to their castle.

Renaud listened as his brothers told him what had happened at Montauban since he went away, and then they listened in their turn to his account of his exploits abroad. Hearing that his faithful Bayard had escaped the king's revenge and was living in the forests, Renaud wished to go and find him. One night, when all the others were fast asleep, he got up, put on some simple clothes and, unseen by anyone, went downstairs and out to the gate. There he called the guard, who approached and, recognising Renaud, asked:

"Where are you going, my lord? It is not safe to go out unarmed like this. I'll call your brothers . . ."

"No, friend, do not do that," said Renaud mildly. "Tomorrow morning just tell them that I send my greetings and wish them to remember me with kindness." Renaud pulled a gold ring off his finger and gave it to the guard, saying: "Take this ring as a token of my friendship. You have served me well." The guard could not keep back the tears as he thanked Renaud for his gift and took leave of him.

The sun came out next morning, and the brothers awoke to find Renaud's bed empty. They asked one another where he had gone, they searched everywhere, but their eldest brother was not to be found at Montauban. He had left his breast-plate, his shaft and his lance, his sword and shield, iron boots and golden spurs behind. They questioned the guard, who told them what he knew and showed them the ring. Mounting their horses, the three brothers looked for Renaud all that day in the neighbourhood, but when evening came they returned to Montauban without having found the slightest trace of him.

Renaud was a long way away by then, walking through deep forests by day and along the roads by night; he lived on mulberries, garlic, and wild apples, he drank water from the streams and slept in the shade of the rocks.

Thus he made his way to the Forest of Arden, that huge forest with a river on either side. And one morning he at last heard the distant beat of hooves, and the breeze carried to his ears the sound of a horse neighing.

Renaud smiled and, walking quickly towards his desired goal, he continued his journey, his heart full of joy and peace.

H UON AND AUBERON

Huon and Gérard, the two sons of Seugin, Duke of Bordeaux, were on their way to Paris, to the king's court. Both were very young — Huon a mere lad, Gérard scarcely more than a child. The sun was shining brightly, and Huon sang as he rode, his spirits undaunted even though he was covered with dust from head to foot. Gérard, on the other hand, rode his horse in silence, his head bent, for he could not rid himself of an evil presentiment as he listened to his brother's merry voice.

When they reached a small wood on the outskirts of Paris, a band of armed riders suddenly appeared from a hiding-place and came riding towards them. One of them attacked Gérard, who had neither a sword nor a lance and was taken quite unawares. Before he was able to raise a hand in his defence, the young lad was struck down from his horse and remained lying in the grass. Huon now turned upon the attacker, striking out ferociously with his sword and piercing the other's heart. At this the other riders fled, and the skirmish was over. Huon saw to his relief that Gérard had not been seriously hurt and helped his younger brother into the saddle. But alas, the dead assailant was none other than Charlot, the king's son. The traitor, Amaury, had set him against the two brothers, falsely claiming that they refused to submit to the king's authority. The king had to punish Huon but, being a just ruler, he commanded Amaury to fight with the lad, to show which of them had been in the right.

Huon and his adversary fought in front of the entire royal court, and their duel seemed endless. A hundred times they charged at each other on horseback, and then they fought on foot, with only their swords in their hands, and still the issue had not been decided. But then Huon struck Amaury down with his sword, thus proving to the court that he had been falsely accused and had every right to defend himself against Charlot's attack.

The king, however, was loth to accept such a decision, and he sent Huon on a mission to far-away Babylon; Huon was to carry a message from the king to Gaudisse, the mighty emir of all the heathen. But he was also to cut off the head of the first heathen he met in the Babylonian ruler's palace, to kiss the emir's daughter three times, and to bring the French king the emir's beard and three of his molars as a trophy. Should he fail to accomplish these incredibly cruel and difficult tasks, Huon's own life would be forfeit.

Huon set on his journey. He rode and rode; he had never been so far away from sweet France and he felt very homesick for both his country and his mother. As he travelled through yet another foreign land he sighed, his head bent low and tears filling his eyes. All his companions were sorry for him; they had never seen their master so sad and forlorn before.

They were riding through a dense forest on their way to the Red Sea when, all of a sudden, a small dwarf, no taller than a three-year-old child but with a face as beautiful as the sun, appeared among the trees in front of them. His shoulders were draped with a glittering cloak embroidered with gold, and in his hands he held a bow with a silken bow-string. A horn made of gold and ivory hung round his neck.

"*Mon Dieu!*" exclaimed Huon. "Who is this creature coming towards us so unexpectedly?"

"It is a forest gnome and, doubtless, a sorcerer," his companions warned Huon. "Do not speak to him, in case we fall under his spell."

They halted, and the little man addressed them in these words:

"I greet you, who have entered my forest, and would have you greet me in return as your good friend."

The riders turned their horses round and took another path, to escape from any wicked magic tricks. But the dwarf raised his hand and touched his heart. At once a terrible storm broke out, the gale uprooted trees, birds were tossed about helplessly in the sky, and wild creatures of the forest scampered past, trying in vain to find some shelter from the raging elements. Huon and his men also fled, but they came to a wide river that had overflowed its banks and they could not find any means of crossing it. Turning back, they wandered about the forest for many wearying hours, until they found themselves back where they had started, with the little man standing in front of them and gazing at them silently.

"Sir," said Huon, "tell me why you have seen fit to molest us."

"It is all on your account," replied the dwarf. "I have the power to see inside every human soul. And as I see nothing but goodness and loyalty in you, I wish to offer you my services and my aid. Of course, you do not know, nor can you guess, who it is speaking to you. I am

Auberon; my father was a great warrior, my mother the fairest of all forest fairies. I was their first and only son, and when I was born four fairy godmothers came to my cradle. The first was not particularly wise, for she decided that I should be a dwarf all my life; I stopped growing at the age of three, and shall never grow any bigger than I am now. Yet, wishing to give me something good, she also decreed that I should be the most handsome of all creatures, as beautiful as the sun itself; and my face has always been as you see it now. The second godmother endowed me with the power to read people's hearts and minds; I no sooner look at someone than I know all his deeds and dreams, his wisdom as well as his crimes, his glory and all his sins, even those he is yet to commit and whose horror he is unconscious of. The third godmother gave me something even better than that: I am able to appear wherever I choose, in the most distant corner of the world or on a desert island far out in the middle of the ocean; and I can conjure up a splendid palace with tables laden with food and drink of every description whenever I please.

"The fourth fairy godmother also had a good heart, and she gave me a most unusual gift: in all the world there is not a single bird or beast who would not obey me when I speak. Even the most bloodthirsty of wild beasts becomes as gentle as a lamb at my command. And I shall never grow old, but shall remain as I am today. When my time to die comes, I shall have a seat at God's feet."

Huon was amazed to hear all this, and even more surprised when Auberon went on:

"I know you haven't eaten for three long days and that all your men are tired to death. Come, then, why don't you eat and drink your fill?"

No sooner had Auberon said this than a magnificent palace stood in front of the astonished knights, who went inside the great hall and found everything prepared for a feast, with whole rams being roasted on spits, and goblets filled with the choicest wines.

Huon felt a thrill of fear at sight of such miracles, and he asked Auberon for his permission to leave. But the dwarf had two more gifts for the young Frenchman before he left: a goblet, and a horn of gold and ivory.

"He who has a pure heart and lives in God's grace can drink from this goblet whenever he wishes and never drain it; as soon as it touches his lips, it fills up to the brim with wine."

Huon took the goblet from Auberon and put it to his lips, to try for himself. And, sure enough, as he lifted the goblet to his lips, it became full of wine and Huon drank thirstily. Then Auberon handed him the horn of gold and ivory that he had worn round his neck, and said:

"If you ever need my help, just blow this horn and I shall come to your assistance wherever you may be. And now you can leave. I shall detain you no longer."

They parted company and Auberon vanished. Huon, his mind full of the strange encounter, rode on with his companions. As he was little more than a boy, he could not resist the temptation to test the horn's magic powers. He blew it, and it was as if a great storm were approaching; they heard the thunderous beat of horses' hooves and the clatter of swords, and suddenly there stood in front of them ten thousand riders, all armed, with Auberon at their head.

"Forgive me," cried Huon, "I don't really need your help as yet!"

Auberon smiled. "I forgive you," he said, "but I feel sad when I think how many similar mistakes you will make in your life. Farewell. Continue your journey and keep well. And do not forget you're taking with you not only my goblet and my horn of gold and ivory, but also my heart."

They parted company, and Huon travelled on to Babylon, where, with Auberon's assistance, he successfully carried out all the tasks set him by the King of France, before returning home with the beautiful Esclarmonde, the daughter of the Babylonian king.

TRISTRAM AND ISEULT

In a time long ago there lived in Cornwall a king by the name of Marc, and his nephew Tristram. The boy served his uncle as a harp player, hunter and faithful vassal. He accompanied the king to the council chamber as well as to the hunt. At night he slept with the other counsellors in the royal apartments, and when the king felt sad Tristram played on the harp for him to raise his spirits and drive away his sorrow. When he grew to manhood, Tristram carried out many heroic deeds on behalf of his sovereign, thus showing him his respect and his gratitude.

One day the mighty Irish lord Morholt proclaimed King Marc his

One day the mighty Irish lord Morholt proclaimed King Marc his vassal and demanded that he pay a heavy tribute: three hundred talents of copper the first year, three hundred talents of silver the second year, three hundred talents of gold the third year and, most cruel of all, three hundred maids and youths from Cornwall's leading families in the fourth year. King Marc refused, and Morholt at once began to prepare a large fleet to attack Cornwall, to make the Cornish ruler obey his will by force of arms. But the young Tristram sought King Marc's permission to challenge Morholt in single combat and, matching himself against the Irish lord on a barren island, he split Morholt's skull with his sword.

Tristram did not survive the duel unscathed, however, being badly injured by the poisoned head of Morholt's lance. For seven days and seven nights Tristram floated on the sea all alone in a small boat without sails and oars. He became so weak that he could not even lift his arms and he had to leave his tiny vessel at the mercy of the wind and the waves. He would have died if he had not been discovered by some fishermen on the dawn of the eighth day. They took him ashore and placed him in the care of their mistress, who was the only person in that port who knew of every healing herb and was able to cure every sickness and injury. Her name was Iseult the Goldenhaired and it was she who, with her medicines, saved Tristram's life.

When he had fully recovered, Tristram returned to Cornwall, where King Marc showered him with favours and tokens of great friendship. Tristram was held in such esteem that all the barons and counsellors who were close to the king began to fear that he might be appointed successor to the throne. Conferring together in secret, they urged King Marc to marry, recommending that he choose a well-born maiden who would give him a son to succeed him when he died. Tristram, too, added his voice to the barons', hoping to convince them that his affection for the king was based on pure and unselfish motives. King Marc gave in to their entreaties, promising to give them his final decision within forty days; but he was at a loss as to where to look for his future queen. As he paced to and fro about the palace, lost in thought, he suddenly caught sight of two swallows flying in through the window. One of them dropped a long hair at the king's feet — it gleamed like like a ray of sunlight that pierces the clouds.

Marc picked the hair up and admired its beautiful colour and fine texture. Then he sent for his counsellors and said:

"I have decided to take your advice. However, I shall take as my queen no one else but the woman to whom this golden hair belongs."

They asked who that lady was, being eager to send for her and hold the royal wedding. And when the king revealed that he did not know, they suspected a trick was being played on them and became angry with Tristram once more, for they believed he had planned it. But Tristram remembered Iseult the Goldenhaired and promised to bring her to the king, though he knew that he was embarking on a dangerous expedition.

He prepared a ship and sailed for Ireland, making for the port in which Iseult had saved him from certain death. His journey was fraught with peril and, on arriving in Ireland, he challenged to a duel a monster who had been terrorising the land by demanding daily the lives of several helpless maidens. After a gruelling fight, Tristram killed the monster. When asked by the grateful citizens what he wished to have as a reward for his bravery, he demanded Iseult's hand in marriage for the King of Cornwall. As Iseult was the daughter of the King of Ireland, the monarch himself placed her hand in Tristram's, to signify that he was to take her to his king. Once Iseult became Marc's queen, all enmity between the two countries would be at an end and they would at long last live together in peace and unity.

When it was time for Tristram and Iseult to leave, the Irish queen secretly plucked some herbs, roots and flowers, which she mixed with wine. Then, with the aid of incantations and spells, she made a magic potion. Calling to the maid-servant, Brangien, who was to accompany the queen's daughter to Cornwall, she said to her:

"I am entrusting you with this treasure, in which my daughter's whole future happiness is contained. It is a potion to ensure eternal love.

Those who drink it together, or even just moisten their lips with it, will be joined for the rest of their lives and no one will ever part them, by fair means or foul; they will remain together even in death. You must conceal this little bottle carefully and, before their wedding night, when the king and Iseult are alone together, pour some of the potion into their wine, destroying the rest. No one else must touch it, otherwise there will be untold misfortune."

Brangien promised to do exactly as her mistress bade her. She hid the bottle and looked after it as if it were her most prized possession.

When the time came for them to set sail, there was a sad leave-taking, and the farther they sailed from the Irish shores, the greater grew the distress in Iseult's heart. She would not speak to anyone, not even to Tristram, so unhappy was she at the thought that he was taking her away to become the wife of an unknown king who had for so many years been her father's enemy.

The voyage was long and the seas were rough, but then one day the wind died down and the sails drooped from the yard-arms in the heat of the sun. Tristram gave the order to go ashore on the nearest island, to rest after their arduous journey. All the sailors were glad to obey, and only Iseult and her youngest maid remained aboard. Seeing that, Tristram went back to the ship and tried to relieve Iseult's depression. But she remained sad and silent. The sun rose higher in the sky and the heat grew more oppressive, and so Tristram asked the young maid-servant for a cup of wine. The girl at first could not find any, but then she brought out a bottle with a dark red liquid in it, which she poured for them. This, however, was not ordinary wine but the magic potion which Iseult's mother had prepared for her daughter's wedding night. The thirsty Iseult drank deeply and then handed the cup to Tristram, who finished the wine, leaving not a single drop.

Brangien returned at that moment, and she saw Tristram and Iseult standing in the middle of the cabin, looking into each other's eyes; she spoke to them, but they did not hear her — it was as if they were the only two people in the world, alone in the middle of a huge desert.

Until that moment Iseult had wished fervently that she might learn to hate Tristram, but after drinking the potion she could not bear to be absent from him for even a second, her eyes brimming with tears whenever he had to leave her. Tristram was unhappier still, for he had hoped to bring King Marc a queen to show him his respect and fealty, and he suffered at the thought that Iseult would never be his own and that by loving her he was betraying his sovereign.

Only Brangien knew what had happened. For two whole days she watched them as they refused all food and drink, walked about as in a dream, hearing no one and speaking to no one, and seeking every opportunity they could find to be in each other's company. On the third day Tristram came to Iseult and asked her what made her so sad.

"Everything makes me sad," she replied, "the sky and the sea, as well as my every thought. Why did I ever have to meet you? Why did I cure you of your mortal wounds? Why did I not turn my back and leave you to die? And, having been saved, why did you have to return to Ireland?"

She went on lamenting for a long time, and Tristram's heart all but broke at the sight of her misery.

"Why are you so sad?" he asked again. Then Iseult looked in his eyes and replied simply: "I am sad because of my love for you."

They spoke no more; stepping forward, they embraced each other. Brangien threw herself down at their feet and confessed what she knew: that they had been enchanted by the magic potion in their wine, which should have been drunk by King Marc and Iseult on their wedding night, and that there was no power on earth which could lift the magic spell.

Tristram and Iseult listened to her, then they gazed at one another and embraced once more, this time as if they were trying to capture a whole lifetime, as if they could not bear to part.

And while their ship approached the Cornish coast, Tristram and Iseult, clasped in each other's arms, stood on board, anticipating the events to come — their misfortune, their love, and their death.

THE GREAT LOVE OF AUCASSIN AND NICOLETTE

Count Bougart of Valence made war against Count Garin of Biaucair, overrunning his domain and finally besieging his city with a hundred knights and ten thousand soldiers, who launched one attack after another against the town walls.

Count Garin of Biaucair fought valiantly, but he was distressed by his only son, Aucassin, who refused so much as to touch a sword. Aucassin would not take part in tournaments; he wanted neither to ride nor to fight, for he was deeply in love with a beautiful girl called Nicolette, and he could think of nothing else but his beloved. Both his father and mother pleaded with him, protesting that Nicolette was a common Saracen captive, but all Aucassin would say in reply was:

"I shall gladly take up arms and fight in the remotest part of the world, if only you give me Nicolette, whom I love."

His parents offered him the noblest daughters of France, but Aucassin would not deign to look at any of them. None, he felt sure, could compete with Nicolette — not even the Empress of Istanbul, the Queens of Germany or of Spain. Seeing that nothing would avert Aucassin from his wilful choice, his father went to one of his knights, in whose house Nicolette dwelt, and he asked the man, in the name of God, to kill the girl, for otherwise Aucassin would never be cured of his passion. The knight, however, was loath to slay Nicolette, but he promised to send her where she would never be seen by anyone again. He took the girl to the top floor of his palace and sealed the door of the chamber, which had one small window looking out over the garden and admitted only a little light and air.

The news of Nicolette's disappearance soon spread throughout the country. Some asserted that she had fled abroad; others said that Garin of Biaucair had her murdered so as to free his only son from his deep attachment. As soon as Aucassin heard the rumours he went to Nicolette's foster-father and asked him what had actually taken place. The knight carefully replied:

"My lord, Nicolette is not for you. I took her captive in a foreign land and have brought her up as if she were my own daughter. Now I would like to find her a husband who could earn a living by honest toil. She is not fit to be your wife. Marry a lady of noble birth and do not try to gain Nicolette by force, or your soul will go directly to hell."

"I have no desire for heaven," rejoined Aucassin. "All I want is Nicolette, nothing more. What would I do in paradise? That is a place for the sick and the lame, for old men in worn capes, for the naked and the barefoot who are dying of cold and thirst and hunger. What would

you have me do in such company? In hell I shall find wise masters and
brave knights who fell in battle or tournament, gay young lads and
noble gentlemen. There they have gold and silver and precious furs,
harp-players and minstrels and pipers by the dozen. With such as these
I wish to be, but only with my love Nicolette at my side."

The other grew sad at the young man's blasphemous obstinacy, saying:
"Go with God, for I cannot help you. Were I to give you Nicolette, your
father would have me burned, and Nicolette as well. You yourself
would have to fear for your life. I have no choice but to obey the
count's wishes."

During this time the enemy had laid siege to the finest and best fortified
castle in the land, and when Count Garin of Biaucair learned about this
he again urged his son to take up arms against their foe lest he lose his
entire heritage.

"I shall gladly take up arms and fight in the remotest part of the world,"
said Aucassin, "if only you give me Nicolette, whom I love."

His father became very angry at this and walked away in a rage. Aucassin
raised his head and called him back.

"Father," he said, "I'll go and fight the enemy, but under one condition:
that if I return alive and victorious, you'll allow me at least to see Nicolette. I'll speak just two or three words with her and go. All I want is
to assure myself that she is alive and well."

His father agreed, and Aucassin took the field, riding out of the city in
the saddle of his finest horse, well armed and well clad with a helmet
on his head and his sword at his side. It was not of the enemy and the
ensuing battle that he thought, however; his mind was full of Nicolette
as he rode, head bent and eyes on the ground. His horse carried him
straight into the thick of the fray, and since Aucassin sat in the saddle
as one in a dream, he was soon unhorsed and would have been killed
by his enemies — but before it was too late Aucassin recovered, realising
that if he let himself be put to death he would never set eyes on Nicolette again. The thought of her put fresh life into him, and the blood
coursed faster in his veins. Aucassin drew his sword and fought like

an enraged boar being mauled by mad dogs in the forest. He knocked ten enemy knights from their saddles, wounded seven of them, and finally captured Count Bougart of Valence. Bringing the prisoner to his father, he said:

"Here is the enemy who has caused you so much humiliation, Father. For twenty years the war did last, and only I have been able to put an end to it. In return I ask you to fulfil the promise you made me before I went to battle."

"I know of no promise," replied his father. "As for Nicolette, I'd rather have her burned at the stake than permit her to become your wife."

And the count gave immediate orders for Aucassin to be cast in the deepest dungeon and kept there in chains until he abandoned his foolish plan.

In the meantime Nicolette was thinking of her beloved, day and night. In the end her longing made her overcome all fear and throw precaution to the winds. One moonlit night in May she tied several sheets together, making herself a rope long enough to reach from her little window to the ground. Climbing down it, she gathered her skirts up to avoid the dew on the grass, and hurried to the dungeon in which Aucassin was being kept prisoner. She heard him at once, lamenting and calling out her name, and she called to him in reply and threw a lock of her hair through a grille in the dungeon wall.

Nicolette's escape was soon discovered and soldiers were told to search the streets of the city, with orders to capture and kill her. A guard, from his vantage point on the battlements of the tower, watched Nicolette as she spoke with her beloved Aucassin, and he also saw the soldiers approach and wanted to warn her, but there was not enough time for him to run down to where she knelt, pressed against the cold stone of the dungeon wall. The guard therefore started singing an ancient song, whose words conveyed a warning, and Nicolette understood. She hid in the shadows until the soldiers had marched by, before taking leave of Aucassin and, under cover of the darkness, she then ran to the castle walls. Finding a place where the wall was broken, she jumped down into the deep moat. She injured herself when she fell and began to bleed badly, but still she did not give up and, scrambling out of the moat, looked round for a suitable hiding-place. Some way off she saw the dark silhouette of a forest. She felt sure that it would be full of wild beasts and snakes, and even of boars and lions, but she was convinced that it would be safer there than within the walls of the city. She therefore made her way to the edge of the woods, where she lay down by a brook and fell asleep.

Some shepherds found her there next morning, and Nicolette begged them: "In the name of God, go quickly and tell Aucassin, the son of Count Garin of Biaucair, that a doe is waiting for him in the forest. Let him come at once and catch her. Once he has taken her, he will not give away a single one of her hooves for a hundred talents of gold, nay, not even for five hundred, not for anything in the world."

The shepherds only laughed, unable to believe that there might be such precious game in their forest. Only when she had given them a little money from her purse did they promise to deliver her message if they chanced to meet Aucassin. They would not go into the city, however, for they were afraid of Count Garin's wrath should they be caught trying to communicate with his imprisoned son.

Nicolette thanked them and walked deeper into the forest. In a little clearing among the bushes she started building an arbour of leaves and lily blossom, in which to welcome her beloved.

The news spread that Nicolette had disappeared again. Some asserted that she had fled the country; others said that she had been murdered on the orders of Count Garin, who wished to save his son from making an unequal marriage. As soon as the count heard the rumours he had Aucassin brought out of the dungeon. Aucassin, however, did nothing but mourn his loss; his grief was unrelieved by splendid feasts and the company of all the brave knights and most beautiful maidens of the land. He wandered by himself through deserted halls and along lonely paths, lamenting his lost Nicolette. One day he wandered as far as the edge of the forest, where the shepherds were resting, eating bread and drinking wine and being merry together. Seeing how sad Aucassin was, they tried to cheer him with a song about a blue-eyed, fair-haired girl who had given them money for their bread, wine and cakes. It occurred to Aucassin that the girl might be none other than Nicolette, and he asked them to repeat their song, but the shepherds would not; only when he had brought out his purse and given them a handful of gold coins did they tell him about the white doe he was to hunt. They told him if he managed to catch her, he would not give her up for anything in the world.

Aucassin knew at once who the doe was meant to be. He hastened into the forest, cutting his way through brambles and thorns, but he failed to find the doe. It was growing dark when he came across a bedraggled man, walking towards him along a path that wound its way between the trees. The man was very ugly and blacker than a charcoal pile, and he used a huge cudgel as a stick to support him. When he saw that Aucassin was weeping, the man asked him why he was so sad.

"Why should I not weep," replied Aucassin, "when while hunting I have lost my white greyhound, the most beautiful creature in the world?"

"So much grief for a mere dog?" said the man incredulously. "Surely your father has enough money to buy you a whole pack of dogs in place of the one you have lost. What am I to say? I am in the service of a squire, and I was ploughing with four oxen when one of the animals, the finest of the four, went astray. My mother is very poor, for the squire has taken everything from her; she sleeps on the straw and I am wandering about the woods to escape the squire's revenge — if he catches me he will have me hanged. I cannot go home until I have paid him for the loss of his ox. And you're weeping for a dog! Cursed be he who holds you in esteem!"

At this Aucassin gave the man twenty pieces of gold from his purse to pay the squire, and they parted company.

"Thank you, my lord!" the ploughman called after him. "May you too find what you're looking for!"

Aucassin went on, and before long he saw in front of him a small arbour made of leaves and lily blossom. And in it he found his beloved Nicolette.

They kissed and embraced each other fondly, and their joy knew no bounds. Unwilling to fall into the hands of Aucassin's father, they decided to seek refuge in a foreign land.

Early next morning they set out on their journey, travelling over hill and dale before they reached the sandy shores of a great sea. There they embarked on a ship which took them far away from France, where their love had not prospered. But the sea did not prove to be any kinder to them; a storm came that drove their ship to harbour in the distant land of Torelor. The king of that country was involved in a merciless war; his knights on one bank of a river and the enemy, on the opposite bank were throwing rotten eggs, wild apples, and loaves of sugar into the water. The side which managed to pollute the river more would emerge victorious. Aucassin drew his sword and easily turned the enemy to flight. Then they feasted for many days at the castle of the Torelorian king, Nicolette by Aucassin's side. He was beginning to hope that his luck had turned at last, but fortune still refused to smile at him. A large Saracen fleet sailed into the harbour and sacked the town, taking many prisoners. Aucassin and Nicolette were captured and, to their great dismay, separated. The ship in which Aucassin found himself sank in a storm, and he, saving himself on a piece of wreckage, managed to return to his native land. While he had been away his father had died of old age, and so Aucassin inherited a title and many lands, becoming a wise and kind ruler. But he was full of an immitigable sadness, and continued to lament the loss of his Nicolette.

Nicolette was living in a distant city, for the Saracen emperor had recognised her as his only daughter, who had been captured by his enemies in a battle many years before. He wanted to give his daughter in marriage to a heathen prince, but Nicolette would not marry anyone but her beloved Aucassin. Secretly, she dressed up as a wandering minstrel and, having smeared her face and hands with the juice of a herb that turned her skin quite black, she boarded a ship sailing for France.

Despite many difficulties she at last came to Aucassin's castle, where she was asked to sing before the sad count. Nicolette gladly consented and, on being presented to Aucassin, she sang a long ballad about a lonely girl at the court of the Saracen emperor who was pining away for her distant lover.

The minstrel's song made Aucassin grow more sorrowful. Taking the singer aside, he entreated her to tell him everything she knew about the unhappy girl of her song. And when he had heard the story, he asked the minstrel to bring the girl to him, for he was waiting for her and would wait until the end of his days.

Nicolette promised to do so, and went out. Smearing her face and hands with celandine juice, which made her skin white again, she returned to Count Aucassin, who this time recognised his beloved.

They embraced one another, and the very next day their wedding was solemnly celebrated. They lived happily together for very many years, and their great love is still recounted in song and legend.

SPANISH
LEGENDS

The night is at an end, morning comes in full glory;
tell me what tale you'd like to listen to, what story?
The lonely cock is crowing, to show the night is done;
my horse I wish to mount, and ride towards the sun.

THE HONOUR AND LOVE OF RODRIGO OF VIVAR

Rodrigo of Vivar was a young nobleman who had been brought up at the king's court and had, since his earliest boyhood days, shown many virtues. It was a happy event when he took up his sword and became a knight, for there was not a braver man to be found in the whole of Spain. King Fernando loved Rodrigo and wished to have him constantly by his side. The Moors were a permanent threat, always waging war against Spain, but they feared young Rodrigo like the plague.

Only rarely did Rodrigo visit his native Vivar and, when he did so, he saw with sorrow how his father, Diego Lainez, was growing feeble with age. He could not bear to part from the old man, and he always left him with the same entreaty:

"If ever you have need of me, dear Father, just send for me and I'll come and help you, whatever the circumstances. You are no longer young, and your life is more precious to me than gold. Should it become necessary to lift a sword in defence of our family honour, do not ride out against the enemy yourself. Many are the battles you have survived, countless the engagements you have fought — now it is my turn to stand up and fight."

Rodrigo's father always nodded his white head, but he did not think that he would ever have need of his son's assistance.

As time passed, Rodrigo continued to serve his king, and during his absence unpleasant things happened in Vivar. The proud and self-willed Count Lozano offended Diego Lainez by his high-handed behaviour. He was made bold by his knowledge that the old man could no longer wield a sword and face him in armed combat. Rodrigo's father felt his humiliation keenly; he became dispirited and was unable to raise his eyes from the ground. He could neither eat nor drink, and he avoided all his old friends so as not to make them share his disgrace.

But when his shame gave way to despair, Diego Lainez sent for his son.

"My dear son," he told him, his voice feeble and dull, "you alone can avenge my humiliation and wipe out the dishonour attached to me and our house. Put your courage to good use and win back our family pride."

He described how Count Lozano had insulted him and, giving Rodrigo his blessing, handed him a sword.

Young Rodrigo knew that the count was a formidable and brave adversary, a man of considerable influence, with many friends who would take his side in a quarrel. His anger had been aroused, however, and he was not afraid to fulfil the task his father had set him.

"Have no fear, Father," he reassured the old man. "I am the blood of your blood, and a sense of justice urges me to fight. I shall either avenge the wrong done to you, or perish like a knight."

Buckling on his sword, he hastened to Count Lozano's house. As soon as he saw the count, he called out to him in front of all his guests:

"Do you think, Count Lozano, that you are brave just because you dare to bully an old man? Has it not occurred to you that the honour of his house cannot be besmirched in this way? I would have you know that I have come to wash away our disgrace with your blood. I have sworn to have your head, and I have come to fulfil my promise."

"Leave this house at once, insolent boy!" the count shouted at him. "Go, or I shall have you whipped like a naughty page!"

But the challenge had been uttered, and the two rode out to face each other in accordance with knightly conduct.

Count Lozano sat on his horse proudly as, watched by all the assembled knights, he took up his position. A fierce duel followed, Rodrigo dealing the mortal blows. The count fell, and the young avenger severed his opponent's head from his body, to take to his father as proof that the dishonour incurred by their family had been wiped out. And as the duel had been fought honourably, according to the rules of Spanish knighthood, the knights who had witnessed it allowed Rodrigo to depart in peace.

Rodrigo then spent some time with his father, to comfort him in his old age. The young man rode out every day to hunt in the forest and he quickly gained the respect of every knight in the neighbourhood, while all the noble maidens admired his manly beauty.

Shortly after the duel King Fernando went to the nearby town of Burgos, where he was to sit in judgement over disputes between his knights. Count Lozano's young and lovely daughter Jimena came before the king. She was dressed all in black, her face veiled with black lace. Kneeling in front of the throne she made her plea.

"Our lord and king, my mother and I are living in great shame. The knight Rodrigo of Vivar, who killed my father, goes out to hunt every day with his hawk and his falcon, and I cannot help but see him daily

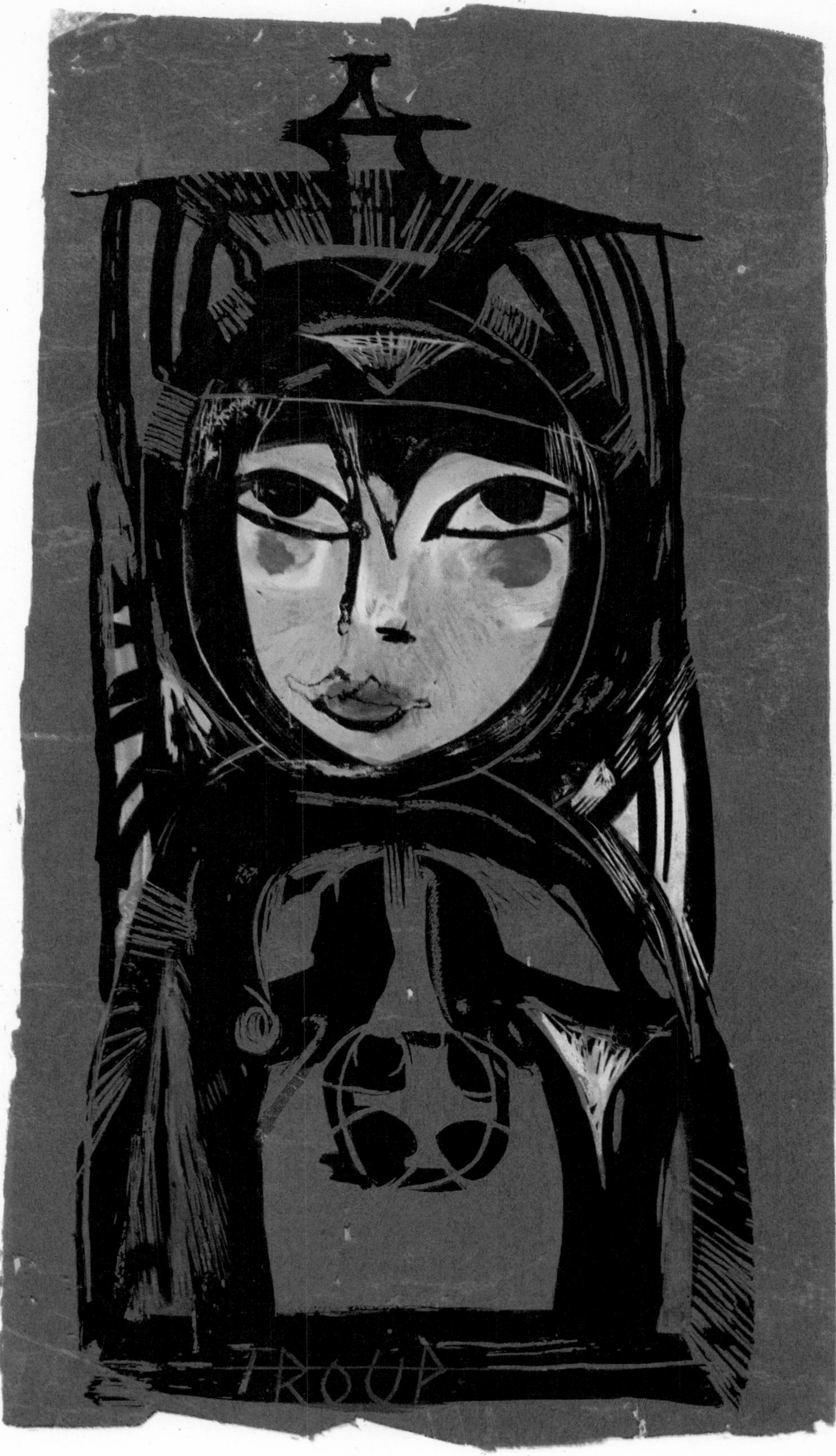
TROUP

as he rides past our house, gazing at my window. Those eyes of his plague me by day and by night, for I see them even in my dreams. If you are king, then put an end to my affliction, for a king who does not dispense justice had better not mount a horse and put on golden spurs; such a king ought not to eat bread, because he is not worthy of it."

The king was greatly disturbed by this indictment, and knew not what to do for the best. If he punished Rodrigo, he would incense all his knights and courtiers, yet if he failed to do so, his conscience would be troubled by the sorrow he caused the beautiful Jimena.

The king hesitated, unable to reply. Finally, he explained his predicament to the girl.

"If that is how things stand," the count's daughter replied, "give me Rodrigo for a husband, my lord. He has killed my father and caused me much unhappiness — let him then make me happy by becoming my faithful husband."

King Fernando rejoiced at this, marvelling at such feminine wisdom. He gladly agreed to Jimena's request, and sent a special messenger to Rodrigo, whom he asked to join him in Burgos without delay.

When Rodrigo arrived with his retinue, the king went out to meet him, saying:

"Welcome, Rodrigo of Vivar. I have good news for you: the noble Jimena is willing to forgive you for killing her father, since justice was on your side. However, to make her forgiveness complete, I would ask you to marry her. I shall then show you the extent of my esteem by giving you a number of richly-endowed estates."

When the king had finished speaking, Rodrigo bowed and said:

"In this, as in everything and always, my lord, I shall do as you command. I shall be happy for Jimena to become my wife."

On a Sunday morning, when the sun had risen over the horizon, Rodrigo fulfilled his promise, leading Jimena to the altar. When he saw how radiantly beautiful his bride was, he glowed with pleasure. And as love drives out all enmity and amends wrongs, Jimena, too, knew no happier day than that, her wedding day. It was a joyful occasion for all, including the king, who attended as Rodrigo's groomsman.

When, during the ceremony, the bride put her hand in his, Rodrigo said solemnly:

"Dear Jimena, my wife, I have killed your father, but it was in the honourable combat of one knight against another. I have killed the man who was closest to you — let me now give you another man, myself, to serve you for the rest of my days in all justice and love."

Hearing these words, all those present were overjoyed and had nothing but praise for Rodrigo.

"How well he has expressed the reconciliation of honour and love," whispered the knights and nobles. "How highly he prizes justice. It was for a just cause that he fought Count Lozano to the death. And, having honourably achieved victory, he has put away all hatred. In him, as in a true knight, honour and love have both come into their own."

King Fernando prepared a great feast in his palace at Burgos. All the streets through which the wedded pair passed on their way back from church were strewn with flowers, and gay rugs were hung out of every window. There were musicians and singers everywhere, and jugglers and acrobats performed their amusing tricks. Grain was thrown on the bride and groom from the houses that lined their route, and the king, laughing, also tried to catch some of the golden shower, which was meant to bring good luck.

People talked of that magnificent wedding feast for a long time, but then other events occurred which provided new matters for discussion: the heroic exploits of Rodrigo of Vivar. In the unending struggle waged by the Spaniards against the Moors for the liberation of Spain he became his country's foremost champion, admired by friend and foe alike. His countrymen gave him the name of Campeador, which means Warrior, while the Moors called him Cid, or Lord. The once unknown knight Rodrigo of Vivar became Spain's great national hero, Cid Campeador.

THE CID'S EXPULSION FROM CASTILE

When the good King Fernando died, he was succeeded by King Sancho, and he in turn by King Alfonso. Cid Campeador then served his third master, and he served him faithfully and well, as a good vassal. He had fought hundreds of battles against the Moors; his fame had spread not only through Spain but also throughout the kingdoms of the enemy. Again and again he had ridden out to battle armed with two lances and two swords, one of which he carried at his side and the other hanging from his saddle.

His wife Jimena sincerely loved her husband Cid Campeador, and she loved and looked after their two little daughters, Elvira and Sol.

But complete happiness can never last forever. Cid Campeador had been sent by his king to collect the tribute of the Moorish kings in Andalusia, and he had carried out his mission honourably before returning to court. Envious courtiers, however, accused him of having defrauded the king by keeping part of the money for himself. King Alfonso was taken in by this lie, for he did not realise that the Cid's accusers were jealous of his triumphs and glory. The king became very angry and sent the Cid a letter, expelling him from the land.

With a heavy heart, Cid Campeador read the letter, according to which he had nine days to leave the Kingdom of Castile. Knowing that he was the victim of a terrible injustice, and at the same time being aware that it was not the king but his jealous courtiers who were to blame, the faithful vassal decided to obey, however untrue the charges that had been made against him.

He therefore called all his male relatives and vassals to Vivar and told them what had happened and what his plans for the future were.

"Within nine days I shall obediently leave Castile," he said. "Those of you who wish to accompany me may the good Lord repay for loyalty; those who decide to remain I shall part from as a friend."

His cousin Alvar Fáñez replied on behalf of all those present.

"We'll go with you, Cid, and never leave you as long as we live. We wish to serve you as your devoted vassals in whatever you undertake."

The others confirmed his pledge with their oaths, and the Cid thanked them, his heart full of gratitude. Without more delay he set out into exile at the head of his people, leaving his palace at Vivar empty, all the doors open and the gates unlocked. His eyes filled with tears, and, to make matters worse, he saw a crow fly across their path from left to right: this was a bad omen that foretold misfortune. Nevertheless he gave his horse rein and dug his spurs into its flanks, his sixty companions urging their horses forward likewise.

As they were nearing Burgos, a crow crossed their path from right to left, and the Cid nodded joyfully. "Let us not be afraid, my friends, a good omen follows the bad. That means that though we may now be expelled from Castile, one day we'll return in honour and glory."

When the companions all entered Burgos, the townspeople ran out of their houses, or at least leaned out of windows, to get a good look at them. The same words of admiration came from every mouth:

"What a fine vassal — if only his master were as good!"

And they would very much have liked to invite the Cid into their homes and offer him hospitality, but not one person in the town dared to do so, for the day before a message had come from the king, warning that whoever gave the slightest comfort to Cid Campeador would have the king's wrath to fear.

The Cid and his retinue stopped outside an inn, but they found the door securely locked from the inside. Though his men called loudly, no one replied; only a small girl of nine came up to the Cid, saying:

"Campeador, you will find no door open to you in Burgos. The king will punish anyone who helps you. Such are the punishments that none of us dares take you in. We should lose our property and our homes, as well as our two eyes. You cannot hope for anything from us in our predicament. May the Almighty Himself help you with His holy grace!"

Having heard the girl out, the Cid turned his horse round and galloped right through the town to the Church of the Holy Virgin, where he dismounted, went down on his knees and prayed fervently. Then he delayed no more but took his people out of Burgos through the far side of the city.

They forded the river and pitched camp on the opposite shore. Though only a short distance from the city, they encamped as if they were far out in the wilds, knowing they would have to contend with hunger, since they were without food.

Just when his retinue was beginning to lose heart and the Cid himself was weighed down with worry, they saw a cart driving towards them from the city. In front of it rode a stalwart knight, but none of them could recognise who it was, as he was too far away.

"Who can it be that dares come to us like this?" they asked one another,
looking at the approaching rider.

The Cid was the one to recognise him at last. It was none other than
a noble citizen of Burgos, Martín Antolínez. He entered their camp,
followed by the cart, and, advancing towards the Cid, addressed him as
follows:

"Campeador, I bring bread and wine for you and your people. I have not
bought any of it; all the supplies I have here are my own. I shall be
accused at court of having helped you and, should I remain in Burgos,
I could not hope to escape the king's wrath. I'll therefore come with
you, follow you wherever you go, and willingly fight on your behalf
as your vassal. If I survive, then sooner or later the king is bound to
forgive me and realise that I am his friend. And if I cannot gain forgiveness, then I'm not worth a pinch of salt."

Cid Campeador was overjoyed to hear this, and replied gratefully:

"Martín Antolínez, knight of the mighty lance, if I live, I'll owe you
a double debt, for your help comes at a most difficult time. As you
can see, we have no supplies of our own. I have neither silver nor gold,
and much hardship lies ahead for me and my men. From now on we
have no choice but to procure everything we need by force of arms."

"Campeador," said Martín Antolínez after a short pause, "there's no
need for you and your men to starve and suffer want. I know of a way
you can easily come by some money. You have been slandered as
having kept part of the king's gold from the Moorish tribute from
Andalusia. The money-lenders will therefore believe us when we tell
them you have the gold, and they will not hesitate to lend us money.
Then, when you gain rich booty in the lands of the Moors, you can
return your debt and will have cheated no one."

"Very well, Martín Antolínez, I shall do as you say. I'll get ready two
coffers covered in red leather and fastened with gilded locks. These
we shall fill with sand to make them heavy and offer them to the
money-lenders as security, telling them they contain gold."

When the sun set that day and darkness covered the land, Martín Antol-

ínez rode back to Burgos, where he sought out two money-lenders, Raquel and Vidas. They were just counting their profits when he knocked on their door.

"Raquel and Vidas, my dear friends, let us speak together in secret, for I wish to discuss a most confidential matter. Both of you give me your hands and promise not to betray anything of what I tell you, and I shall make you rich for the rest of your lives."

The money-lenders anticipated great profits, and they swore to keep silent.

"Listen, then," Martín Antolínez continued. "Cid Campeador went to Andalusia to collect the Moorish tribute, and he kept the most valuable part of it for himself. As you know, he has been accused of cheating the king and now has to leave the country. He has two coffers full of pure gold, which he cannot take with him lest he betray his identity. The king has withdrawn his favour and protection from him, and the Cid must not stay in Castile. He wants to send these coffers to you for safe keeping for a year, asking you to lend him as much as you consider right in return for such a treasure. You must, however, promise not to open the coffers until the year is out."

Raquel and Vidas conferred together before replying:

"We are money-lenders and have to look to our profits. We know that Cid Campeador has brought much wealth back from the Moors in Andalusia, and we understand that he does not wish to take his treasure with him — uneasy is the sleep of those who possess much gold. We shall, therefore, accept these coffers and hide them in a place where not even the devil himself would ever find them. Only tell us how much the Cid wishes to borrow and what interest he offers us for a year's loan."

"Cid Campeador does not ask more than is reasonable, for his main interest in this transaction is to place his gold in safe keeping while he is out of the country. He needs six hundred marks."

"Agreed."

"Then give me the money — there is no time to lose."

COLLEGE OF THE SEQUOIAS
LIBRARY

"No, no," protested the money-lenders, "this is no way to do business. First you must take, then give."

"In that case come with me to the Cid, and we shall help you take the coffers away and conceal them from Moor and Christian alike."

And so the money-lenders set out with Martín Antolínez to the Cid's camp, making a detour to avoid being seen by the people of Burgos.

When they had been ushered into the Cid's presence, they kissed his hands and swore that they would not touch the locks on the coffers for a whole year. They also promised that when the loan was returned to them twelve months hence, they would not ask an extortionate interest.

The coffers were then loaded on to mules, and Raquel and Vidas rubbed their hands together, thinking they had not concluded so profitable a deal for many a month.

Under cover of darkness they carried the coffers inside their house, followed by Martín Antolínez, who received from them the promised six hundred marks — three hundred in silver and three hundred in gold. Having accepted the money, he asked how much he would get as a reward for having negotiated the transaction.

"Here is thirty marks for you," said Raquel and Vidas. "You have earned it, and your tongue deserves to be locked with a golden key. You are our trusted friend and must never divulge any of this to anyone."

Once more that night Martín Antolínez of Burgos went out to the camp of Cid Campeador. The Cid received him with open arms.

"Is that you, Martín Antolínez, my faithful vassal?"

"Yes, it is indeed, Campeador, and I bring you good tidings. You have gained six hundred marks, and I thirty."

"I hope that one day I shall be able to repay all that you have done for me!" Campeador exclaimed.

The night was still young, but there was no time to spare.

"Campeador," said Martín Antolínez, "let us wake all your men, strike tents, and leave here as quickly as possible. If I may advise you, it would be best for us to hear the cock crow in the monastery of San Pedro de Cardeña, rather than here. Your wife, Doña Jimena, and your daughters will be at the monastery, waiting to bid you farewell. Let us make haste to leave the Kingdom of Castile — nine days is a short time."

The Cid took his friend's advice, and his retinue was soon on the road, riding fast, to put as much distance as they could between themselves and Burgos.

Martín Antolínez went in the opposite direction alone, going back to the city to take leave of his wife and to instruct his servants of their duties during his absence.

"Ride on," he called out to the Cid's troops, "I'll be with you again before daybreak."

And they galloped through the early morning mist, sixty banners fluttering in the breeze.

The first cock was crowing and the red sky in the East was heralding the dawn when the Cid and his people arrived at the monastery of San Pedro.

The abbot welcomed his guests, offering them food and shelter.

"Thank you, Abbot," replied Campeador, "but we shall prepare our food ourselves. As you know, I have to leave this country, and I have come to take leave of my dear wife and my daughters. Here are fifty marks for what you have spent on them so far, and another fifty for the time I shall be away. Whatever you spend over that amount, I shall repay your monastery fourfold when I come back."

Doña Jimena appeared, accompanied by her two daughters, Elvira and Sol, and their nurses. Doña Jimena knelt in front of her husband, sobbing bitterly.

"Campeador, oh, Campeador, why did the malice of the envious have to drive you out of the country?"

"Doña Jimena, my sweet wife, I love you as I love my own soul, but there is nothing to be done — we must say goodbye."

They heard the sound of horses' hooves ringing in the courtyard; Martín

Antolínez had arrived, but he was not alone. He brought with him a hundred riders who had gathered in Burgos to accompany the Cid into exile. The Cid went out to greet them, whereupon they all kissed his hand, thus becoming his vassals.

And the Cid then addressed his retinue, which had grown so unexpectedly, saying:

"You are about to depart from this land, my faithful friends, leaving behind your property and heritage. God willing, these losses will be made good to you in time, with interest. It is now six days since I was expelled, which leaves only three in which to be out of the country. That is very little for the journey that awaits us. Prepare yourselves as well as you can and provide yourselves with everything that is necessary. I have very little money, but each of you will receive his share. Get ready, and at cock-crow tomorrow saddle your horses. The abbot will say Mass for us in the morning, and then we shall set out on our journey."

The day passed, and the night, and the dawn drew near.

When the cock crowed, the Cid's followers saddled their horses.

And when the cock crowed a second time, they made their way to chapel.

At their head walked Cid Campeador with his wife, Jimena. No one prayed to God more fervently than she did, her prayers all having one plea in common:

"Oh Lord, protect my Cid Campeador, and though we have to part now, grant that we may soon be reunited in this life."

The Mass over, the Cid's men mounted their waiting horses.

The Cid embraced Doña Jimena, who wept as she kissed his hands — her sorrow made her quite bereft of reason. The Cid stroked the heads of his two little daughters, gazing at them for a long time, as if unable to tear his eyes away. And then he embraced his wife once more.

At last Alvar Fáñez said to his cousin, Cid Campeador:

"Oh, Cid, you who buckled on your sword at such an opportune hour — where is your proud spirit? Where is your courage? It is high time to take to the road."

Those were their final words spoken in the monastery of San Pedro.

Their arms gleamed in the sun, their banners fluttered gaily. Cid Campeador and his followers rode hard towards the borders of Castile. They travelled all that day without pause, and the following night many more riders joined them, resolved to leave their homeland with the Cid.

The Cid slept in his tent — his sleep was short but untroubled. The Archangel Gabriel came to him in a dream and said:

"Go out and do battle with the enemy; fight as no man before you has ever fought, Campeador. Fortune will smile on you for as long as you live."

Well pleased with his vision, the Cid awoke on the morning of the ninth day, the last vouchsafed him by the king. And on the ninth day he left the Kingdom of Castile. Though only he had been expelled, he went accompanied by some three hundred warriors. Three hundred banners waved above the heads of his followers. Such is the might of justice, which rallies all the brave and fearless under its flag.

This was but the beginning of a glorious campaign. Having been expelled from the land by his king, Campeador nevertheless continued to fight faithfully for his sovereign, as befits an honest vassal. He won for King Alfonso and his country vast territories that had previously been under the rule of the Moors. He gained great riches for himself and was easily able to return the money he owed Raquel and Vidas; he sent it back with interest, as well as with an apology for having to misinform them about the contents of the coffers:

"However, you must know, Raquel and Vidas, that apart from sand those coffers contained the value of my word as a knight. It was on this word that I took from you the loan which I am now returning."

The tale of the unjust expulsion of Cid Campeador, a tale that began so sadly, came to a glorious end.

The Cid continued to celebrate one victory after another, the most famous of them all being his conquest of Valencia.

THE CID'S RECONCILIATION WITH THE KING

As the powerful and wealthy lord of Valencia, Cid Campeador one day called his cousin Alvar Fáñez to him, and said:

"Do you recall, my dear cousin, with what a small band of men we left Vivar, all of us unhappy outcasts? Yet look what glory and riches we have today. But for all that, my soul still lacks much for complete happiness and peace."

"I shall undertake anything that you wish to be done," replied Fáñez.

"I wish to send you, Alvar Fáñez, to King Alfonso in Castile. If you are willing to go, select a hundred of my horses and take them to the king as a gift from me. Kiss his hand in my name and on my behalf request him to allow my wife Jimena and my daughters to come to me here in Valencia. If he gives his consent, then go to the monastery of San Pedro and bring my wife and daughters, with all honours due to them, to this land we have won for ourselves."

Alvar Fáñez picked a hundred horses without delay, and a hundred men got ready to accompany him. Before their departure, the Cid sent his dear cousin a thousand marks in silver, saying:

"Half of this is the amount I promised to the Abbot of San Pedro; use the other half as you see fit."

The magnificent procession then set out for Castile.

King Alfonso dwelt at Carrión at the time. He was on his way to church when the Cid's delegation arrived in the city.

Alvar Fáñez knelt before the king and, kissing his hands, said to him:

"Have mercy, our lord and king, for the love of God! Cid Campeador kisses your hands, a faithful vassal of his good master, trusting in your magnanimity. A hundred saddled horses he sends you, requesting that you accept his gift, for he has always remained your vassal and acknowledges you as his liege lord."

At this the king raised his right hand, crossed himself, and then replied:

"By Saint Isidore, I would have you know that my heart rejoices at the valorous deeds and famous victories of Cid Campeador. I accept the horses he has sent me as a gift."

Hearing the king speak so benevolently, Alvar Fáñez said:

"Permit me to speak further, Your Majesty. The Cid asks you in your mercy to allow his wife Jimena and his two daughters to leave the San Pedro monastery and go to him in Valencia."

"He has my consent," replied King Alfonso. "I shall see to it that Doña Jimena and her daughters have everything they need, and shall give them my protection all the way to the frontiers of my kingdom. Once over the border, it will be your duty, and the Cid's, to protect them."

Before Alvar Fáñez could express his thanks, the king turned to his courtiers and told them, speaking in a loud voice so that all should hear:

"Listen to what I have to say: let no one harm the Cid or his men in any way whatever. All the property confiscated from those who went into exile with him shall be returned. I want them to know that they have nothing to fear from me because they have served me well, as good vassals."

Alvar Fáñez kissed the king's hand, and King Alfonso added:

"Anyone who wants to leave the country and join the Cid has my permission to do so. More profit will arise out of clemency than would ever come from further cruelties."

The king sent his royal herald to accompany and serve the Cid's delegation, whereupon Alvar Fáñez took his leave.

Among those who joined the Cid's followers were the two young Counts of Carrión, Diego and Fernando. On the way to the San Pedro monastery they rode up to Alvar Fáñez and tried to ingratiate themselves with him.

"We know that you have always been faithful to your friends and we ask you to befriend us now. Please convey our compliments to the Cid and tell him that he may count on us. We shall gladly serve him and, believe us, he will not regret accepting our support."

Having said this, they returned home to Carrión.

But their words were not sincere. They were not thinking of serving the Cid, but rather of partaking in his wealth. And they did not reveal their chief purpose, which was to court the Cid's daughters so that one day they should inherit his possessions.

Alvar Fáñez and his men continued their journey to the monastery of San Pedro, riding fast and with light hearts.

They were joyfully greeted by Doña Jimena, whose delight increased still further when Alvar Fáñez told her:

"I bow to you in all respect and humility, Doña Jimena. May the good Lord keep and protect you and your daughters, Doña Elvira and Doña Sol. Cid Campeador sends you his greetings — he is well, rich and powerful. The king, in his mercy, has given consent for you and your daughters to leave this monastery and the Kingdom of Castile, to join your husband in Valencia. With your permission, I shall accompany you on your journey. When the Cid sees you in the best of health and as beautiful as ever, believe me he will soon forget the bitterness he knew in this country."

"May God grant that it be so!" replied Doña Jimena.

Alvar Fáñez then sent three knights to Valencia with the following message: By grace of His Majesty the King, Doña Jimena, Doña Elvira, and Doña Sol, with all their ladies-in-waiting, will arrive in Valencia two weeks from hence.

And while the three knights set out for Valencia, many others hurried to Alvar Fáñez, sixty-five of them all told, requesting that they be accepted into the Cid's service. Every one was gladly accepted.

Alvar Fáñez gave the abbot the five hundred marks for the monastery, using the rest of the money to provide Doña Jimena's retinue with all they needed for their journey to Valencia.

Full of gladness and impatience they rode their horses at great speed. They travelled quickly and without the least difficulty to the frontier of the kingdom. Wherever they stopped for the night they were well provided for, the king having placed all his resources at their disposal. The royal herald, who accompanied them, witnessed the great loyalty shown to Cid Campeador by the whole nation, as ever more riders, with their banners flying, kept arriving to join Alvar Fáñez.

On the fifth day they crossed the Castilian border at Medinaceli.

The Cid, who had been advised of their coming, sent a hundred horsemen to meet them, with his faithful followers Muño Gustioz, Pedro Bermúdez, Martín Antolínez, and the Bishop of Valencia, Jerónimo, at their head.

And when the two retinues met and approached the city together, he sent out another two hundred riders, to whom he said:

"I myself shall stay here, in this beautiful city which I have conquered, and I shall welcome Doña Jimena and my two daughters by the city gate."

And so it came to pass.

The Cid gave orders for the walls and gates of Valencia to be well guarded, to prevent the enemy from taking advantage of the occasion for an unexpected assault on the city. He then had his horse Babiec saddled, the horse he had only recently won from the King of Seville, and in full armour the Cid rode out of the gate to await his wife and daughters.

As soon as they arrived he dismounted, embraced Doña Jimena and both his daughters, Doña Elvira and Doña Sol. Tears of joy were shed to the accompaniment of cheers from his assembled followers.

"Doña Jimena, my beloved wife — my dear daughters, who are as precious to me as my own heart and soul — come with me and enter beautiful Valencia, the city I have conquered for you." Thus spoke the Cid, leading his wife and daughters into the city.

They went up to the battlements of the highest tower and looked out over the surrounding countryside. Below them lay the city in all its splendour, with the harbour and sea, fields and gardens. They all joined their hands in prayer, thanking God for His goodness and bounty.

They then settled down to live happily together.

Doña Jimena's joy was marred only by further wars against the Moors. It could not have been otherwise, for the wealth of Valencia tempted the Moors to make repeated attempts to conquer that city. Yet the Cid and his knights fought them back every time, their most famous victory being that over King Yúsuf and his fifty thousand warriors, whom they routed.

After that triumph the Cid sent a new deputation to King Alfonso. Alvar Fáñez and Pedro Bermúdez this time presented the king with two hundred saddled horses as a gift from Cid Campeador.

The king received them most graciously, and said:

"Hear me, Alvar Fáñez and Pedro Bermúdez: I expelled Cid Campeador from the kingdom, causing him much hardship. He nevertheless went on serving me as a good vassal, and I made my peace with him in my heart long ago. If the Cid wishes it, I shall gladly meet him. Moreover, I have some news that I desire to give him. Diego and Fernando, the Counts of Carrión, would like to marry his daughters. I would therefore ask you to be my messengers and carry this news to him on my behalf."

The Cid's delegates thanked the king and took their leave of him, returning to Valencia.

As soon as Cid Campeador heard the king's message he wrote him a letter, in which he said that he was willing to meet King Alfonso anywhere he wished. Two knights took the Cid's message to the sovereign, who replied:

"Greetings to Cid Campeador. Tell him that we shall meet on the banks of the river Tajo three weeks from now. If it pleases the good Lord to keep me alive and well by that time, I shall not fail to be there."

And both sides made their preparations for the journey and the great meeting to come.

King Alfonso gave orders for adequate supplies to be sent to the meeting place, and he himself set out at the head of many horsemen. The gayest among his followers were the Counts Diego and Fernando of Carrión, who joined his retinue with a large company of their own men and rode along full of gleeful anticipation. They were con-

vinced that, with the king speaking on their behalf, their plan could not fail.

The king arrived a day earlier than the Cid.

When the Cid came, he rode forward with fifteen of his finest knights. Then he jumped down from his horse and knelt in front of the king.

"Mercy, my king and liege! On bended knee I, your faithful vassal, beg your indulgence, with all those present as my witnesses."

"Arise, Cid Campeador, and kiss my hands as my faithful vassal, but not my feet as a supplicant. I make my peace with you and return you to my favour with all my heart. From this happy day you are free to enter my kingdom whenever you please."

"Thank you, King Alfonso, my liege. I give thanks to the Almighty, to you, my lord, and also to these warriors who have come with me."

Still kneeling, the Cid kissed the king's hands. When he rose to his feet, he and the king embraced each other.

"And now, my lord and king, may I ask you to be my guest."

"No, that would not be right," replied King Alfonso. "You have only just arrived, whereas I have been here since yesterday. Therefore, allow me to play host today; I'll be your guest tomorrow."

Thus the Cid and all his followers came to be the king's guests that day.

And also on that same day Diego and Fernando, the Counts of Carrión, came to the Cid and bowed before him.

"We greet you, Cid Campeador, you who buckled on your sword in a fortunate hour. We are your sincere and honest friends."

To which the Cid replied:

"May God grant that it really be so."

King Alfonso stayed with the Cid all the time, not leaving him for an instant, so pleased was he to have his faithful vassal by his side again.

The day passed, and the night, and then a new dawn brought the sun to the sky.

The Cid gave orders for food to be prepared for everyone, and his word was obeyed so zealously that the fare enjoyed by those present was such as none of them had tasted for many years.

Finally, on the third day, Bishop Jerónimo said morning Mass, after which they all assembled in front of the king, who said to them:

"Hear me, knights, lords and counts, I have a request to make of Cid Campeador. May it please God that nothing but good will come of it. I ask you, Cid, to give your daughters, Doña Elvira and Doña Sol, in marriage to the Counts of Carrión. They beg you to do so, and I, too, intercede on their behalf, since I would consider such unions to be most suitable and honourable. Let all those who are present here, on your side as well as mine, plead the same cause with you."

The Cid listened attentively to the king's words, and then replied:

"I had not intended my daughters to marry just yet, for they are very young. The Counts of Carrión are of noble birth and make dignified suitors for my daughters, nay even for daughters of nobler families than that of a mere knight. I therefore leave my daughters in your hands — marry them to anyone you consider suitable, my lord; I shall be more than satisfied."

"Thank you, my good Cid, thank you for permitting your daughters to marry the Counts of Carrión. With your consent, then, I shall marry Doña Elvira and Doña Sol to Count Diego and Count Fernando. Three hundred marks in silver will be my contribution to the weddings. And I beg you to receive the counts among your followers. When we part now, they shall accompany you on your journey home. And if they stay in Valencia, they, like your daughters, will be as your children."

The Cid accepted Diego and Fernando of Carrión as members of his family, and he kissed the king's hands.

The betrothal had been sealed, and Cid Campeador took his leave of King Alfonso.

Returning to Valencia with his future sons-in-law, the Cid went to Doña Jimena and told her what had been decided.

"Whatever you decide," replied Doña Jimena, "is always for the best. Yet I cannot help fearing that the proud Counts of Carrión will think our daughters are not good enough for them."

"You must know, Jimena, that it is not my will that has led to these betrothals. But King Alfonso pleaded and insisted so much that I could not possibly refuse, and I have entrusted our daughters into his care. Believe me, it is the king who is giving them away in marriage, not myself."

"May God grant them happiness," replied Doña Jimena.

Shortly afterwards Valencia witnessed two splendid weddings.

The Counts of Carrión thus achieved their aim. And no one would then have guessed how harshly they would one day treat their wives, Doña Elvira and Doña Sol.

The Counts of Carrión had been living in Valencia for two years when one day a strange thing happened.

In the heat of noon the Cid was lying asleep on a couch when a lion escaped from its cage and began to prowl about in the palace. All his friends quickly surrounded the sleeping Cid in order to protect him, but his two sons-in-law showed cowardice. Fernando hid under the couch, while Diego ran away, shouting: "Oh, Carrión, I'll never set eyes on you again!"

The Cid awoke and, seeing his followers grouped around him, asked:

"What's happening? What do you want?"

"A lion has burst from his cage," they told him.

The Cid got up and, unarmed as he was, advanced towards the lion. The beast stopped roaring, hung its tail, and the Cid put his arm around the creature's neck and led it unresisting back to its cage. Everyone marvelled at the Cid's courage.

He then asked after his sons-in-law, but no one would tell him anything. Neither of the brothers replied when their names were called, but in the end they were discovered, pale and frightened. Fernando was under the couch and Diego in so shameful a place that it is best not to mention it. They became the laughing-stock of everyone at Court, and were only saved from worse ridicule by the respect everyone had for the Cid.

Fernando and Diego felt deeply humiliated by the incident.

But not long afterwards, when King Búcar and his army marched against Valencia, they displayed their lack of valour once again. They protested to each other:

"We married the Cid's daughters in the hope of gaining riches. It seems that we forgot to think of what we might lose; we may fall in battle, and our wives will then become widows."

The Cid soon learned of their attitude and he went to them and said:
"Listen to me, sons-in-law, stay here in the city and conserve your
strength. I shall confront the Moors by myself and, with God's help,
defeat them."

In the meantime King Búcar sent the Cid a message demanding that he
evacuate Valencia forthwith, giving up the city without resistance.
Should he fail to do so, he would be crushed by King Búcar's army.

"Go and tell Búcar that within three days I shall do whatever is necessary," Cid Campeador told the king's messengers.

The next day he gave orders for all his men to prepare for battle and
to ride against the foe. Diego and Fernando came forward, asking him
to grant them the honour of being the first to strike a blow against
the Moors. Greatly pleased, the Cid agreed; he and all his warriors
were quivering with impatience, and he did not realise that his sons-
in-law were trembling with fear.

When the Cid had grouped his forces, Fernando of Carrión rode forward against the Moor Aladraph, but as soon as his adversary attacked,
the count turned tail and fled. Pedro Bermúdez, who had been close
behind him, came to his aid and killed the Moor. Turning to Fernando
he told him:

"Say that it was you who killed this fellow. I'll bear you out."

Pedro Bermúdez did this out of love for the Cid, whom he wished to
save from yet another disappointment.

A fierce battle ensued, in which the Cid's followers fought so bravely
that they completely routed the enemy. The fleet-footed Babiec carried
the Cid right up to King Búcar, and the Cid killed him, thus getting
possession of the Moor's sword Tizona, which was worth a thousand
marks in gold. The Cid's army returned to Valencia with rich spoils.

When he next saw the Counts of Carrión, the Cid addressed them joyfully.

"Well, my dear sons-in-law, nay, my dear sons, you have acquitted yourselves with honour in this battle. I'm satisfied with you, for you have
begun well and next time you may do even better."

There was much booty brought to Valencia after King Búcar's defeat, and the Counts of Carrión received a generous share. Nevertheless, they were not at all happy, for they enjoyed little respect among the Cid's followers, who had never seen them fight and who suspected that stories of the counts' merits were only invented for the sake of the Cid. And of course people had never forgotten the incident of the escaped lion.

And so Diego and Fernando said to themselves:

"Having gained all we wished to gain, why should we stay here any longer? We have enough wealth to last us for the rest of our lives. Should we wait for another battle to begin? Are we to suffer the whispered taunts of the Cid's men? We'll do far better to return home to Carrión. We can take our wives with us and then get rid of them — being of noble birth we can marry again, next time taking brides who will be our equals in origin."

They wasted no time in putting their plan into action. They both went before the Cid and Doña Jimena, and they asked for permission to leave for Carrión with their wives, Doña Elvira and Doña Sol.

"We should like to show them our county and make them a gift of some villages."

"If that is your wish, dear sons-in-law," the Cid told them, "I'll not hinder you. Our daughters are your lawful wives; go then and show them the county of Carrión. Take these two swords, Colada and Tizona, both of which I won in war, and keep them, for you are my sons. I shall also give you three thousand marks, horses, and mules, as well as a quantity of other goods. Let Castile, Galicia and León see with what riches the Cid blesses his children."

The counts accepted all these gifts, and they made their preparations to leave. Doña Elvira and Doña Sol kissed their parents' hands and received their blessings. Their cousin, Félix Muñoz, was to accompany the two young ladies to Carrión and then return to Valencia to report on their journey and safe arrival.

It was a sad parting between daughters and parents, but no one guessed what terrible things lay ahead in the near future.

On the first day of their journey, they came to an ancient oak forest at Corpes, where they spent the night. In the morning, when all the others were about to start out again, Diego and Fernando expressed a rather peculiar wish: they sent the rest of the train on ahead, while they remained behind with their wives.

As soon as their companions had disappeared from sight, Diego and Fernando committed an outrageous act. They stripped their wives to their chemises, and tying them securely to the huge oak trees, they whipped them with horse-reins until the girls were wracked with pain. The counts behaved like two madmen and they showered their wives with curses.

"No villages will you get in Carrión," they shouted. "You'll get nothing but these blows and these ropes. Here you'll stay tied up until the wild beasts and birds of prey come to rend your bodies. When the Cid and all his people learn what has happened to you, they'll stop laughing at us over that business with the lion! That'll put an end to all the ridicule at the expense of the Counts of Carrión!"

"For God's sake," moaned Doña Elvira and Doña Sol, "take the swords which our father gave you and cut off our heads! Let us die like martyrs by the cold steel of Colada and Tizona and make a quick end to this."

They continued to plead with their husbands until pain and anguish made them lose consciousness.

The treacherous counts then left their wives at the mercy of the wild creatures and hurried after their retinue.

When they caught up with the rest of their company, however, Félix Muñoz, seeing that the counts were alone, turned back and searched the forest, with a terrible sense of foreboding.

When he at last discovered the limp bodies of his cousins tied to the trees, he exclaimed in horror:

"Can these be my dear cousins? Is it really you, Doña Elvira and Doña Sol? What an outrage the Counts of Carrión have committed! May the Lord wreak His most dreadful vengeance upon them!"

The two young ladies were so weak that they could not so much as open their mouths to reply. Félix Muñoz brought a little water in his hat from a nearby stream and gave it to them to drink. He then put his cousins in front of himself on his horse and left the forest with all speed, since there was a danger that when the counts noticed his absence they might set out in pursuit. Spurred on by his rider, Muñoz' horse carried the unfortunate ladies to safety.

When he came to learn of the terrible treatment the Counts of Carrión had meted out to his two daughters, the Cid at once sent messengers to the king, instructing them to tell Alfonso everything that had occurred. He also instructed them to add:

"You yourself, my liege, married the Cid's daughters to Diego and Fernando of Carrión, and thus the shame arising out of this treachery falls on you as well as on the Cid."

The couriers rode by day and by night to give his message to the king without delay.

"Yes, it was indeed I who married the Cid's daughters to the Counts of Carrión," the king replied. "I did so believing that I was acting for the best. Now I wish those marriages had never taken place. Tell the Cid that my heart is full of sorrow and anger. Let him make haste and bring his knights to Toledo. Three weeks from today we shall sit in judgement there, and justice will be done. Out of my love for the Cid I shall convene the court and hold solemn trial. Give him my word!"

The day before the trial the Cid met King Alfonso on horseback. He was about to dismount and pay homage when the king stopped him by saying:

"No, do not dismount, Cid, let us rather stay as we are. For that which grieves you grieves me likewise. May tomorrow's hearing bring you justice and peace of mind."

The following day the king invited the Cid to sit by him, but Campeador gave thanks for the honour and remained seated among his own people.

King Alfonso then opened the trial. The Counts of Carrión did not dare to raise their eyes to meet the fearful look of the Cid, who stood up to deliver the indictment against them.

170 "I thank you, my king and liege," he said, "for having called this assembly on my behalf. May it please you to hear what I demand of the Counts of Carrión. Not that they should have to answer to me for having dishonoured my daughters, for it was not I but our king who gave them away in marriage. I ask that they return my swords, Colada and Tizona, which I won in battle. These I presented to them as to my sons-in-law, which they no longer are."

The two swords were handed to the king, who gave them to Cid Campeador. The Cid received them and at once presented them to two of his faithful followers: Tizona to Pedro Bermúdez, Colada to Martín Antolínez.

Then the Cid voiced his second demand:

"I gave the Counts of Carrión three thousand marks in silver. I now ask them to return this amount, for they are no longer my sons-in-law."

The Counts protested at this, for they had already spent the money. The court decided that Diego and Fernando were to give the Cid horses, mules, and other goods to the value of three thousand marks and they were to do so immediately, in front of the king.

Finally the Cid presented the third point of his indictment: the betrayal and disgrace of Doña Elvira and Doña Sol.

The spokesman of the proud counts rose to his feet and said arrogantly: "You have received back your swords, you have been recompensed for the money you gave the counts. You can ask no more. The Counts of Carrión are of noble birth, and your daughters were not their equals. The counts were therefore in the right when they got rid of their wives, who were not worthy of them, of their noble house and blood."

Pedro Bermúdez now asked to speak, saying:

"I know your nobility and your worth, Don Fernando. You fled before the Moor Aladraph like a cowardly dog, and when I killed him you claimed the victor's honours. I kept silent about this, not wishing to grieve the Cid while he was still your father-in-law. But now I must speak the truth in the hearing of all. So much for your noble blood, Fernando of Carrión!"

Turning to Fernando's brother, Pedro Bermúdez went on:

"And as for you, Don Diego, perhaps you will recall the incident of the lion. Where did you run, where did you hide yourself when the lion broke out of its cage? You know best what sort of place your nobility chose to conceal itself in when danger threatened, I do not dare give that place its proper name here. And is it you who dare to claim that a hero's daughter is not of sufficiently noble birth for him to marry?"

At that moment the doors opened to admit two messengers — one from the ruler of Navarre, the other from the King of Aragón. They came before King Alfonso to convey their masters' requests. The King of Navarre and the King of Aragón wished to marry Doña Elvira and Doña Sol, who would thus become the queens of those two kingdoms. King Alfonso turned to the Cid, who knelt in front of him, and, kissing his hands, said:

"I give thanks to God that these messengers have come, and I ask you, my liege, to marry my daughters to the kings of Navarre and Aragón. I leave it in your hands to amend what happened that should not have happened."

The king then replied to the messengers, promising to arrange the weddings while he was still in Toledo.

All those present rejoiced to hear this, only Diego and Fernando and their followers were greatly dismayed.

"Behold how justice prevails," said Alvar Fáñez. "Doña Elvira and Doña Sol are to become queens, and the Counts of Carrión will have to kiss their hands, being less noble than they. In any event I say to the Counts of Carrión: You are a couple of cowards and traitors! Let anyone who thinks I'm wrong face me with a weapon in his hand, as my name is Alvar Fáñez."

The Counts had no choice but to accept this challenge. King Alfonso suggested that the duel take place the following day, but Diego and Fernando replied that this was impossible, as the Cid had taken their horses und arms. It was therefore decided to hold the duel three weeks later in Carrión, Pedro Bermúdez, Martín Antolínez and Muño Gustíoz being chosen to represent the Cid, while on the counts' side, Asúr Gonzáles, their kinsman, was to fight.

The Cid himself refused to go to Carrión, the home of his former sons-in-law. Instead he asked the king to guarantee the safety of his knights in the domain of the treacherous counts and, thanking the king and his judges, he prepared to return to Valencia.

Before he left, the king asked to be shown the famous horse Babiec in full gallop. When the Cid had done so, he offered to give Babiec to the king, but Alfonso replied:

"By Saint Isidore, I declared that in all my kingdom there is no better knight than you, Campeador. If you were to give up Babiec, he would never again find such an excellent master. Thank you for the honour, but I cannot accept the gift. Such a splendid and exceptional horse is yours by right. I am honoured and content to have such a vassal on such a horse."

The Cid then took leave of the king, as well as of his three chosen knights.

"Acquit yourselves in the duel like the valiant knights I know you to be, so that I may receive good news of you in Valencia."

Martín Antolínez replied on behalf of all three:

"Why do you say this, Cid? You may perhaps learn that we have fallen, but never that we were defeated."

Pleased by this answer, Cid Campeador journeyed to Valencia, and the king to Carrión.

There, three weeks later, the duel was held.

The duelling ground was marked out, and the king named the judges. Those knights who were defeated at the point of a sword would be proclaimed the losers.

The huge crowds which assembled to witness the tournament were not allowed nearer than six lances' lengths on every side.

The judges drew lots to decide which trio should enter from the left and which from the right, placing themselves in the middle. When everything was ready for the duel to begin, the judges withdrew and left the adversaries facing each other, three on either side.

Each of them raised his shield and lowered his lance and, eyes fixed on his opponent, dug his spurs into his horse's flanks. The six knights clashed with such force that it seemed that they must all fall dead to the ground, but this did not happen.

Pedro Bermúdez was matched against Fernando, who hit his foe a number of times, but always only on the shield. Pedro Bermúdez had a better aim, and he drove his lance into Fernando's chest close to the heart. Had the count not been wearing three breast-plates he would have died instantly. As it was, he fell from his horse, badly wounded. Thirsting for revenge, Pedro Bermúdez waved Tizona in the air, about to deal the last, mortal blow.

"I'm defeated!" cried Fernando, and so the blow did not fall. The victor rode away from his vanquished enemy and stood in front of the king.

Martín Antolínez and Diego of Carrión fought together, each breaking his lance on the other's shield. The Cid's knight grasped Colada firmly in his hand and split Diego's helmet right down to his skull. He raised his sword once more and was about to strike a second blow when Diego cried out in terror:

"Oh, God, defend me from this sword!"

And, with that cry, he galloped away, being judged defeated.

The king then called the victorious Martín Antolínez to him.

The most ferocious duel took place between the last couple of contestants. Asúr González, a kinsman of the Counts of Carrión, finally penetrated the armour of Muño Gustíoz but did not succeed in injuring him; while Muño Gustíoz' lance pierced his adversary's chest, with such force that it went in as far as the shoulder-blade. Asúr González tumbled from his horse and lay senseless on the ground.

His father then declared him defeated to save him from the death blow.

The duel was over. The treachery of the Counts of Carrión had been avenged.

The king saw how angry the counts and all their adherents were, and he advised the victors to leave Carrión that same night, for he was afraid that otherwise they might be waylaid as they returned home to Valencia. They took the king's advice and left town secretly in the night.

When they arrived in Valencia with the news of their victory, the Cid smiled happily and thanked all three for the way they had defended his honour.

Their weddings having been arranged, Doña Elvira became the Queen of Navarre and Doña Sol the Queen of Aragón.

King Alfonso not only married them to nobler husbands than before, but he also made them very happy.

When the hour of the Cid's death approached, the hero was able to close his eyes in peace and tranquillity. His loyalty and bravery had helped Spain to regain vast territories, his daughters had become queens, and his fame had ascended like the sun over all the land.

It is said that to this day on the heart of every Spaniard there is inscribed in letters of gold the name of Rodrigo of Vivar — Cid Campeador.

THE SEVEN INFANTES OF LARA

Ruy Velasquez was a knight who had killed five thousand Moors in battle and who had taken, at least, three hundred captives. His memory would have been truly glorious if he had died immediately after his heroic deeds, or if he had died without committing the treachery with which he soiled his name forever.

But his treachery was baser than any other. It was the betrayal of his own kinsmen.

Ruy Velasquez married a beautiful noblewoman, Lambra. The wedding took place in Burgos, and the wedding feast was held at Salas. It was a memorable occasion, outshining all similar feasts both in length and splendour, for it lasted a full seven weeks.

Guests were invited from near and far, and Salas was crowded with visitors. The company included Ruy's sister, Doña Sancha of Lara, and her seven sons, the seven Infantes of Lara.

Only her husband, Gonzalo Bustos, did not attend, not because he did not want to, nor because he refused the invitation. He failed to come because he was in Cordoba, having been taken prisoner several years earlier by the mighty Moorish king Almanzor.

Being without her husband, Doña Sancha was all the more afraid for her sons, who were now her only pride and joy.

When she arrived in Salas and found the town full of merry wedding guests, she gave her seven boys good advice:

"I want you to enjoy yourselves, my sons, but I beg you to keep your wits about you. Do not abandon yourselves to the fun and merry-making at once. First, take your weapons and go to the inn you have been assigned. Stay there for the time being. Festive occasions such as this frequently produce quarrels and fights. Look after yourselves, my sons, and especially you, Gonzalo Gonzales. You're the youngest and you know how fearful I am for you."

Her sons obeyed her, and went straight to the inn, where they found the tables already laid and their food prepared. They ate and drank, and then started playing chess.

But the youngest brother, Gonzalo Gonzales, did not find the game to his liking. He asked for his horse to be saddled and rode into the town. There was so much to see everywhere, so much to enjoy. The young man came to a square in which his uncle, the bridegroom, Ruy Velasquez, was demonstrating his strength, throwing his lance high over the tower.

Seeing this, Gonzalo took his own lance and did likewise. Being very young and inexperienced, he did not succeed nearly so well, his lance flying low and falling quickly to the ground.

His uncle's bride, the young and beautiful Doña Lambra, saw him throw, and turning to her ladies she said out loud:

"Choose whomever you please, but I wouldn't give my husband Ruy Velasquez for five such as this one."

And laughing, she pointed at Gonzalo.

The youth's mother, Doña Sancha, overheard this and she was very annoyed at the ridicule to which her son was being subjected. Raising her head proudly, she called out:

"Be quiet, Doña Lambra, no more of this! I have not five but seven such sons, and each one of them is worth more than anyone else. You wait until they hear how you have spoken — things will go ill for your husband then!"

"You be quiet!" retorted Doña Lambra. "Imagine boasting that you have seven sons! Even a sow can have a litter of seven!"

Now it was Gonzalo's turn to be angry when he heard what Doña Lambra said.

"How dare you, Aunt Lambra!" he exclaimed. "You brazen creature, with a tongue like a serpent! Stop this at once, or I'll cut off the hem of your skirt, as they do to harlots!"

Doña Lambra said no more, but she was mortally offended. She called to her husband, Ruy Velasquez, and told him what had just happened.

"If you don't avenge this insult," she said, "I swear that I'll give up the Christian faith and seek satisfaction from the Moorish god."

"Rest assured, my dear," replied Ruy, his face white with rage, "I'll avenge the insult, and I'll avenge it most terribly. All my nephews, all seven Infantes of Lara, will pay for it in a way that will go down in history."

And he began to act on his plan.

He did not show his anger, and when the wedding feast was at last over, he invited his nephews to extend their visit. While they were staying with him he persuaded them to accompany him on an expedition against the Moors. He had no intention of fighting the Moors. Instead he made a secret pact with them, intending to send his nephews to their doom.

Trusting their uncle, the Infantes of Lara rode out to battle with their
followers. As they advanced through the Arabian valley they were
terrified to see that they were surrounded on every side by countless
riders, who advanced towards them, shouting and waving banners
bearing the sign of the crescent.

"What is this?" the Infantes asked one another, unable to believe their
eyes.

"Death to the Infantes! Death to the Infantes of Lara!" was the thunderous
reply. "We'll avenge Ruy Velasquez! Death to the Infantes!"
With these shouts the Moors drew nearer and nearer.

The Infantes were rallied by their tutor, the old Nuño Salido, who had
brought them up and taught them everything they knew.

"My dear sons, oh why have I lived to see this day! Have I reached my
old age only to witness your destruction? Must I watch you die? My
heart will surely burst as I do so. We cannot escape. Our death is near.
The traitor Ruy Velasquez has set his trap exceedingly well. However,
let us fight like heroes and make the heathen pay a heavy price for our
lives. Above all, let us not regret that we have to die. We shall die
together and it will be a heroic death."

With tears in his eyes Nuño Salido then embraced one young man after
the other. No sooner had he done so than ten thousand Moors came
charging upon the Infantes and their mere two hundred followers.

"Saint James, stand by us now!" they called out to the sky. And then
they fought as well as they knew how, each of them raking on twenty
of the enemy. They all killed countless Moors, whose bodies soon
covered the ground. But their own losses were also heavy, and finally
not one of the two hundred was left. Nuño Salido had fallen, and only
the seven Infantes fought on. Isolated in a sea of enemy troops, they died
one after the other, and the Moors cut the heads off their dead bodies.

The Moorish tide swept over them. The traitor Ruy Velasquez could
well rejoice, so terribly had his revenge been accomplished.

Several days after this dreadful battle the Infantes' father, Gonzalo Bustos,
sat at table with King Almanzor. The king quite often asked his noble

prisoner to come and talk with him, for his sister had a son by Gonzalo Bustos. This son of the king's Spanish prisoner and the Moorish princess did not know who his father was, of course. He was a half-caste, by the name of Mudarra.

While Gonzalo Bustos sat sadly in the king's chamber, a huge platter was suddenly brought in, covered with a lid.

"Lift the lid and look underneath," King Almanzor told him.

Gonzalo lifted the lid — and found the severed heads of his seven sons, the Infantes of Lara. For a moment the unfortunate man remained frozen with horror. Then he burst into tears. His grief was so profound that even King Almanzor was moved by it.

Gonzalo Bustos picked up the head of his eldest son, talking to it as if his son were still alive. Then he took the head of the second son and spoke to it, doing the same with each of the seven, all the Infantes he had last seen as children.

King Almanzor was so affected by this heart-rending scene that he released his prisoner that same day. Gonzalo Bustos returned home to Spain, but he was only a shadow of his former self, a body without spirit.

Mudarra meanwhile had grown to manhood and the question of who his father was loomed ever larger in his mind. He paced about the royal palace, finding no peace anywhere. Seeing how the secret tormented him, his mother finally relented and told him:

"Your father is Gonzalo Bustos."

"In that case I am the son of a worthy father," Mudarra replied, "and I know what my duty is to him and to myself."

Mudarra said no more but set off at once for Spain to avenge the death of his brothers, the seven Infantes of Lara.

He travelled up and down the country, looking for Ruy Velasquez, until one day he at last found him, resting under an oak tree during a hunt.

"God be with you, sir, under this green oak," Mudarra greeted Ruy.

"And you, good knight," replied the traitor.

"May I enquire after your name and your family, noble sir?"

"My name is Ruy Velasquez. Doña Sancha is my sister, and Gonzalo Bustos my brother-in-law."

"I am Mudarra Gonzales, Gonzalo Bustos is my father, and I had seven brothers, the seven Infantes of Lara. You killed them, you foul traitor! And now God will help me to kill you."

And Mudarra cut the traitor's head off with his sword.

One day, Gonzalo Bustos was sitting in front of his house at Salas, bemoaning the cruelty of life.

"Ah, what am I today? Nothing but a fruitless tree! No, not even a tree, just a shorn trunk standing lonely in the field! Why have you left me, my dear sons? Why did that traitor Ruy Velasquez send you to your deaths? Your blood is ever fresh in my mind and will never dry."

Then he sat motionless, gazing out over the broad plain.

Suddenly he saw a rider on the horizon. It was a young and handsome Moor, on a fine thoroughbred. He came nearer and nearer, until he stopped in front of the unhappy Gonzalo Bustos. The young rider bowed, saying:

"I have come to seek you out and I am happy to have found you."

On the lance which the rider held in his hand was a banner with a green cross on a blue field. From one of the straps of his horse's harness hung a severed head.

"I hope I'm right in thinking that you are Gonzalo Bustos," said the young Moor.

"Yes, I am," replied Gonzalo. "What is it you wish?"

"If you are Gonzalo Bustos, then accept this severed head from me. It belonged to a traitor by the name of Ruy Velasquez."

"Oh!" exclaimed Gonzalo, realising that his sons had been avenged. "But tell me, who are you?"

"The avenger of my seven brothers — I am Mudarra, your son."

And then Gonzalo Bustos called out to him in a voice grown suddenly rich and strong:

"Come to me, my son, so that I may embrace you. This day brings to a happy conclusion all my obligations in this world."

GERMAN LEGENDS

These ancient legends tell us of heroes staunch
and brave who fought in many battles, and who sought
no quarter nor gave any. Now listen to tales of their
glory, undimmed by time, tales that have the power
to move us to wonder and to tears.

BLACKSMITH VÖLUND

Long, long ago there were three brothers, three princes, the sons of a king. They did not live in a royal castle, nor did they rule over any kingdom; they lived together in a remote forest, skiing and hunting.

The eldest of these three brothers was called Slagfin, the middle one Egil, and the youngest Völund. All of them were strong and brave; all three were excellent hunters. Völund was also a skilled blacksmith and goldsmith, using various metals to fashion things that no one else could make. Völund happened to be the king of the dwarfs, who are accomplished smiths, and was more than just a prince or an ordinary human being, for he possessed supernatural powers.

The three brothers went everywhere together, skiing and hunting, but in the end they tired of this nomadic life and settled in Wolf Valley, where they built themselves a house. They had been there for some time when a strange thing happened.

Going out to hunt early one morning, the brothers came to Wolf Lake and, as they walked quietly through the woods, they saw three beautiful maidens sitting on the lake shore, spinning flax. The brothers stopped in their tracks, amazed to see three such beauties there in the wilderness. They wondered where the maids might have come from.

It was only when they took a closer look that the truth began to dawn on the brothers. Each of the three beautiful maidens had a garment of swans' feathers lying near her, which meant that they had flown there. The maidens were none other than Valkyries — who chose which warriors were to fall in battle and become companions of the god, Odin, at the great hall, Valhalla.

The brothers were enchanted by the three beauties, and they caught them and took them home to their house in Wolf Valley. Since the three maidens were also princesses, the three princes decided to marry them.

For seven years they all lived happily together, but when the eighth year came, the Valkyries began to pine and fret, and in the ninth year they flew away.

The three brothers were very sad, but they could not feel angry with their wives, for Valkyries must always be present at any war and they must always go where any fighting is in progress. Slagfin and Egil put on their skis and prepared to leave home. Völund looked at them in silence, but he made no preparations to depart.

"What is this, Völund?" his brothers asked him. "Aren't you coming with us to look for our wives? Did you not love your wife that you do not wish to go and seek her?"

"Of course, I loved my wife, and I'm as sad as you are. I miss her just as much as you miss your wives. But I know that it is useless to try and find them. Their wings leave no trace in the sky; there's nothing for us to follow. Once love is gone, there is no recovering it. Therefore, I shall stay here and wait — perhaps my wife will come back of her own accord. If she does, I'll receive her with open arms; if she does not, it means that our love is dead."

His brothers did not argue with him, and so they made their farewells and left.

Völund remained all alone in their house in Wolf Valley. He did not sit at home moping, however, but spent his time working busily, setting precious stones in gold and making beautiful rings. In his thoughts he remembered his beloved wife, hoping that she would come back to him one day.

The months passed, however, and still she did not come, and Völund kept adding one ring after another to his collection.

Nothing in this world remains a secret forever, and after a time people discovered that Völund was living alone in the wilderness of Wolf Valley. Eventually, the news reached King Nidud, in whose domain the valley lay.

"Ah, is that so?" said the king to himself. "The clever blacksmith is all alone in the forest; his brothers are far away and cannot come to his aid. Now I can make him my slave."

And his wife said to Nidud:

"This is your opportunity, my lord! Take Völund by force or by subter-fuge and make him work for you. You will not find a better blacksmith, nor a better goldsmith anywhere in the world. He excels over all mankind in every manual skill, for he is the king of the dwarfs, as everyone knows. This is your opportunity. Do not fail to grasp it!"

King Nidud accordingly sent his soldiers to Völund's house. Not daring to go there in the daytime, for they knew all about his supernatural powers, they went to set a trap for him at night, when he was in the habit of going out hunting.

Fully armed and carrying stout shields, the king's men entered Völund's house in Wolf Valley. Looking round the hall, the first thing that caught their attention were the rings which Völund had strung on a strand of cord. They were exactly seven hundred in number, and the king's warriors rejoiced to find so splendid a treasure. Never before had they seen such fine gems. They took down the rings and examined them, all seven hundred. Then they hurriedly put them back on the cord, so that Völund should not suspect anything, but in their haste they overlooked one ring. They then hid themselves out of sight and waited for Völund to come home.

It was very late when Völund returned from the hunt, tired and hungry. He lit some dry brushwood in the fireplace, threw in a few logs, and roasted some bear's meat for his supper. Having eaten, he sat down on a bearskin and, taking down the rings, counted them while he thought about his absent wife. Discovering that one of the rings was missing, he wondered how this was possible, but could find no explanation for the mystery. Finally it occurred to him that perhaps his dear wife had come back in secret and had taken the ring to tell him that she was near. His heart lifted at this thought, and he went on sitting there on the bearskin, day-dreaming, until sleep overcame him and, to his misfortune, he fell into a deep slumber.

As soon as they saw that he was asleep, the king's soldiers crept forward and bound Völund with thongs of leather, chaining his hands and feet with heavy shackles.

Thus fettered and helpless, Völund was led before the king.

"Hear me, Völund," said Nidud to the captive king of the dwarfs, "I own Wolf Valley and all this land. Therefore I also own you and everything you have, as well as all your skills. Stay at my court and work for me."

Völund was overcome by rage, and had he not been chained, King Nidud might have fared badly. After some time Völund calmed down again, and only the whites of his eyes still flashed with fire.

The queen saw this and said to her husband:

"Beware, Nidud, do not forget that everything that lives in the forest is wild — Völund, too, is wild, and he inspires fear. His eyes shine like a tiger's; if you set him free, he'll leap from your grasp. And look how he grates his teeth in fury! He cannot bear the sight of our daughter Bödvild, who is wearing one of his rings, and he is angry that you have buckled on his sword. You must have Völund crippled — once he's lame he'll not be able to run away and he will work for you until he dies."

Nidud acted on his queen's advice.

He had Völund crippled and confined him to an island in the middle of a lake. There Völund was put to work, fashioning pieces of armour and jewellery for the king. There as Nidud's prisoner, he toiled day after day, full of hate and sorrow, finding his only pleasure in the fruits of his work, and the astonishing skill of his two hands. And no one was allowed to visit him but the king.

All the time Völund sang one single song, over and over again.

"My sword gleams and glitters at Nidud's side,
My sword, whose blade I have sharpened well,
My sword, which with my two hands I have wrought
And fashioned into a fine weapon.
From this exquisite sword I've had to part
Never again shall I wear it.
All my skill cannot mend a broken heart,
Which bleeds because my wife's red ring
Instead of on her finger is now worn
By Bödvild, daughter of the king."

All the time Völund sat in his workshop, hammering and cutting metal, singing and musing unhappily, a forlorn, crippled artist.

But then one day his opportunity for revenge against the king came. The king's two young sons rowed in secret across the lake to Völund's island, curious to see him at work, and longing to find out how he made those wonderful weapons and ornaments. They stood in the doorway of his workshop and watched him, their eyes round with amazement. Völund noticed his unexpected visitors and invited them in, demonstrating his skill and divulging the secrets of his craft. The two boys looked on with gleaming eyes and listened in rapt silence. Then they begged Völund to show them the precious things he made. So Völund took them to his secret chamber, unlocked the wooden chest with his key, and spread before the king's sons the most exquisite ornaments of pure gold they had ever seen.

Seeing how thrilled they were, how eager to possess some of these magnificent articles, he said slyly: "Why don't you come again, and pay me another visit. You can have all this gold, if you wish. I shall keep it here for you. But now you must go back home. Don't breathe a word to anyone that you have been here. I shall look forward to your next visit, and when you come I shall give you anything you ask for."

The boys did as Völund told them, revealing to no one that they had visited the blacksmith on his island. And as soon as they could they made another clandestine trip across the lake.

Völund took them to his secret chamber and there he opened the wooden chest. The boys leaned over it, trembling with expectation. Then Völund slipped out of the chamber and imprisoned the boys there.

When the boys failed to return home, panic broke out at the royal court. But as no one knew of their visit to Völund's island, no one looked for them there.

Only Völund in his island workshop knew the truth, and he laughed in secret glee at his success.

There was only one thing more that irked him: the infuriating knowledge that Bödvild wore the ring he had made for his wife. And he wondered how he was to wreak his vengeance upon the princess as well.

One day it so happened that a clasp he had made for Bödvild was broken. Bödvild took it and secretly made her way to the island.

"I do not dare tell my father or mother about it," she said to Völund. "Be so kind as to mend the clasp for me and make it whole again."

"Yes, I'll mend your clasp for you," replied Völund. "I'll mend it in such a way that it will be even more beautiful than before. You, too, when wearing it will seem more beautiful to your father and mother, and more pleasing to yourself. Sit down and wait while I go to work."

The cunning craftsman offered Bödvild some beer, filled her cup again and again, and, trying to win her over, he said to her:

"You are wearing my wife's ring; why don't you become my wife?" And Bödvil consented.

Only afterwards did Bödvil realise what she had done and, utterly dismayed, she left the island. Her clasp was whole again, but she had become Völund's wife. She left as secretly as she had come, telling no one of what had happened.

Satisfied, Völund lived on in his lonely island workshop. But there was still one more thing that troubled him. True, he had his revenge, had made the king pay for enslaving him and the queen for her treacherous advice — but how did all that help him since his legs were crippled?

"Oh, if only my legs were well again, and I was able to walk and run, to jump and dance; if only I were my old self again!" lamented Völund all the time. And then he had a brilliant idea.

He would never be able to walk properly again, but perhaps he could fly. He thought about this and set to work, making himself a cloak of birds' feathers in the shape of a pair of wings, to carry him soaring up into the air.

When he had successfully tested his new invention for the first time he laughed long and loud. Then he soared up into the sky, leaving the island in the middle of the lake, leaving the place of his captivity. He flew straight to the castle, to king Nidud's royal residence.

Bödvild looked up at the sky and quivered with fear when she saw Völund. Nidud's wife also looked up at the sky and was so amazed she could not utter a sound. Völund alighted on the castle wall and looked through the window of the king's bedchamber.

"How now, Nidud, how are you, my king? Still awake and not sleeping, King Nidud?"

"No, I'm not asleep; my nights have been sleepless ever since my sons vanished. I have not slumbered all this time. My head is heavy, and cold as stone. Come closer, Völund, and help your king. Tell me — you are no ordinary mortal, you are the king of the dwarfs — tell me then, what has befallen my dear sons? What has been their fate, and where are they now?"

Völund replied carefully:

"Before I tell you what you wish to know, you must swear an oath."

"What oath do you want me to take, Völund? Is my royal word not enough for you?"

"Repeat after me, Nidud, the words of this oath: By the ship's prow and the edge of the shield, by the sword's blade and the horse's hoof, I do solemnly swear that I shall not harm Völund's wife, nor his child, even if they should be found to live inside this castle, in these royal halls."

King Nidud longed to hear about his two boys, the princes, and he therefore made no protest but repeated the oath after Völund.

And having thus sworn, King Nidud waited for Völund to speak. Völund did not spare the king as he revealed the truth:

"Listen, then, vile king. Listen to my speech. Go to the smithy you have set up for me; there you will find both your sons imprisoned in a secret chamber. For having imprisoned me, for having made me, a free man, your slave, I have punished you by making your sons prisoners on the same island. I did that so that they would know what it is like to lose one's freedom, so that they would know how bitter it is to be a prisoner. And I did even more than that. I have talked your proud, beautiful daughter Bödvild into becoming my wife, the wife of a man you had humiliated. Be kind to Princess Bödvild, be kind to your daughter, for you have so sworn. Bödvild will become the mother of a child, and I am the child's father. Treat them both well, in accordance with your oath. That is all I wanted to tell you, King Nidud. That is all."

At this the king burst into tears and, however much his instinct prompted him to reach for his sword, he did not move. He sat there as if paralysed. It would, however, have been quite useless to try and lift a weapon against Völund, who could simply soar up to safety in the sky.

And the king continued to lament:

"What have you done, Völund? No one can hope to catch you on horseback; no one can slay you with a sword. I have no archer who could bring you down from your cloudy heights. Oh, what have you done, Völund?"

Up in the sky the lame Völund laughed, waved his wings in farewell, and vanished forever.

And that is the end of the story of blacksmith Völund, whom the king unjustly deprived of his freedom. Such was his revenge on King Nidud. For not even the most mighty can do wrong, not even the most powerful rulers can enslave free men. He who uses and misuses force must expect that he will get his due.

Hamdir and Sörli

It was a dull and cheerless morning; the sky was the colour of red blood. It was one of those mornings when all the sorrows and griefs, all the affliction and anguish of mankind come awake.

When she rose from her bed that morning, Queen Gudrun, the widow of King Jonacre, called for her sons, Hamdir and Sörli.

"Come here, my beloved sons," she said to them, her face a mask of grief. "Come here and listen to what your wretched mother has to say. I must tell you what you already know. I must remind you of what happened in the past. You once had a sister by the name of Svanhild, a dear and well-loved sister.

"The Goth King, Yörmunrekk, married her and took her away to his court, promising to love and cherish her as his good wife.

"This he promised, but he did not keep his promise; he failed her most miserably. The king committed a terrible crime. Turning a gullible ear to the slanders of the wicked, he became angry with Svanhild, whom malicious tongues accused of being unfaithful to him, and he sentenced her to death. When I think of it, the tears stain my face and my heart cries out in my breast with the darkest despair. He dared to put to death my daughter Svanhild, your sister! How reluctantly I parted with her, oh my poor Svanhild, who was the sun on my horizon. And how beautiful she was! My anguish knows no bounds when I think of her golden hair, her lovely face and graceful figure.

"Do you understand, my sons? Do you see what sorrow ails me? I stand here as lonely as an aspen in the forest, betrayed and friendless, like a pine-tree with its boughs cut off. All my joy has fallen away from me like the leaves falling from a willow in the heat of a summer's day. Do you see? Can you understand my grief?

"No, no, I can see you understand nothing of this. You do not care in the least about your sister's tragic fate, about your mother and your family. Are you truly the sons of a king? Or has the royal blood been drained from your veins? You are the last descendants of a famous line — do you intend to live out your years in shame and disgrace? Do not tell me you are powerless! Do not pretend that you lack the strength to take revenge! Who else, if not you, can avenge the death of your sister? Who else is likely to lift a sword on Svanhild's behalf? Am I, your mother, to go down on my knees before you and beg?"

"No, you do not need to beg, Mother, nor need you exhort us to action," Hamdir replied. "There is not the slightest reason why you should doubt our royal blood and our nobility, or our courage and determination. We come from noble stock and our hearts are royal. We shall go to the court of King Yörmunrekk and exact vengeance for our sister Svanhild. Have our arms brought to us and our horses saddled."

Hearing her son's words, Gudrun left the room with a smile. She went to the armoury and found the royal helmets, which she then took to her sons.

And when the two brothers had buckled on their swords, Sörli said: "Have you no more to say to us, Mother, before we set out to meet our fate?"

But Gudrun remained silent and did not speak.

And when the two princes had mounted their horses, Sörli went on: "Hear me, then, Mother, hear me speak that which you, in your anxiety, cannot bring yourself to utter. You are now mourning the unhappy Svanhild, and you will soon be mourning us, your two sons who sit here in the saddle, with the sign of Death already upon us."

Gudrun was unable to reply through her tears, and yet she was happy that her sons were about to avenge her daughter's murder.

Hamdir and Sörli left their home and cantered through a rocky gully on their Hun horses; they were young and handsome, and they burned with anger against the treacherous Yörmunrekk.

No sooner had they vanished from sight than Gudrun fell prey to a terrible anxiety. She was appalled at herself for having sent them out alone and feared that they would not come back. She hastened to the chambers at the back of the palace, where Hamdir's and Sörli's half-brother lived, the strong, courageous Erp. Lamenting loudly, she begged him to mount his horse and follow the two heroes, to join them and aid them in battle.

The valiant Erp did not have to be asked twice; he jumped into the saddle at once and, fully armed, rode after his brothers.

Not wishing them to know that he had been asked to help and that their mother was fearful on their behalf, he took another, shorter road and, having outdistanced them, turned his horse round and met his brothers, pretending to be surprised at the encounter. Hamdir and Sörli, however, guessed that Gudrun had sent Erp to aid them, and their pride was deeply wounded.

Erp rode unhurriedly towards them and, when they met, lifted his shaggy head, exclaiming:

"Ah, is it you, Hamdir and Sörli? Where are you going? May I accompany you? Perhaps I can be of help to you in whatever you intend doing."

Hearing this, Hamdir scowled and said:

"In what way could this hairy fellow help us?"

"I can help you most ably and faithfully, as one leg helps another," replied Erp.

Now it was Sörli's turn to scoff.

"And in what way can one leg help another, may I ask?" he said.

And Hamdir added contemptuously:

"You speak of helping us? Do you mean to tell us how to go about our business, we that have set out to fight of our own free will?"

Erp went pale with rage and retorted:

"No, I do not mean to tell you anything, for what is the use of talking to cowards."

Upon hearing Erp's offensive words, Hamdir lost his temper. He drew his sword, and raised it high above his head.

"You have spoken most ill-advisedly, Erp, and you will pay with your life for your impudence. We need no one to fight our battles for us. We are riding out like men to meet our Fate and we shall accept no help from anyone. Let not Fate think that we mean to evade it, let it see that we accept what is to come. You must die, Erp, for you thought us timorous in the face of destiny."

And saying this, he fell upon Erp and the two young men engaged in furious battle. Erp fell dead and Hamdir and Sörli continued on their journey, going forward to meet their Fate. But Hamdir's cruel deed had lessened his strength by a third.

Hamdir and Sörli smoothed their robes, cleaned their swords, and arrayed themselves in a fashion befitting a king's sons. The castle of

King Yörmunrekk came into sight. And the brothers' desire for revenge spurred them to greater speed. They rode on, with the cranes calling ominously overhead.

As they approached the castle they saw that gallows had been erected on either side of the road. The sight chilled their blood, and the two brothers galloped furiously towards the castle, a venomous hatred filling their hearts.

King Yörmunrekk and his thanes were carousing in the great hall. His warriors were drunk and they made so much noise that they failed to hear the approaching horsemen. They knew nothing of the two avengers who were riding at full speed towards the castle gate. Only when the watchful guard blew his trumpet did the warriors recover themselves, and some ran out to find two strangers entering the courtyard.

The warriors hastened to report to their king:

"Quick counsel is needed," they said, "for the avengers are here. Hamdir and Sörli have come in full armour, with their helmets on their heads, their eyes flashing with anger. It is Hamdir and Sörli, whose sister Svanhild you had put to death."

King Yörmunrekk chuckled and stroked his beard. Intoxicated with wine and eager to fight, he shook his brown mane of hair, gazing at his white shield and twirling a gold cup in his hand.

"Let my precious brothers-in-law come in!" he cried. "Bring them to me at once! I shall be happy to receive Hamdir and Sörli in my hall — I'll bind them both with bowstrings and hang them on the gallows!"

All the company blanched at these words, but King Yörmunrekk's mother, sitting on her high throne, said to him:

"Quite right, my son. You are right to invite Hamdir and Sörli into the hall, since you have nothing to fear from them. What can these two hope to achieve, alone, against all of us? Can they overcome and kill all the ten hundred warriors inside this castle?"

No sooner had Yörmunrekk's mother uttered these haughty words than the fearless avengers, Hamdir and Sörli, burst into the hall and began

to fight. Like a couple of fierce lions they hacked at their enemies, their swords dealing terrible blows. Before the king's thanes had come out of their stupor and lifted their weapons to defend themselves, the hall was filled with the clamour of battle; goblets rolled on the floor, and Yörmunrekk's men went down, wounded and dying.

But Hamdir and Sörli had not come to kill henchmen; their revenge was aimed at the king himself. And so they cut their way through the ranks of the king's warriors, getting closer and closer to Yörmunrekk on his high throne. Hamdir was the first of the two brothers to reach him. Flinging a number of Yörmunrekk's followers aside, he struck out with his sword and wounded the king in the legs. The king groaned with pain and his men stood aghast. Sörli now came charging towards the royal throne, and his furious sword wounded the king in the arms. The king's warriors cried out in horror. They threw themselves upon Hamdir and Sörli, pressing in upon them to kill the two brothers in a concerted attack. However, the fine armour worn by Hamdir and Sörli kept them from all injury. They continued to fight unharmed, though completely encircled and heavily outnumbered by their adversaries.

Hamdir laughed in triumph to see so many of their enemies lying dead at his feet. And he shouted like one possessed at sight of the wounded king.

"You invited us in, King Yörmunrekk!" he cried. "You invited the brothers, Hamdir and Sörli, into your great hall! You wished to bind us with bowstrings and hang us on the gallows! What do you see now, murderer of our sister? What are you now, treacherous Yörmunrekk? Nothing but the wreck of a man, wounded both in arms and in legs!"

And King Yörmunrekk shouted like a wounded bear:

"You must use stones, you must stone them, otherwise you cannot hope to win! Neither sword nor lance will avail against Hamdir and Sörli. Fate will not allow them to die by the iron! Take up stones against them, my men! With stones avenge your king!"

Hearing Yörmunrekk's words, his warriors began to hurl stones at the two brothers, from the front and behind, from the left and from the right. And as the stones fell thicker, Hamdir and Sörli jumped and dodged to avoid them, but it was clear that they would be defeated in the end.

Amidst that shower of stones, Sörli called out to his brother:

"It was not wise, Hamdir, to jeer at the king as you did. Look what advice he has given his men, what terrible advice! Truly did he say that the iron could not suppress us, but the stones will pound us to death!"

"Be quiet, my dear brother," replied Hamdir. "Do not rebuke me. I did worse than this. I did wrong to kill Erp. Had the brave and stalwart Erp lived, had he come with us to Yörmunrekk's castle, we should surely have won today. As I wounded the king in the legs, and as you wounded him in the arms, so Erp would certainly have cut off his head. I did wrong to fall upon our brother like a bloodthirsty wolf. I ought not to have killed the valiant Erp."

As he spoke, Hamdir was separated from Sörli in the ferocious fray. And as they sank under the hail of stones, fighting to the last, the brave Hamdir cried out to Sörli:

"We have fought well, standing on the enemy corpses like eagles perched on boughs. Have no regrets, my brother, do not be sorry, for we have won fame for ourselves and now we must die. We stepped out intrepidly to meet our Fate, and Fate has ordained that the end should come like this."

Just then Sörli fell where he was, by the front wall of the banqueting hall. And he had not touched the floor before Hamdir, standing by the other wall, likewise fell dead, each of them lying on a mountain of bodies.

Such was the dreadful outcome of the journey taken by the two brave brothers, Hamdir and Sörli, against ten hundred enemy warriors. Bitter were the tears shed by Queen Gudrun, their unhappy mother, when the sad news was brought to her.

Yet something has survived Hamdir and Sörli: an ancient song. It spreads their fame even now, for the song says that a brave man should always trust his Fate and that he cannot gain a victory if he commit an evil and unjust deed when blinded by false pride.

SIEGFRIED AND THE TREASURE OF THE NIBELUNGS

The Frankish king, Siegmund, ruled the town of Xanten on the lower Rhine. He was an old man and looked forward to the day when he would pass on his crown to his son Siegfried. But Siegfried refused to succeed his father while the old man still lived, and instead he set out by himself to see the world.

On his travels he came to the Forest of Saxony, which was inhabited by the dwarfs who were guarding the treasure of their deceased king, Nibelung. A ferocious dragon had made his dwelling in the rocks just above the place where the treasure was hidden, and so Siegfried the hero fought the dragon and killed it. When he bathed in the dragon's blood, he became immune to every blow. Only one single spot on his body was left vulnerable — it was just below his left shoulder-blade, where a linden leaf had lodged when he took his bath.

The dwarfs were amazed by Siegfried's valour. They came to him and asked him to share out the treasure between Nibelung's two sons. As a reward for his services the dwarfs offered Siegfried the sword Balmung. But when it came to the actual division of Nibelung's wealth, an argument arose when one of the king's sons accused Siegfried of unjust dealing. The argument led to a brawl, and the dwarfs fell upon Siegfried, who killed both Nibelung's sons and all their followers.

Still the danger was not over. Siegfried was attacked by an invisible enemy, who strucked at him again and again from every side. But then Siegfried succeeded in grasping the invisible adversary, who materialised in his true form and began to beg for mercy.

"I am Alberich, Nibelung's treasurer. Spare my life, and I shall guard the treasure that is now yours by right," pleaded the dwarf. "And I'll give you this magic cape which makes its wearer invisible." Siegfried received Alberich's oath of loyalty, took the magic cape from him, buckled on his sword Balmung and set out for his home town. In Xanten, King Siegmund held a great feast in his famous son's honour, hoping that Siegfried would at last become king in his place.

This was not to be, however. At the feast the minstrels sang about the most beautiful maiden in the world, the Burgundian princess Kriemhild, and as he listened, Siegfried resolved to see her for himself.

"My dearest son," replied his father when Siegfried had revealed his intention to him, "do not think of wooing her. The Burgundians are very mighty and proud. Princess Kriemhild has three brothers, every one of them a hero — Gunter, Gernot, and Giselher. Their vassal is a giant of a man, the dangerous Hagen von Tronje. All four of them guard Kriemhild at the court in Worms, and she herself refuses all suitors."

These words only served to increase Siegfried's curiosity and determination. With a mere twelve men he left Xanten, sailing up the Rhine, and within seven days he had reached the town of Worms.

King Gunter, and his brothers Gernot and the youthful Giselher saw the strangers arrive and wondered who dared to come to them like this, unannounced. Hagen guessed that it was Siegfried, whose fame had already travelled round the world. This was confirmed by the stranger, who jumped down from his horse and introduced himself by saying:

"I am Siegfried, son of the Frankish king from Xanten. Does the Burgundian king wish to fight with me for his honour and his land?"

"If you are Siegfried the hero, I wish there to be friendship and peace between us," replied King Gunter. But Hagen shouted wildly:

"I accept your challenge and shall repay you for your insolence!"

Just then the young Giselher stepped forward and welcomed Siegfried in a most friendly fashion. He was followed by Gernot and Gunter, who were happy to have the famous hero at their court. Hagen, being a faithful vassal, had no choice but to do as his lords did.

A month went by in friendly merriment, with tournaments, feasts and hunts succeeding one another. During all this time Siegfried had seen no sign of Princess Kriemhild. King Gunter and his brothers had become genuinely fond of him, and when the month had passed, they begged

him not to leave them, but to stay in Worms for as long as he pleased. Siegfried remained, but even after a whole twelvemonth he had not so much as glimpsed at the royal maid.

He had given up all hope by that time and was preparing to leave, when war was declared on Burgundy by the Danish king Lüdegast and the Saxon king Lüdeger. King Gunter had only a thousand men at his call, while the enemy marched against them with an army of forty thousand. Siegfried could not leave his friends at such a time. He offered them his services, and was put in command of the Burgundian vanguard. At Odenwald he overpowered and captured the Danish king Lüdegast, and when the main force led by Hagen arrived on the battlefield, Siegfried helped to defeat the Saxons, whose king Lüdeger he led back, a captive.

Then at long last Siegfried came to meet the beautiful Kriemhild. During the big feast in celebration of their victory, Gunter brought his lovely sister into the banqueting hall and introduced her to the valiant guest of honour, Siegfried. It was a splendid moment, for they fell in love at first sight. Throughout the two weeks of the festivities, the dragon-slayer was constantly by the princess' side, their mutual affection turning into a lasting bond.

Siegfried kept delaying his departure. And then King Gunter turned to him with an unexpected request:

"There is an isle called Iceland," he told Siegfried, "which is ruled by Queen Brunhild. Not only is she incomparably beautiful, she is also prodigiously strong. Whoever wishes to seek her hand in marriage must first defeat her in throwing the javelin, hurling a stone, and jumping. If he fails, he forfeits his life. I do not want any other woman for my wife, and I'll gladly risk my life in the attempt to obtain her. Come and sail with me and Hagen to Iceland — if I succeed in wooing Queen Brunhild I shall reward you royally."

"I'll gladly accompany you, King Gunter, but you for your part must promise me the hand of your sister Kriemhild."

King Gunter agreed, and they set sail down the Rhine, Gunter, Siegfried and Hagen, each accompanied by a dozen men. After a long sea voyage they reached Iceland and beached their boat on the shore. On being presented to the queen, they were surprised by the unforeseen turn of events.

Queen Brunhild recognised Siegfried at once and she was convinced that it was he who had come to fight for her. She therefore spoke to him:

"Brave Siegfried, I welcome you to my court, but I warn you: Go back, for you cannot defeat me, and I should regret your futile death."

In the frosty silence that followed her words Siegfried said:

"Forgive me, gracious queen, but it is not I who come to fight with you. I only accompany the noble King Gunter, whose loyal vassal I am — it is he who will defeat you and take you for his wife."

The queen went pale and she replied coldly: "Know then, Gunter, that you and all your men will pay with your lives for your audacity."

She then commanded all the visitors save the king to lay down their arms and leave them on board their ship. Below decks Siegfried put on the magic cape of the Nibelungs and, being invisible, he went to the place where the contest was to be held.

Brunhild raised a huge javelin above her head and hurled it at King Gunter. All the onlookers gasped with amazement as the king's shield resounded with the blow and they saw that the shield was pierced right through, but their wonder was even greater when they saw that Gunter had remained standing, calm and unshaken. This was because the invisible Siegfried had stopped the javelin in its flight; and, holding it in his powerful hand, he flung it back at Brunhild, with, of course, the blunt end forward so as not to kill her. The queen's shield was split in two and she fell on her knees.

Fuming with rage, she jumped to her feet and continued the duel. Twelve men brought a mighty rock. Brunhild picked it up, threw it six times twelve feet, and with one tremendous leap jumped on top of it. Gunter's rock, thrown by the invisible Siegfried, flew even farther, and, with the hero's aid, the king's jump was longer than Brunhild's.

Humiliated by her defeat, Queen Brunhild stood up and, turning to her people, said: "From this time on you are the subjects of King Gunter."

No one but Gunter himself knew the secret of his triumph. In the general flurry and excitement of the occasion Siegfried's absence went unnoticed. The contest over, the hero reappeared among the Burgundians.

Everyone was congratulating King Gunter, and Siegfried was equally happy, for by helping Gunter to achieve victory he too had won the bride he desired.

Preparations were made for the journey back to Worms. The ships sailed from Iceland, and before long the brave seafarers were being welcomed home, together with their prize — Brunhild, the future Queen of Burgundy. Two weddings then took place, more magnificent than any others ever witnessed, and those present did not know whom to admire more — Gunter and his Icelandic bride or Siegfried and Kriemhild.

Though she was beautiful and radiant, Brunhild was not truly happy. She could not help thinking how incredible it was that only Gunter should have succeeded in besting her. She suspected that she had been tricked in some way. And she thought it strange that Gunter should give his sister in marriage to Siegfried, who was only his vassal.

When the wedding feast ended at midnight all the guests went to their respective chambers. As soon as Gunter had locked the door of their bed chamber, Brunhild clutched him firmly in her arms, bound him with her girdle and hung him on a hook on the wall.

Next morning the vexed Gunter told Siegfried what had happened, for he was afraid that Brunnild would do the same on the following night. Siegfried advised him not to lock the door that night and to put out the candle as soon as he entered the room. Evening came, and Gunter did as Siegfried had told him. Siegfried, in his magic cape, slipped into the royal bed chamber, and when Brunhild was about to tie Gunter up again, Siegfried fought with her and overcame her. Then he seized her girdle and her ring, and left the chamber with his two trophies.

Siegfried made but one mistake; he gave the girdle and the ring to his wife Kriemhild, not only telling her what had just occurred, but also revealing to her the secret of Gunter's victory in Iceland.

Brunhild at last believed that it really was Gunter who had defeated her, and they were both happy. Siegfried was able to leave Worms with his bride, and he took Kriemhild home to Xanten. Before the year was out, Brunhild gave birth to a son, who was named Siegfried the Younger after his uncle. And when a boy was born to Kriemhild, they called him Gunter the Younger after the King of Burgundy.

The years passed, the two royal babies grew into boys, and it seemed that Fate meant to be kind. And yet one day Brunhild fell prey to her old suspicions, and she started to question her husband, saying:

"Why does Siegfried not come to pay homage to you any more, as is his duty? Did you not tell me in Iceland that he is your vassal?"

She kept plying Gunter with questions such as these, growing more insistent day by day. And in the end Gunter replied to his wife:

"You are right, we have not seen our sister for all of ten years, and it is time that Siegfried, too, came to see us."

Couriers were sent to Xanten, bearing Gunter's invitation to Siegfried. Kriemhild was very homesick by this time, and Siegfried therefore gladly agreed to go. They sailed up the Rhine accompanied by old King Siegmund and a large Frankish retinue. There was much rejoicing in Worms at the reunion. Brunhild, however, was plagued by doubts. Her misgivings increased when she saw how proud Kriemhild had become. And Siegfried's wife grew even prouder as her husband distinguished himself at one tournament after another.

"Siegfried is the foremost and the greatest of all heroes and kings!" exclaimed Kriemhild after one of his many victories.

"Do you mean to say by this that he is greater than my husband?" cried Brunhild, blazing with anger.

"Yes, he is greater than all other men because he saved the world from the dragon."

"You speak very boldly for a vassal's wife!" Brunhild rebuked her sister-in-law, her face red with hatred.

After that moment the two women did not exchange another word. But when they met next day in front of the church, their quarrel flared up anew. Kriemhild was about to enter first, using her privilege as a guest, but Brunhild held her back.

"How dare you!" she cried. "Your husband is Gunter's vassal and you owe me every respect — you cannot enter the church ahead of me."

At this Kriemhild burst out laughing in her sister-in-law's face, telling her the whole truth: how Siegfried had defeated her in that contest in Iceland, as well as in the royal bed chamber. And she strode into the church without another look at Gunter's queen.

After Mass, Brunhild demanded some proof of Kriemhild's assertion. Kriemhild then produced the queen's girdle and ring.

In despair Brunhild made Gunter question Siegfried in her presence, and when Siegfried denied everything, she insisted that he swear an oath. Siegfried resorted to perjury in order to avert catastrophe.

On the surface all was well again. Brunhild, however, guessed that Siegfried had lied to her, and she turned to Hagen for help.

"The traitor and perjurer must die!" said Hagen.

The two of them persuaded Gunter not to interfere with their plan, and Hagen sent a message to Siegfried, alleging that Danish and Saxon forces were marching against Burgundy. Then, while Siegfried prepared for war, Hagen called on Kriemhild, telling her that in the forthcoming campaign he wished to ensure the safety of her husband, for which reason he would like her to mark Siegfried's vulnerable spot on his clothes so that he could be safeguarded. Fearing for her beloved husband, Kriemhild took a yellow thread and sewed a cross on Siegfried's shirt, just below the left shoulder-blade. Hagen needed nothing more.

Hagen's messengers now brought fresh news: the Danish and Saxon armies had withdrawn. Siegfried was annoyed, for he had wanted to fight, and the other lords also felt restless. Gunter therefore called them together, as he had been advised to do by Hagen, and said:

"My faithful lords, since the cowardly enemy did not provide us with an opportunity to show our mettle in war, I wish to invite you to a great hunt at Odenwald."

His invitation was received with joyful cheers, and the very next morning they all set out for the hunt. Only Kriemhild did not share the gay mood of the hunters — she had bad dreams during the night.

Odenwald resounded with the noise of hunting horns and the cries of the hunters. When they gathered together for their meal they discovered that they had no wine. The wine had been sent on ahead, apparently because a much later halt had been intended; actually it was all part of Hagen's plot.

"Oh well," remarked Hagen, "we shall have to make do with water. I know of a fine stream nearby. Let the one who gets there first be the first to drink. I wonder if it will be the king, Siegfried, or myself."

Siegfried laughed.

"You two run ahead; I'll rest here in the grass meanwhile. I shall follow a little later, in full armour. We shall see who'll win the race."

Gunter and Hagen started off at once, without their arms. Siegfried ran after them carrying his spear, shield, and sword.

There was still no sign of either Gunter or Hagen when Siegfried stopped by the stream. He waited and did not drink, giving precedence to the king. When Gunter had drunk, Siegfried laid aside his weapons, bent over the stream, and drank deeply. This was the moment Hagen had been waiting for — he threw Siegfried's sword away and picked up his spear, lifting it behind the hero's back, on which he could clearly see the yellow cross marking the hero's only vulnerable spot. With all his strength he thrust the spear into Siegfried's body at that very place, and pierced his heart. Wounded, Siegfried raised himself to kill the treacherous assassin, but his sword had gone. He therefore picked up his shield and struck Hagen down, but did not kill him.

Siegfried himself now fell to the ground, cursing Hagen and the king.

His last words, however, were a plea:

"Gunter, protect Kriemhild, my beloved wife."

Siegfried's body was placed on a shield, and someone asked:

"How shall we explain away this death? Perhaps it would be best to say that Siegfried was killed by robbers."

"Certainly not," replied Hagen. "I killed Siegfried and I take full responsibility for the deed. Siegfried was a perjurer and he mortally offended our Queen Brunhild. This is his reward."

That night the hunters returned to Worms, and Hagen put Siegfried's body on the threshold of Kriemhild's chamber.

Finding her dead husband in the morning, Kriemhild lamented so loudly that her cries could be heard all over the town. The old King Siegmund and his men came hurrying to her, their swords drawn. King Gunter reasoned with them, urging them not to fight. The Frankish warriors heeded Gunter's advice, and lifting their ruler's corpse they carried it into the church.

Huge crowds poured into Worms from near and far to pay homage to the famous hero. Yet these demonstrations of respect and admiration for her dead husband could not console Kriemhild.

Then the two she had been waiting for entered: Gunter and Hagen. Hesitantly they approached her husband's coffin. At that instant Siegfried's body began to bleed anew. This was proof of what Kriemhild had already been told and had so far been unwilling to believe. She swore by Siegfried's memory that she should avenge his dastardly murder.

She spent three days and three nights alone with her dead husband. Only then was Siegfried buried with all due honour and ceremony.

As soon as the dead hero had been interred, the old King Siegmund and all his retinue prepared to return home. Expecting her to come with them, the old king said to Kriemhild:

"Come, my daughter, it is time to leave the dead and attend to the living. Xanten needs its queen. Siegfried's son needs his mother."

"No, my lord, do not ask me to go back with you. My husband has not left me a country to govern but rather a crime to avenge. Bring up my son yourself so that he may one day be a famous king and hero. Farewell, go in peace, and do not think ill of your wretched daughter who must remain here."

Kriemhild would say no more. But her words were the beginning of a terrible ordeal for the Burgundians and for Kriemhild herself.

KRIEMHILD'S REVENGE

Widowed and unhappy, Kriemhild lived in Worms, a lonely, desolate woman. For four years she went nowhere but to church, and of her three brothers she saw only Giselher. Time and time again she was reminded of a dream she had once had long ago, when she was still a very young girl: she had dreamed that she had a beautiful falcon which was killed by two eagles. The falcon – which was Siegfried – was the joy of her life. The dream had thus been a prophecy which had now come true in such a dreadful fashion.

Kriemhild asked nothing of life any more; nothing pleased her; she had

nothing to hope for. She only lived so that she might avenge Siegfried's death, but no opportunity came her way. Gunter was still the
King of Burgundy, and Hagen his foremost vassal. The hapless widow
was quite powerless against them.

Realising this, Kriemhild came out of her isolation, pretending to have
forgiven Gunter. She even gave her consent for the treasure of the
Nibelungs to be brought to Worms, and she sent her brothers Gernot
and Giselher to the dwarf Alberich, asking him to hand over the
treasure. Alberich agreed to do this, for after Siegfried's death it belonged to Kriemhild by right.

When the treasure was brought to Worms everyone was astonished at
Kriemhild's wealth. No one had ever seen so many fine weapons, so
much gold and silver, so many precious stones and glittering gems. But
Kriemhild did not rejoice in her treasure for its value and beauty — to
her it was a means by which she might accomplish her revenge.

This soon became clear to the wily Hagen, who one day said to Gunter:
"Can you not see what is going on at your court, my lord? Kriemhild is
at the court, lavishly distributing the treasure of the Nibelungs. Do you
think she does it out of the goodness of her heart? Not a bit of it — she
is thus gaining supporters, winning the less devoted of your subjects
over to her side in the hope that they will help her destroy us. Unless
you wish to lose your throne and your life, you must have the treasure
taken from her."

These words struck fear in Gunter's heart, and he agreed that Hagen
should relieve Kriemhild of the Nibelungs' treasure. Hagen seized it
and took it away on board a ship, sailing up the Rhine to his domain.
There he secretly hid the treasure.

Discovering the theft, Kriemhild was desperate — the man who had
killed her dearly loved husband had now deprived her of his legacy. Her
soul was drained of everything but a ferocious thirst for revenge.

Time went by and still the hour of reckoning did not come.

But one day a delegation arrived in Worms sent by the king of the
Huns, Etzel, led by a Christian knight, Count Rüdeger of Belcharn. He

brought rich gifts for King Gunter, as well as the following message: "King Etzel, the mighty ruler of the Huns and lord of many Christian knights, sends his greetings to the famous King Gunter. There is great sorrow in King Etzel's heart, for his wife Helche has just died. No one but you, King Gunter, can help the grieving king. Only your sister, the lady Kriemhild, can dispel his sorrow by her beauty and sweetness. We have been sent to you to ask for her hand in marriage."

Gunter stood amazed, not knowing what to say in reply. He would have been quite glad to get rid of Kriemhild, but the decision could only be made by his sister herself.

He therefore asked Count Rüdeger for three days in which to consider King Etzel's request.

Of course Hagen came and warned King Gunter:

"Beware, my lord! Etzel is very powerful, and if Kriemhild becomes his wife, she will try to persuade him to destroy you. You know that she wishes nothing else than to be revenged on us. I advise you to refuse. Do not tell Kriemhild why Etzel has sent his messengers to you. And as for Rüdeger, you can say that Kriemhild does not wish to marry his lord and king because Etzel is not a Christian."

This time, however, Gunter did not listen to his vassal's counsel and left the decision to his sister.

Kriemhild at first pretended that she was loath to leave her native Worms. On the following day she said she had changed her mind and would marry Etzel. Pleased to hear this, Rüdeger told her:

"Yours is a wise decision, noble lady. For Etzel is a mighty king, and his love for you is genuine. And what does it matter that he is not a Christian? I swear that I, as well as the other Christian knights at Etzel's court, will always stand by you."

"Thank you," replied Kriemhild. "Your promise fills me with gladness. But you must also swear, dear count, to be ready at all times to avenge any and every wrong that is done me."

"This I swear most readily and I shall keep my word like a knight," Count Rüdeger said, bowing before his future queen. He could not

guess what he was taking upon himself by his oath, not knowing what
Kriemhild was contemplating.

Kriemhild then asked Gunter to return the treasure of the Nibelungs to her, as she wished to take it with her as her dowry. But Hagen refused to give it up to her.

"Think twice before you allow it, my lord," he told the king. "She wants the treasure so that she can assemble allies against us. I certainly have no intention of handing over the treasure."

Kriemhild was very angry, but eventually she left without the treasure. Her brothers spared no cost in equipping her for the journey, and her departure was a festive occasion. To keep her company in the alien land to which she was going she was given a hundred beautiful girls and a splendid retinue of knights.

The large procession travelled through forests and over mountains towards Passau, and from there straight to Belcharn, where Kriemhild was made welcome by Rüdeger's wife and daughter, who both wished her every happiness. King Etzel rode as far as the town of Tuln to meet his bride. Waiting for her at the city gates, he was immediately enraptured by her beauty. The twenty-four princes who accompanied him were equally dazzled by her.

A splendid wedding was then held in Vienna; the festivities lasted a whole fortnight. Among those who took part in the feasts, tournaments and games was the famous Goth king Dietrich of Berne, who happened to be Etzel's guest at the time. Kriemhild had heard about this hero and was delighted to find that he was a friend of her husband's. She did not feel in any way lost in her new environment, since there were many Christian lords among Etzel's vassals, and King Etzel himself was by no means a barbarian.

After the wedding ceremonies the royal pair and all the members of their court went aboard ships and sailed down the Danube to Etzel's seat, Etzelburg. There Kriemhild came to know the full extent of the Hun emperor's wealth and power; only there did she really become a queen.

Before the year was out Kriemhild gave birth to a son named Ortlieb. Etzel glowed with pleasure and could not do enough for his wife and baby son. Kriemhild might have been truly happy then with a new and contented life. But happy she was not. There could be no happiness for her while her soul continued to burn with the desire for revenge, while she heard inside her an implacable voice reminding her of that terrible crime committed long ago. She still mourned Siegfried in secret; her heart was still full of hatred for his murderers. She brooded over ways of achieving her revenge until she at last decided on a plan.

One day she came to Etzel and said:

"Think, my dear lord, how long I have now been your wife and mother of your son — yet there are still some who doubt my noble origin. Nor do I blame them for it, since how can they know who I am and where I have come from, Worms being far away and nobody here knowing my royal brothers. Please invite my brothers to come and visit me. Let them see for themselves how well I am looked after; let them marvel at your great power. And let all the Huns see my brothers, so that in the future no one should question my noble birth."

King Etzel gladly agreed to her wish, and sent messengers to Worms to invite the three brothers and their followers to be his guests. Kriemhild urged the messengers to make sure that Hagen came as well, for it was Hagen whom she particularly wanted to have in her power.

When the messengers had delivered Etzel's invitation in Worms, the brothers Gunter, Gernot and Giselher were overjoyed.

"If we have been invited to the feast of the summer solstice at Etzelburg, it means that our sister Kriemhild is not angry with us any more," exclaimed the youngest of the three, Giselher. Gunter and Gernot shared his exultation.

The royal brothers rejoiced, as did the entire court at Worms. Only one man did not rejoice with the rest, but wore a dark scowl. This was none other than Gunter's chief vassal, the giant Hagen von Tronje. King Gunter noticed his strange demeanour and asked Hagen what ailed him.

"Nothing, my lord," replied Hagen, "I am well. It is you who must fear the future. Don't you see what lies behind that invitation? Do you not know your own sister well enough to guess that she is luring you to your destruction? It is nothing but a trap. If you wish to stay alive do not go to Etzelburg."

"No, Hagen, you're wrong, believe me. You're wrong, but by all means stay at home so as not to raise Kriemhild's anger. We, however, shall go."

Hearing this, Hagen flew into a rage, shouting:

"Has Hagen von Tronje ever abandoned his king? I know I am not wrong. The invitation is a ruse. The king of Burgundy will go to his death, but if you do not heed my advice, my lord, and are set on going, I, your faithful and obedient vassal, will come with you and die by your side."

Having said this, Hagen went to prepare for the journey, supervising the armourers and delaying Etzel's messengers as long as possible. He wished to keep Kriemhild in a state of uncertainty and make it harder for her to plot against the Burgundians. He was quite convinced that they were going to their doom, yet his spirit knew nothing but duty and fealty.

Their preparations completed, they set out on their journey: the three brothers, Gunter, Gernot and Giselher, accompanied by a large and magnificent train of knights, at whose head rode Hagen, followed by the brave Dankwart, and Volker the musician, who handled a violin with as much skill as he wielded a sword.

Seeing them leave, Queen Brunhild moaned aloud in sudden anguish, fearing that she would never see them again. But her voice was drowned in the clamour of trumpets and flutes.

They marched through Bavaria and came to the river Danube. Before they crossed to the other side, Hagen met three water-nymphs, who prophesied the outcome of the expedition.

"It will end badly, Hagen," the water-nymphs told him. "None of you will escape with your lives, none of you save the chaplain."

This only confirmed what Hagen already suspected, but still he wished to put the prophecy to the test. And so, as they crossed the river Danube,

220 he picked up the chaplain and threw him into the water where the current was at its strongest. Though he did not know how to swim, the chaplain was saved by being washed up on the river bank.

"The prophecy will come true," said Hagen to himself. "The chaplain is destined to survive, therefore he did not perish in the river. The rest of us will die."

The expedition went on its way in a joyful mood, and a few days later they were welcomed by Count Rüdeger and his wife and daughter at his castle in Bechlarn. Their stay at the castle was not long, but it was most cordial. Young Giselher fell in love with Rüdeger's daughter and asked her father for her hand in marriage. They were betrothed on the following day, and it was agreed that on Giselher's return journey he would come for her and take her with him to Worms. But then the time came to proceed to Etzelburg. Count Rüdeger joined Gunter's expedition and accompanied his Burgundian guests to King Etzel's capital.

It happened that the great king of the Goths, Dietrich of Berne, was a guest at Etzelburg again, and suspecting that Kriemhild was plotting to destroy the Burgundians, he rode out to meet and warn them.

"Return home while there is still time; do not go to Etzelburg. Kriemhild still grieves for Siegfried and is preparing to destroy you, Burgundian heroes."

"We are not cowards who take flight whenever danger threatens, King Dietrich," replied Hagen with a laugh. "This will not be the first time that we have looked Death in the face. And anyway, we're already in sight of Etzelburg."

It was true enough. Within a few minutes they saw the walls of the city ahead of them.

As the large procession approached, more and more curious onlookers flocked to see the spectacle, and most eyes were fixed on the huge Hagen. They rode into the courtyard of the castle, and immediately the heavy gate closed behind them with a rumble. They stood in the courtyard, an oppressive silence all round them.

Kriemhild emerged from the reception hall. Proud and cool as ice, she scanned one after the other with a severe look on her face, bowing almost imperceptibly to Gunter and Gernot. Giselher was the only one she embraced and kissed.

"Who invited you?" she hissed at Hagen. "Do you expect me to kiss you by way of welcome?"

"No, I expect no cordiality from you," replied Hagen firmly. "Perhaps only a little courtesy, according to established custom."

"If you are so particular about established custom," retorted Kriemhild, "then I suppose you have brought some gifts. Have you brought me the treasure of the Nibelungs?"

"Have no fear on that score — the treasure is safe. One does not bring gifts where one has to carry arms."

Kriemhild went pale with anger and withdrew.

Thus ended the strange welcome. The Burgundians agreed among themselves that come what may, none of them would part from their weapons, and that they would all keep their heavy armour on.

Dietrich of Berne repeated his warning, promising that if any fighting broke out, he and his people would not join in.

Hagen and Volker sat down on a stone bench in the courtyard, and Hagen placed the sword Balmung on his knees.

When Kriemhild saw Siegfried's sword, she came up to Hagen with a large band of Hun warriors and, beside herself with rage, cried:

"How dare you come here? Who asked you to come, who? Tell me!"

"My king was invited, and I am duty bound to serve him."

"You killed my husband. Tell me why you did it!"

"Because he blemished the honour of my queen."

Kriemhild ordered the Huns to attack Hagen, but they were frightened of the giant and his mighty sword and they cravenly retreated.

The day ended, and it was the eve of the summer solstice.

King Etzel held a feast in the big banqueting hall. He knew nothing of Kriemhild's lasting sorrow for Siegfried, nothing of her great hatred and of the true purpose of her wish to have the Burgundians invited to Etzelburg for a visit. He was very friendly to all his three brothers-in-law, and he was pleased that now none of the Huns would have cause to doubt Kriemhild's exalted origin.

He found it very strange that his guests never for a moment laid aside their arms and that they even came to the banqueting table in full armour.

"It is a custom in our land," said Hagen when Etzel asked him about it, "that wherever we are guests, we keep our arms about us for the first three days of our stay."

Kriemhild heard this curious and untrue explanation, but she did not say a word. King Dietrich of Berne also heard it and understood, but he too said nothing.

After the feast the Burgundians were taken to a large chamber with only a single door, where they were to spend the night. They were all very tired by this time, yet many of them had no thought of sleep. It was quite obvious by then that Kriemhild meant to have them killed. Hagen and Volker especially were certain of this, and therefore they did not go to bed but instead kept guard outside the chamber.

All was quiet, nothing moved anywhere, until midnight. Then dark shadows slithered stealthily about, and vague shuffling noises could be heard. The Hun soldiers were gathering to attack the sleeping men. Hagen and Volker, standing in the darkness under the arch of the doorway, watched and listened carefully without making their presence known to the soldiers. When the Huns were ready they advanced like a silent black wall towards the entrance. Just then the two Burgundian knights stepped out of the shadows, and the moon lit up their heroic figures. This was something the Huns had not expected. They drew back in alarm and crept away as softly as they had come. The rest of the night passed uneventfully, with Hagen and Volker continuing their vigil.

When the following morning Etzel took Kriemhild to Mass and saw the Burgundians still fully armed, he expressed his astonishment that they went to church as though they were going into battle. But his guests had no intention of relinquishing their armour and weapons, for they

knew that only Hagen's and Volker's foresight and intrepidity had saved them from being massacred in their sleep. King Etzel knew nothing of Kriemhild's intrigues, which she was careful to keep secret from him. And so, suspecting nothing, he gave orders for a tournament to be held, a tournament that would have finished in a battle between the Burgundians and the Huns, if Etzel's prudence and magnanimity had not averted the disaster.

The Hun lords felt themselves slighted, and Kriemhild was quick to make use of this, entering into an alliance with Blödel, one of Etzel's leading nobles, to whom she promised some rich land and the most beautiful maiden in the country for his wife if he would assassinate the Burgundian knights.

Blödel waited until everyone had gone to attend a feast before he assembled his men. Then they burst unexpectedly into one banqueting hall, in which some of the Burgundians were sitting at a table, headed by Dankwart. The Burgundian knights were badly outnumbered, but the valiant Dankwart did not allow this to daunt him. He cut off Blödel's head before the Hun could raise his own sword. The hall ran with blood as one warrior after another went down in the terrible slaughter. There were seven Huns to every Burgundian, but even that was not enough. In the end all of Dankwart's men were killed; he alone survived and cut his way through to the main banqueting hall and to his king.

Etzel and Kriemhild sat at the head of the table. She was holding her little son Ortlieb on her lap. With them feasted the rest of the Burgundians, Dietrich of Berne, and Etzel's lords.

When the bloodied Dankwart appeared in the doorway, bringing his dreadful news, Hagen leaped from the table and drew his sword.

"Stay by the door, Dankwart!" he shouted in a mighty voice. "Don't let anyone either in or out. Those who wanted bloodshed shall have it!"

And with those words he struck at those around him. Before the rest of the company had recovered from their surprise, Volker too was on his feet, and together with Hagen he began to slay the Huns. When Gunter, Gernot and Giselher also drew their swords, Kriemhild begged Dietrich of Berne to help her. Dietrich jumped up on the table and called on the Burgundians to stop fighting.

"As a knight speaking to knights I ask you to hold back. Let all those who are of the Christian faith leave freely, as well as these my two friends, whom I shall embrace."

The Burgundians lowered their swords, and King Dietrich embraced Etzel and his wife Kriemhild.

These two, and all the knights, then left the banqueting hall, and the Huns remained at the mercy of the Burgundians. The entrance was now guarded by Volker and Dankwart, while the others, led by Hagen, massacred the Hun nobles. They threw the dead bodies out on to the staircase, to make room inside the hall for the battle that was to follow.

Hun warriors now came running into the courtyard from all directions.
A terrible sight met their eyes: they saw the staircase strewn with the corpses of their foremost lords and a bloody battle being waged inside the banqueting hall.

Just then Hagen appeared in the doorway of the banqueting hall, and he called out to Etzel in derisive tones:

"You are a king, are you not, Etzel? You are the ruler and protector of the Huns. If so, take up your sword and come and fight!"

King Etzel grasped his sword, his face burning red at this insult. But Kriemhild stopped him.

"No, do not go, my dear, your life is far too precious. That insult will be cruelly punished nevertheless." And, turning to the Hun nobles and knights who had gathered in the courtyard, she raised Etzel's shield high in the air and cried:

"Hear me, every one of you! He who slays Hagen will receive the king's shield, filled up to the brim with gold."

The brave Danish knight Iring stepped forward and bowed to Kriemhild.

"Not for the gold but for the honour of my queen I shall undertake this duel gladly."

With his sword and lance he rushed inside and engaged Hagen in a fierce struggle. The palace shook under the fearful blows, but neither of the contestants wavered. Iring therefore left Hagen and attacked Volker, whom he thought an easier adversary. Unable to overcome him, he took on Gunter, and then Gernot, finally killing four Burgundian commoners. The death of these four men lent added strength to Giselher, who knocked Iring to the ground with a single blow. But Iring was not dead — he suddenly jumped to his feet and fled from the banqueting hall. Hagen barred his path at the top of the staircase, where Iring wounded him in the head with his lance and then ran away.

Kriemhild rejoiced that Hagen was at least injured. He, however, stood on the stairs and jeered:

"Your joy is a little premature, for this is nothing but a scratch. If lord Iring has the heart to continue, let him come back. I await him."

Iring did not wait for more but attacked Hagen once again. Hagen killed him with a sword thrust and then plunged his lance into the Dane's body.

All the Danes and Thuringians now swarmed into the banqueting hall to avenge their valiant lord. Not one of them came out alive, though — the Burgundians killed them to a man, throwing their dead bodies out on to the staircase.

A desperate and enraged Kriemhild had in the meantime summoned a large force of Huns out in the courtyard. They surrounded the palace, making an unending succession of assaults upon the handful of Burgundian warriors inside. When evening came corpses were piled high everywhere in front of the entrance to the banqueting hall.

In vain the Burgundians sought to talk with King Etzel; in vain they demanded that they be allowed to come out of the palace and die in the open. Nor did the repeated Hun attacks change anything — the besieged Burgundians did not slacken their resistance, and made the blood of their adversaries flow unceasingly. Etzel therefore recalled his men, and Kriemhild sent a message to her brothers that they would go free if only they yielded up Hagen. This offer received nothing but ridicule; all those inside the hall were determined to lay down their lives together.

"Nothing remains for us now but death," said Gunter when their enemies started to fire burning arrows at the palace.

"There is one thing more," Hagen corrected him, "and that is glory."

The Burgundians spread out along the walls, covering themselves with their shields, as the ceiling of the banqueting hall burst into flame. Hungry, thirsty and exhausted after a day of battle, they spent the night of the summer solstice in the heat of the burning palace.

That night Etzel came to the conclusion that his men would not defeat the Burgundians. At dawn he called to Count Rüdeger and urged him, as his obedient vassal, to take up arms against the enemies.

Rüdeger hesitated, saying that he found it hard to fight those among whom was Giselher, his daughter's betrothed.

"You forget that you swore to avenge every wrong that was done to me!" exclaimed Kriemhild.

And so Rüdeger buckled on his sword and led his retinue to the razed palace. Seeing him approach, the Burgundians rose to welcome him as a mediator, for it did not occur to them that he might be coming to fight against them. Rüdeger stopped and spoke to them with a heavy heart.

"Hear me, all of you, and understand what I say. Among you is Giselher, my son-in-law, and you have my friendship on your side. Yet I have come here to engage you in battle, for I am bound by a double oath: to Etzel I have sworn a vassal's fealty; Kriemhild has my word that I'll avenge any and every wrong that is done to her. Therefore, my friends, prepare to fight."

"We understand, count," replied Hagen, "and we have nothing but respect for you, since loyalty is a virtue worth dying for. We, too, find it difficult to fight against you — let us at least promise one another that in the forthcoming engagement you and Giselher will not stand opposed."

"That I promise. And now to the attack!"

Count Rüdeger and his followers entered the ruins of the palace, their swords held ready in their hands. The fight was a short one. Gernot and Rüdeger slew each other. The rest of the count's warriors were killed down to the last man.

Dietrich of Berne learned of Rüdeger's death, and his eyes filled with tears, for they had been close friends. He sent his knight Hildebrand to enquire how the death had come about and to demand Rüdeger's body.

As the sun slowly rose in the sky, Kriemhild's lamentations could be heard from the royal chambers:

"The faithful Rüdeger dead? How can it be? Will no one be found to avenge Siegfried's death? And who will there be to return the treasure of the Nibelungs to me?"

Dietrich of Berne, the King of the Goths, heard these words, and yet he hesitated. It did not seem an honourable thing to do to fall upon men

who fought so valiantly against such odds. But while he reflected, the wounded Hildebrand appeared in the doorway.

"It is true," he said. "Count Rüdeger is dead. He was killed by Gernot."

"And you, I see, are wounded," replied Dietrich of Berne.

"Yes."

"Then have all my knights called together; call all the Goths and send them out to fight the Burgundians."

"The only two Goths left at Etzelburg are we, my lord," Hildebrand replied. "The others fell in the skirmish that followed my request that the Burgundians surrender Count Rüdeger's body."

Dietrich of Berne was rooted to the ground with amazement, his heart contracting with sorrow for his faithful followers. But then he took up his sword, Eckesachs, and, accompanied by Hildebrand, ran out into the courtyard.

"My lord, only two of the Burgundians remain alive, Gunter and Hagen," Hildebrand told him.

"Only two? Then I cannot fight with them."

King Dietrich of Berne entered the charred banqueting hall, propping his shield against the wall by the door, as a sign that he wished to parley.

"Listen to me, Gunter and Hagen, who have killed my Goths. You have done enough fighting, and all your men are dead. I cannot take arms against you after what you have lived through today. However, if you will surrender and trust your lives to me, I guarantee that you will return to your homeland."

To this Hagen made the following reply:

"Now you listen, King Dietrich and lord Hildebrand. It is not our custom to entrust our lives to any but our weapons. We are not destined to return to Worms; we're here to fight and to die. I shall consider it an honour to match my sword against the brave King of the Goths, if he is willing to accept my challenge."

Upon this Dietrich of Berne seized his shield and sprang to the attack. The duel was fierce but unequal, for Hagen was much spent by the battles he had fought that day and Dietrich was fresh and strong. He therefore spared his opponent as much as he could, not wishing to take his life. Their two swords, Balmung and Eckesachs, clashed until the sparks flew on every side. But in time Hagen's strength deserted him, and this was the moment Dietrich had been waiting for. He threw his sword aside and clutched Hagen in his arms so that he could not move. Binding him, he handed Hagen over to King Etzel as his prisoner. Then he defeated Gunter, who had also grown weak by this time, though he had lost nothing of his determination and courage.

The two Burgundian heroes were led away and imprisoned in separate cells. King Etzel and Kriemhild thanked Dietrich for his decisive help, and he in turn pleaded with them for mercy to be shown their captives.

But Kriemhild still thirsted for revenge. She had Hagen brought out of the dungeon and, her voice filled with a terrible hatred, shouted at him:

"You wretch, at last you're in my hands, my prisoner and my prize! Now I can do as I please with you. But if you tell me where you have put the treasure of the Nibelungs you will be pardoned in spite of all the evil you have done."

"I have sworn not to reveal where the treasure is buried as long as a single one of my masters is alive. My king Gunter still lives."

Thereupon Kriemhild had her brother Gunter executed, showing his head to Hagen.

"You are dead, my lord and king," said Hagen, staring at Gunter's head. "You are dead, and it is well. Now no one knows where the treasure of the Nibelungs is to be found except God and myself. And neither of us will divulge the secret."

His words drove Kriemhild into a frenzy. With her own two hands she seized the sword Balmung and with one fierce stroke chopped off Hagen's head.

All those present stood aghast at her deed.

Hildebrand's face grew red with anger. He picked up his lance and thrust it right through Kriemhild.

"Take that, Queen Kriemhild, for daring to lift your hand against an unarmed prisoner. How humiliating it is for a hero such as Hagen to die by a woman's hand!"

Such was the terrible end of the Burgundian heroes and of their sister Kriemhild, the end of the tale of Hagen's fidelity to his king and of Kriemhild's faithfulness to her husband's memory.

The treasure of the Nibelungs even now remains buried somewhere in Hagen's former domain on the upper reaches of the Rhine.

LOHENGRIN AND THE SWAN

When the Duke of Brabant and Limburg was about to die he called his
vassal Friedrich of Telramund to him and said:
"My dear Friedrich, you have always been faithful to me, in peace as
well as in war. Now listen to my last request. When I die, govern my
dukedom and protect my daughter Elsa until the time she takes a husband. Promise me this, and I shall die contented."
"I promise," said Friedrich, and the duke closed his eyes forever.

When the period of mourning was over, however, Friedrich forgot all about his promise, and he fell victim to an overwhelming pride. He became dissatisfied with his position as a mere protector of the dukedom, and he began to woo the orphaned Elsa, insisting that she should agree to marry him. Elsa repulsed his advances, for she had not the slightest intention of becoming his wife. But Friedrich was determined to gain both Elsa and the dukedom. Seeing that he would not achieve his purpose either by promises or threats, he turned to his sovereign, King Henry, with an accusation that Elsa had undertaken to marry him and that she had now broken her word.

King Henry, who knew Friedrich of Telramund for a brave and honest knight, believed the false accusation, and he gave this judgement:

The Duchess Elsa was either to wed Friedrich immediately or send a knight to challenge him — the result of the duel would show whether the impeachment made by Friedrich was true or not.

Elsa searched among her knights for one who would be willing to challenge the plaintiff and fight him for her honour, but none came forward, as they were all afraid of the powerful Friedrich. Alone, forsaken by all, the unhappy Elsa wept bitter tears, falling on her knees in front of the altar and, in her grief, ringing a little bell she had once taken from the leg of a wounded falcon. And though on earth it only gave a faint tinkling sound, it carried through the clouds all the way to Montsalvage, where it sounded like terrific thunder. Its urgent voice was heard by the knights of the Holy Grail, and they hurried to church, where they found an account of the Duchess Elsa's misfortune inscribed on the Grail. Each one of them was moved by this tale of faithlessness and injustice; each one of them was ready to take up his sword on behalf of the wronged Duchess. They were just trying to decide who was to go and fight Friedrich of Telramund when a new inscription appeared on the Holy Grail, giving the name of Lohengrin, son of Percival.

Lohengrin rejoiced at this and took his leave of King Arthur, as well as of his father and mother. He had grasped the reins of his horse and was putting his foot in the stirrups when a snow-white swan appeared, pulling a boat behind it. Lohengrin considered this to be a sign from heaven, and he therefore let the horse go and entered the boat. He refused to take the food the other knights offered him for the journey, saying: "She who is carrying me away will not let me perish of hunger."

The swan swam away, and soon she was out on the open sea. They travelled for five days on end and Lohengrin had not had anything to eat. Then he saw the swan put her head under the surface and catch a fish.

"Since you're fishing for yourself," said Lohengrin to the swan, "would you mind sharing your catch with me?"

The swan put her head under the surface again and, bringing out a wafer, gave it to Lohengrin, who ate it and fell fast asleep.

In the meantime Elsa was living in fear and uncertainty. The time she had been given to find a challenger for Friedrich was almost up. She therefore called together all her vassals from every part of Brabant and Limburg, and told them about her plight. The knights and vassals stood there like so many dumb statues, their heads bowed. Not one of them dared to take upon himself so great a responsibility for the fate of the duchess; not one of them dared to stand up against Friedrich, whose strength and skill were known by everyone. Elsa despaired at this, being convinced that nothing could save her. Only her priest could console her and fortify her faith that the Lord would not surrender her into the hands of the unjust. And then at the very last moment, when all hope seemed lost, a swan suddenly appeared on the river, pulling a boat with a sleeping knight inside it.

"Lo and behold, my lady, the Lord has taken mercy on you and is sending you a saviour," cried the priest. Everyone hurried down to the river, exclaiming:

"A miracle! A miracle!"

The noise woke Lohengrin, who stepped out of the boat and presented himself to Elsa. The swan and the boat were gone before anyone had time to notice their disappearance.

Lohengrin was given a splendid welcome. As soon as he had acknow-
    ledged this enthusiastic greeting, he knelt before the duchess and offered
    her his help. There was much rejoicing at Elsa's court now, for justice
    would not be left unchampioned.
And when Elsa and Lohengrin sat down opposite each other at the ban-
    queting table, their mutual affection blossomed into love.
Lohengrin's contest with Friedrich of Telramund was held in Mainz, in
    front of King Henry and a large gathering of people. The two opponents
    agreed to fight on horseback with wooden shafts.
The contest started. Lohengrin and Friedrich rode out towards each

other, colliding with such force that their horses all but fell under them. On their second encounter, their steeds reared up on their hind quarters, but the riders remained in the saddle. When they clashed a third time, their shafts broke and they drew their swords instead. The audience looked on with bated breath as blow after blow fell like so many lightning flashes, and it seemed as if the contestants' armour would melt with the heat before either of them achieved an advantage. They both fought vehemently and with undiminishing vigour, yet neither could sway the issue in his favour. The outcome was still undecided when suddenly Lohengrin struck Friedrich so forcefully that the opponent's helmet was knocked right down over his face. Friedrich asked for a truce, and Lohengrin replied:

"It would not be consistent with my honour were I to kill you now that you are at such a disadvantage."

Soon afterwards the duel began anew, but this time it did not last for long. Lohengrin attacked his adversary so violently that Friedrich soon begged for an end to the contest. They took off their helmets, and Friedrich of Telramund confessed that he had lied and that the Duchess Elsa had never promised her hand to him as he had alleged.

This incensed King Henry so much that he condemned Friedrich to death by the sword. His courtiers spoke up on Friedrich's behalf, saying that he had not stained his knight's honour in any way except by this one lie, but the monarch's wrath was not to be appeased.

After Lohengrin's victory, which had caused the truth to be spoken at last, he and Elsa became man and wife. Before they were married, however, Lohengrin made Elsa swear that she would never ask him whence he had come. As long as this question remained unasked, Lohengrin would be allowed to stay with her, but if it was once uttered, he should have to leave and would never return. The happy Elsa found no difficulty in making the promise, and the priest joined them in wedlock.

Lohengrin was a wise and firm ruler, and he gave faithful service to his king in the wars against the Huns. He and Elsa were frequently invited to the court, and their happiness was complete when in due course two sons were born to them. The years went by filled with joy and peace, and it never came to Elsa's mind to enquire about her husband's origins.

Then one day King Henry invited them to attend the wedding of his daughter to the Duke of Lorraine. Many tournaments were held during the festivities that followed the wedding ceremony, and at one of these Lohengrin defeated four opponents, one after the other. The king congratulated him on his triumph, and the queen praised him in front of her ladies. She recalled Lohengrin's valour in the wars against the Huns, and Elsa, hearing all this, glowed with pleasure and pride.

Made envious by so much praise of Elsa's husband, who had defeated her own in the tournament, the Duchess of Clèves turned to Elsa and said:

"Lohengrin is without doubt a hero and a credit to all Christendom. What a pity, my dear, that no one seems to know where he comes from. It would almost appear as if he's at pains to conceal his origin because he is not of noble birth."

Her words wounded the Duchess Elsa in her most vulnerable spot. Although the queen began to console her, forbidding the Duchess of Clèves ever to speak like that again, the damage had been done, for a suspicion had been planted in Elsa's heart. Lohengrin soon noticed his wife's dejected appearance and asked her what was the matter.

Elsa tried to make light of it, but on the third day she could no longer conceal her misery, and she asked Lohengrin the fatal question about his origin.

Lohengrin was taken aback, but he calmed his wife and promised to tell her the truth as soon as he returned to Antwerp. He then invited all the lords and knights present to his court in that city, and his invitation was accepted by all, including the king himself.

In Antwerp he assembled his guests and said to them:

"Your Majesty, dear friends. I married the Duchess Elsa on condition that she would never ask where I had come from. Were she to put this question to me, I'd have to leave and never again return. This has now happened. Allow me therefore to tell you all the truth of the matter.

My father was none other than Percival, a knight of the Holy Grail.
And it was the Holy Grail which sent me to help the unfortunate Elsa
to receive justice. Now I must part from you, and I beg you with all
my heart to give every support to my wife and protect my two sons
until they reach manhood. My time has come to depart."

He then had his two little sons brought to him and he kissed them both,
leaving his sword and his battle horn for them. He embraced Elsa for
the last time and gave her a ring he had received from his mother.

The swan then appeared again, with the boat out of which Lohengrin
had stepped many years before. Weeping unrestrainedly, Elsa threw her
arms around her husband, but all her tears could not alter their destiny.
Lohengrin entered the boat, calling out a last greeting, and the swan
sailed away with him.

The duchess fainted into the arms of her ladies in waiting, and the rest
of the noble company stood speechless and overcome. The king himself
looked after the two boys, Johannes and Lohengrin, who grew up into
knights worthy of their father's name. As for the Duchess Elsa, she
mourned her husband and saviour until the day of her death.

The noble knight Tannhäuser had wandered over a large part of the
world, visiting many royal courts and castles and forming many friend-
ships, and during his journeys he had written many excellent songs.
He came to know various countries and towns very well; he wandered
through forests and over mountains, and sailed the rivers and seas. Few
people had seen as many beautiful and wonderful sights as he had. It
would have been thought that he could find nothing new to arouse his
lasting interest. Nor would anyone have believed that there was anything that could divert Tannhäuser from the path of righteousness, for
he had placed himself under the protection of the Virgin Mary, whom
he prayed to constantly during his voyages.

And yet he one day came to a mountain in which Venus, the Goddess of
Love, dwelt with her ladies-in-waiting and hand maidens. Tannhäuser
entered the Cave of Venus, and the goddess invited him to stay and
surrender himself to delight. He hesitated to do so, saying to Venus:

"Forgive me, noble lady, but I am a Christian knight and serve only one
mistress — the Queen of Heaven."

"Beauty," replied Venus, "has nothing un-Christian about it; it is truly
a manifestation of God. Have you not celebrated beauty in your songs?
Stay and be my guest."

It was not Venus' words but rather her charm and that of her companions
which finally persuaded the noble knight to stay. He spent a long time
in the Cave of Venus, knowing nothing but pleasure and joy. He put
the world behind him, forgetting all about his past life and the obliga-
tion he had accepted with his baptism. The goddess rejoiced, hoping
that now the excellent knight would remain with her for all time, but
one day his conscience stirred and he said to Venus:

"Please believe me, my time here with you has been one of great delight.

Nevertheless, I must ask you to release me, for I am plagued with self-reproach, which, being just, cannot be ignored."

"What is this I hear, sir knight? Surely you do not mean to leave us? Do you no longer find it agreeable here? If you will only forget about the world outside and about heaven, I'll give you the most beautiful maiden in my court for your wife."

"I am indebted to you for your kindness, dear Venus, and I feel truly honoured. But my heart and soul have chosen another mistress, the Queen of Heaven. Her I wish to ask for salvation; only she can rescue me from the toils of hell."

Having said this, Tannhäuser would not be deflected from his purpose, though the Goddess of Love cajoled him and pleaded with him to make him stay. When all her blandishments proved of no avail, Venus and her companions attempted to detain him by force. Tannhäuser turned to the Virgin Mary for help, and Venus had no choice but to let him go.

As soon as he had left the mountain he turned his steps towards Rome, making his pilgrimage with humility and repentance in his heart, his eyes fixed on the ground. The closer he came to the Holy City, the stronger grew his hope, and he believed that he would obtain forgiveness through Pope Urban.

And when at last he knelt before the Pope, Tannhäuser meekly confessed his sin:

"I confess to you, Holy Father, that I have spent a whole year in the Cave of Venus. I humbly beg you to give me such a penance that my soul may be saved and that when I die I may look the Lord in the face."

But the Pope pointed to his staff and replied:

"As this dead wood can never grow green and burst into leaf again, so I cannot grant you forgiveness for your terrible sin."

Hearing these words of condemnation, Tannhäuser went down on his knees in front of the altar of the Virgin Mary and wept bitterly. Then he rose and left the Holy City.

"Thus I am expelled and may not serve you, Queen of Heaven. My sin has cast me out forever. What else remains for me but to spend my life in mourning for my past sins."

Three days after the Pope had uttered his cruel verdict, a most wonderful thing happened: his staff was covered with buds, which quickly opened and burgeoned into beautiful green leaves. Pope Urban was confused, for he saw that God Himself had forgiven the knight because of his deep and sincere repentance, and his staunch faith in the mercy of the Lord. And so the Pope sent messengers in every direction, to look for Tannhäuser and acquaint him with the miracle that had occurred.

So it happened that not the Pope in Rome but God in Heaven had forgiven Tannhäuser, the repentant knight.

LEGENDS
OF THE
BALKAN LANDS

The earth had turned red with the blood
of men, when a brave hero came and drew his sabre.
He was afraid of no foe as he fought
for freedom and the faith of his fathers.

T HE BIRTH AND YOUTH OF PRINCE MARKO

The rays of the sun moved across the white walls of Prizren, forced back by the shadow of the Shar-planina mountain. And before long, as on every other night, the stars appeared above the horizon. That night gentle Yevrosima fell asleep in her chamber, and had a vivid dream. She saw a strange, winged dragon holding a sword in its claws, with which it cut down all the Turkish standards in the land, from Kosovo all the way to Stamboul.

Yevrosima was awake early the next day, and before the stars had disappeared behind the mountain she recounted her dream to her husband,

King Vukashin. He thought a while, and then his countenance bright-
ened and he said to her:

"It is not a bad omen, dear Yevrosima, sun of Prizren. What you saw was
our son, who is to be born quite soon. He will be so strong and brave
that even the Turks will bow to him and make him gifts of cities from
the seashore to the banks of the Danube."

Events happened as Vukashin had foretold. A strong and handsome boy
was born to the royal couple. The tsar himself became his godfather ·
and gave him the name of Marko. For three days and three nights wine
flowed freely at Prizren; for three days and three nights the cannon
roared from the castle walls like thunder or like the tumultuous crash
of the sea on the rocks.

The years passed and the young prince grew quickly. At first he only
toddled about the courtyard, then he accompanied his father on his
journeys, and soon he himself went up into the hills among the shepherds and out into the fields among the peasants.

One day he felt he could not stay at home any longer. So he parted
with his father, he parted with his mother Yevrosima, and set out on
a long journey to Prilep Castle, which King Vukashin had given him
as his fief.

He travelled from sunrise till noon, and when the sun stood high overhead, he felt tired and thirsty.

He wandered across the fields and pastures until he found an ice-cold
stream gushing out of some tall grass at the foot of a hill. He bent down
to drink, but before he could refresh his parched throat he saw a beautiful fairy sleeping near the stream. The sun was scorching her delicate
face. Marko knelt down and quickly made a shelter of the wild flowers
that grew thereabouts. Then he picked the fairy up in his arms and was
about to carry her into the shade when she suddenly opened her eyes.

"Where are you taking me, Marko?" she asked him softly.

"Into the shade, so that the sun will not shine on you and mar your
pale beauty," replied the prince, laying her down gently among the
flowers.

"How can I reward you for your kindness, young prince?" she asked.
"Will you choose great wealth or a steel sabre?
A lovely maiden, or Sharats, the splendid horse?"
Marko replied without hesitation:
"Rather than wealth I'll take a steel sabre,
and Sharats, the horse, instead of the maid.
I will need them both in battle."
The fairy then nodded in agreement and took Marko deep into the forest, to where seven dragons guarded her court. She gave Marko a heavy damascene sabre and fetched him the dappled Sharats.

Marko had scarcely got into the saddle when Sharats shot forward, galloping like a whirlwind. Marko just managed to make out the fairy's last words:
"Remember me whenever danger threatens.
Just call me to your aid wherever you may be
and I shall see that no harm befalls you."
As they galloped on, the horse looked round and spoke to Marko, saying:
"Let go of the reins and throw away your gold spurs so you don't hurt my flanks."
Marko dropped the reins and plucked the spurs from his boots.
"Now catch my mane in your left hand and hold the sabre in your right," said the dappled horse.
No sooner had the prince done so than the horse surged forward so swiftly that he scarcely touched the ground with his hooves. Indeed, horse and rider appeared to soar into the air and, in no time at all, Marko found himself in front of the gates of Prilep Castle which his father had given him.

WHOSE IS THE TSARDOM?

In days long ago four great camps were pitched in Kosovo Field next to the little church of Samodrezh: one camp belonged to King Vukashin, over the second fluttered the banner of the mighty Uglyesha, the third camp belonged to Duke Goyek, while the fourth had the emblem of the little Tsarevich Urosh on its tents.

Why had the greatest men in the land gathered there? The first three kept quarrelling and shouted at one another so that no one would have guessed they were brothers. Only the small Urosh kept silent and watched them as they argued. Hour after hour their dispute went on, and now and again knives gleamed in their hands. What was the argument about? Nothing less than which of them was to be the tsar . . .

They could not reach an agreement, and argued endlessly day and night. Finally Vukashin's courier secretly saddled his horse and hastened to white-walled Prizren with a message from his king. Uglyesha wrote, too, and so did Goyek, and even the Tsarevich Urosh eventually took up a pen and sent his messenger, the strongest of the strong.

The four couriers met in Prizren, outside the house of the priest Nedelyko. But the house was empty, for the priest was just serving Mass. The four wasted no time, and rode straight into the church. And there they rudely shouted at the priest, one louder than the other:

"Come with us to Kosovo to decide who is to be the tsar!"

The priest stroked his snow-white beard and, crossing to the church door, asked the impatient fellows:

"Why should I, of all people, adjudicate between the greatest in the land?"

"You were the former tsar's confessor!"

"You have all his papers!"

"But you doubtless know his last will and testament!"

Nedelyko shook his head and said:

"I used to ask the tsar about his sins, not who was to succeed him when he died. But I can give you some good advice: go and talk to Prince Marko — he knew what was in the tsar's mind, for he wrote all his papers. I myself taught him to write, so that he could become our monarch's scribe. Go to Prilep and find out!"

The couriers took to the road again, and rode to Prince Marko's white castle at Prilep. There they knocked on the iron doors, and Marko himself came out to talk to them. They bowed humbly before him, but before he could ask what brought them there, they cried in unison:

"Our masters are quarrelling angrily, and they want you to decide who is to be the next tsar. Make haste and come with us to Kosovo."

Marko agreed to come, and went to take his leave of his mother. Though

Yevrosima knew that her son feared nothing and no one except God, 249
she said to him:

"Whatever your decision, be sure that it is just. You must take neither
your father's nor your uncles' part, even though it were to cost you
your life!"

The prince sought out all the ancient deeds, saddled the impatient Sharats
and, followed by the four couriers, he rode as fast as his horse would
carry him to Kosovo Field.

He stopped his horse outside King Vukashin's tent.

"Welcome, my son," exclaimed the king, his voice oozing honey. "I
know that you, and you alone, will decide justly who is to be the tsar.
And when I grow old," he added in a whisper, "you'll hold the sceptre
in my place."

Marko did not reply to his father's words and was about to leave when
Uglyesha appeared in front of him, as though he had suddenly grown
up out of the ground.

"My dear nephew," he cried, "I'm sure you haven't forgotten how I
used to rock you on my knee, and you'll surely award the tsardom to
me. I shall not fail to reward you for it."

Uglyesha, too, was given no answer, but before Marko had gone a few
paces he was welcomed by Duke Goyek:

"At last you're here, brave youth, to delight your affectionate uncle.
Now I know that I shall be tsar, and I'll shower you with such favours
that no one in the land will be your equal."

Marko did not wait for his uncle to finish speaking but turned briskly
on his heel and slipped inside the tent of little Tsarevich Urosh.

"Marko, my dear cousin," rejoiced the puny tsarevich, rising from his
bed to embrace the prince. They sat down together and talked endlessly,
recalling how Marko had defeated Ban Zadranin, how he had freed
a girl from the hands of twelve Arabs, how he had gone hunting with
the Turks and what had happened then. They had so much to talk about
that they would probably have missed morning Mass, if they had not
heard the church bell ringing.

After the service they all sat down at one table, with King Vukashin at its head, and Marko's uncles, Uglyesha and Goyek, on either side. Little Urosh could hardly be seen among these stalwart heroes. They drank *rakiya* and ate sugar, but it was not a merry feast, for each and every one of them waited tensely for Marko's decision.

The prince rose to his feet, unrolled the ancient parchments, and turned to his father.

"Haven't you a large enough kingdom, King Vukashin? Tend it well so that it prospers, and do not claim a tsardom that does not belong to you!"

Then Marko turned to Uglyesha.

"And do you too wish to be a tsar? Why, you wouldn't know how to be one — just take a look at your own estates and see how neglected they are!"

Uglyesha flushed red, but just as King Vukashin before him he did not say a word.

Marko's gaze then turned on Goyek.

"By what right do you demand the throne of the tsars? Is your duke-dom not enough for you? There is no mention in any of these papers of you as a successor. Here," Prince Marko pointed to the weak Urosh, "is your future tsar! The line of inheritance is a direct one, from father to son!"

Only then did Marko's father and uncles recover from their surprise, and all three began to scold and curse him. King Vukashin was the most violent of all. But they were interrupted by the young tsar, who exclaimed:

"God help you, cousin Marko, that you may become the strongest of heroes, and may your sabre serve you well in every battle!"

And so it came about that the tsar was fairly chosen.

YANKO'S WEDDING

Ban Yanko chose his bride from a land far away from his own home. She was the daughter of King Mikhail of Kotsya. However, Yanko waited in vain for the king's consent — Mikhail was in no hurry. A year went by, then another, nine long years all told.

One day — it was at the beginning of the tenth year — when snow covered the paths below his castle, Yanko heard children's voices under his window.

"Don't you dare! You mustn't think you can do as you please with me, like the king with our ban!"

The children went on squabbling in the courtyard and throwing snow-balls at each other, but Yanko did not wait to hear more. He went straight to the stable and prepared his brown horse for a journey, harnessing him and putting a Turkish saddle on him and a gold-embroidered blanket that reached right down to the ground. Finally he tied the reins to the pommel, so that the horse might walk freely, and, running up into the white tower, he dressed himself in silk and velveteen, put on his plumed helmet, and buckled on his sabre. And then he mounted the horse and galloped out of the castle gate, across the fields and meadows to Mount Romanya, and then over the mountain to the sea.

He crossed the sea without incident and, disembarking in a southern land, he soon arrived at Kotsya Castle. King Mikhail was sitting by the window. Seeing a stranger approach, he looked out to see who it was. Then he shouted to the servants:

"Open the gate quickly, and then get out of the courtyard! I think that Ban Yanko has come!"

Impatient and angry, Yanko did not wait for the gate to be opened; with one leap his horse landed on the wall, with another he stood beneath the castle tower.

Mikhail then had to go down to the dark courtyard to greet the count.

"Welcome, Ban Yanko," he said. "Tie up your horse and come with me to drink a little wine."

But Yanko replied:

"I have no time for wine. You know very well what brings me here. Will you give me your daughter, or must I win her with my sabre?"

"Why shouldn't I give her to you? But do come and drink with me while we talk it over."

Yanko agreed and went into the castle with the king. They drank for one whole day, and then through the next. On the morning of the third King Mikhail said to him:

"Dear son-in-law, it is time you returned home and brought the wedding guests. Bring as many of them as you please, only make sure that there are no drunkards or brawlers among them. Choose wise old men, priests and townsmen."

Yanko again agreed, and without more ado set out on his return journey. As he crossed the castle courtyard, a small window opened in the slim white tower above him and a letter came fluttering down like a white swallow, right in his lap. Eager to see what was inside, Yanko opened it and read:

"Dearest Yanko, my handsome young falcon,
don't ask priests and old men to our wedding,
bring those who know how to use a sabre,
those whose blood still runs fast in their veins.
Do as I say, or you'll not take home your bride,
your body will rot here in the tower."

Yanko looked up at the window, hoping to learn more, but when no one appeared, he spurred his horse and hurried home, to send out the invitations to his wedding.

Yanko sat down and his pen flew over the paper. Ignoring the king's advice, he did as the girl had urged him, for his own heart also warned him that this was the right course to take.

He invited old Father Novak and his sons Gruyitsa and Tatomir, as well as Milosh Obilich. Winged Relya was to carry the banner in front of the procession. And he asked Prince Marko himself to be his best man.

Thus did the ban decide, and couriers sped out of the castle to all four points of the compass: one to Mount Romanya, to old Father Novak, a second to Marko's Prilep, a third to Milosh Obilich at Kosovo, and a fourth to Relya in Pazar.

The festive day came at last. It was still dark when Prince Marko arrived on his horse Sharats, at the head of five hundred agile lads. Yanko took Marko up to his tower, sending food and drink to his men out in the open.

Soon they saw Duke Milosh with five hundred heroes from Kosovo,

and soon after that Relya appeared, waving the banner and with
another five hundred wedding guests.

Only Father Novak and his brigands were nowhere to be seen. The
guests waited three nights for them without avail, and when the sun
rose on the third morning there were many who spoke up in dissatisfac-
tion, saying that the King of Kotsya was not to be trusted, and that
without Father Novak any expedition was as good as lost.

Therefore they all went to Mount Romanya, where Prince Marko called
out in a mighty voice that reverberated through the woods. At once
the undergrowth by the roadside came alive with men. Father Novak
and his brigands suddenly appeared in view.

"Why have you not come for the wedding, brother?" Marko asked him.

"How can I go as I haven't got a single ducat?" replied Father Novak
with tears in his eyes. "It's not right to attend a wedding without
bringing a gift."

"Never mind," said Marko, taking a hundred ducats from his pocket.
Milosh, Relya, and Yanko also gave a hundred each, and the rest of the
guests collected a thousand more among themselves. Novak was satisfied then; he called his five hundred brigands together, and the whole
company set out for Kotsya.

King Mikhail was waiting for Ban Yanko, and looking forward to van-
quishing the wedding guests and putting their gifts in his tower. During
those past nine years he had promised his daughter to nine different
grooms, outwitting every one of them when they had arrived for their
wedding. He had driven out their priests and old men, and filled nine
towers with their gold. He had a tenth tower all ready to receive the
wedding gifts brought by Yanko's guests.

King Mikhail's followers rode out to meet Yanko on Kotsya Field,
where they challenged him:

"Prepare for a heroic duel:
you must be able to throw a rock farther than we can,
or else you will not be allowed to leave this place alive."

Yanko was about to start the contest, but Prince Marko would not let him. He himself threw the rock an incredibly long distance, before rejoining his friends.

The enemy was not yet satisfied.

"You must now jump over this bough, dear ban,

to show that you are worthy of your bride.

Your head is forfeit if you fail this test."

Again Yanko was not allowed to try his skill — it was Milosh who went instead, vaulting the bough with a splendid leap before returning to the other guests.

And then a terrible monster — a three-headed Moor — was led out of Kotsya Castle, and King Mikhail himself called out to Yanko:

"Grapple with him if you want my daughter.

Unless you defeat him, your life is lost."

Without hesitation Relya tackled the monster, but before he could lay his hands on him, he received a frightful blow on the head and collapsed on the ground. The Moor tied him up and threw him into the dungeon behind nine oak doors secured with eighteen chains. Then he returned to the field once more.

In the same way the terrible creature overcame Milosh and Marko, casting them into the dungeon. Yanko was about to fight with the Moor when Father Novak took a hand. He put on nine furs, and three wolves' heads instead of a helmet. Young Gruyitsa handed him his own sabre, saying:

"Your sabre is too long, Father. Before you had had time to swing it, the Moor would be able to smite you. Take mine instead and don't wait for the first blow to fall."

Father Novak weighed his son's sabre in his hand and found that it was light as a feather. Before the Moor could lift his battle-axe and hit him the old man jumped up to him and with one mighty blow cut off all his three heads at once.

Seeing this, King Mikhail's men quickly closed the castle gates, but it was of no use. Father Novak leaped up on top of the wall, followed by all the others. One more jump and he stood outside the dungeon.

With the heavy battle-axe he broke down the nine doors, one after the other. When the last door fell, he found Marko waiting for him with open arms.

In the meantime Ban Yanko struggled up to the top of the tower, duelling with the treacherous King Mikhail. They fought on the stairs and in many chambers, the king retreating but still refusing to give up his daughter. But then, as the king raised his sword for the decisive blow, there was a tinkle of glass, and he stepped backwards into the void. King Mikhail had fallen through a high window and lay dead on the black earth below.

At last Ban Yanko could take his bride home with him.

The terrible battle over, the companions knocked down Mikhail's walls and burned his castle.

The wedding was celebrated at Yanko's castle with wine flowing for half a month before the wedding guests took their leave: Marko with his five hundred heroes went back to white Prilep, Milosh with his five hundred men to Kosovo, Relya and his followers to Pazar, and Father Novak with his sons Gruyitsa and Tatomir returned with their five hundred brigands to Mount Romanya.

Only Ban Yanko remained in his high tower with his beautiful bride, and they lived together and loved each other for very many years afterwards.

THE BATTLE OF KOSOVO FIELD

Like a flock of black crows the Turkish army moved westwards, leaving nothing behind but fire and smoke. There was no one who could halt its implacable advance.

The Turks marched to the West, not stopping until they reached Kosovo Field in Serbia. Then their Sultan Murat took up his pen and wrote to the Serbian tsar, Lazarus, telling him that he wished to rule all the land, and therefore Lazarus must give up the golden keys to all his towns and castles, or else the sabre would decide which of them was to be the tsar of Serbia.

When he received the letter at his castle of Krushevats, Tsar Lazarus was
saddened; he did not want war, bloodshed and sorrow. But seeing that
he had no choice, he sent messengers to every corner of the land to
summon together famous heroes and warriors, such as Milosh Obilich,
the ten Yugoviches, Ivan Kosanchich, as well as many others, then still
unknown, who had never crossed arms in battle before.

It was a splendid sight when, the next day, riders came in through the
castle gate beneath the window of Tsar Lazarus and his wife Militsa.
They kept pouring in, led by one who rode under a banner with a
golden cross — Boshko Yugovich, the tsarina's favourite brother.

As soon as she caught sight of him, Militsa turned to her husband with
her hands joined in entreaty.

"You are taking my nine brothers to Kosovo and only God knows
whether or not they will lay down their lives there. Please leave at
least Boshko behind."

Lazarus nodded, and said with a smile:

"He has my blessing. Let him hand over the holy banner to another in
line and then return home."

Tsarina Militsa ran down from the high tower as fast as her legs would
carry her, not stopping until she had reached her brother. She caught
his sorrel mount by the rein, and told Boshko what had passed between
her and the tsar.

But the young Boshko replied:

"I cannot go home and leave the holy banner to someone else, not if
the tsar were to offer me the whole of Krushevats. Everyone would
laugh at me for being a coward, and as for myself, I want to fight at
Kosovo!"

He gave his sorrel the spurs, and the horse sped through the castle gate
so fast that the dust he raised blotted everything from sight.

Then the nine other Yugoviches rode by — the old Yug-Bogdan riding
first, with his sons behind him, Voyin Yugovich bringing up the rear.

Militsa tried to stop each of them, but not one would look at her. Only
Voyin called out in farewell:

"Go home yourself, sister, for none of us would ever forgive himself if he let others fight for him. That is why we must go to Kosovo Field!"

The flags flew and the war drums resounded at Kosovo when Tsar Lazarus and his nobles sat down for their last meal before the battle. On the tsar's right sat the old Yug-Bogdan, with the nine Yugovich brothers next to him. On his left was Vuk Brankovich, while opposite sat Milosh Obilich, Ivan Kosanchich, and Milan Toplitsa.

They all raised their golden goblets, but the tsar hesitated before proposing a toast.

"To whom shall we drink this cup?" he asked, replying to his own question before anyone could speak: "Yug-Bogdan is the oldest among you, Ivan Kosanchich the most handsome, Vuk Brankovich the most dignified; the voice of my heart says I should drink to my nine brothers-in-law, the Yugoviches . . . For his valour and glory, though, it is Milosh Obilich who deserves the honour. Well then, your health, famous hero . . . to your courage, which will stand you in good stead in the field until the time when you and your men betray me and desert to the Sultan."

Those words angered Milosh so much that he jumped to his feet and cried:

"Thank you, Lazarus, for your toast, but no thanks will you get for your insult. I have sworn in front of everyone that I shall be loyal to you, and I shall prove my loyalty tomorrow at Kosovo ere I die. But heed my warning: the traitor sits on your left. It is not I but Vuk Brankovich who will be disloyal, and if I return alive to your castle of Krushevats, I shall challenge him to a duel to the death!"

Dawn came. It was the Day of St Vitus.

As soon as the sun had shown its face the armies stood and prepared themselves, and when its rays began to warm the earth, scimitars glittered on the sultan's side and the Turks charged into battle.

Yug-Bogdan was the first to ride against them, together with his nine sons, the nine Yugoviches. Each of them had nine thousand men, old Bogdan had twelve. The clash seemed endless. Riders and horses fell on both sides. Yug-Bogdan himself slew seven pashas. But when he fought the eighth, enemies came upon him like a flood and Bogdan was killed. Nor did his sons live to see the end of that day — the Turks slaughtered them, Boshko Yugovich dying last of all.

Then it was the turn of Strahinya Banovich. He fought furiously and valiantly until he fell, as did Ivan Kosanchich and Milan Toplitsa.

Milosh Obilich and his army slew twelve thousand Turks, and Milosh finally drove his lance through Sultan Murat's body there by the river Sitnitsa before he himself closed his eyes for the last time, dying a hero's death.

Tsar Lazarus led seventy-seven thousand Serbians into the battle. His army spread over Kosovo Field like a flock of falcons, taking a heavy toll of the enemy. But just when the Turks were about to quit the field, Milosh's prophetic words were fulfilled. The traitor Vuk Brankovich deserted with twelve thousand riders, and the outcome of the battle was decided.

The outnumbered Serbians defended themselves in vain; the blood shed by so many heroes was shed for naught. They all perished; and where the most broken lances were left pointing to the sky, there Lazarus, the holy tsar, had fought his last.

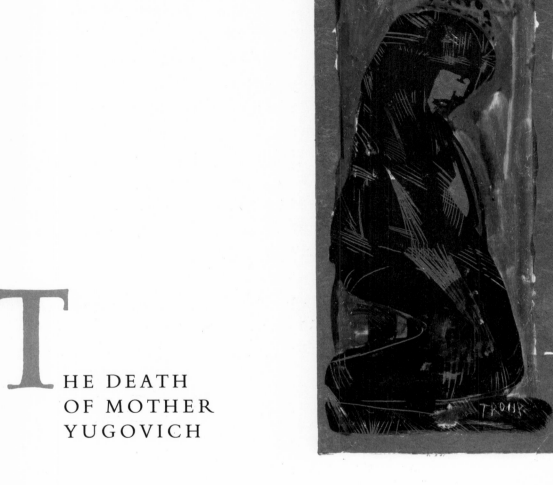

THE DEATH OF MOTHER YUGOVICH

When the armies were fighting at Kosovo Field the mother of the Yugoviches could not find comfort anywhere. She asked God to lend her
the eyes of a falcon and the wings of a swan. She wished to go and see
for herself how the battle was going.

And God granted her wish. Mother Yugovich flew to the scene of the
battle.

She did not have to search for long. Eight Yugoviches lay close together
on a little hillock, and old Yug-Bogdan, their father, next to them. And

above their bodies she saw nine lances, and on them nine falcons. By the lances stood nine horses neighing and nine dogs baying.

Mother Yugovich did not shed a tear. Her heart became as heavy as a stone. Yet her eyes were searching for her youngest son, Boshko Yugovich.

At last she caught sight of him: in the flat Kosovo Field he was fighting the Turks, dealing blows to the left and to the right, sparing no one. The next moment the scene disappeared in a cloud of dust, and there was nothing for Mother Yugovich to do but to return home and deliver to everybody the sad tidings.

The nine dead bodies were lying in the Kosovo Field, the widows and orphans were weeping at home, yet Mother Yugovich did not shed a tear. While her youngest son was still fighting for freedom against the Turks, there was no time for mourning.

It was nearly midnight when a sad horse's neighing could be heard from afar. Everybody ran out into the courtyard. Boshko's white horse was returning home, alone, without his master.

Boundless was the sorrow of those standing in the courtyard. Yet one pair of eyes remained dry — the eyes of Mother Yugovich, for there was still hope in her heart.

And when morning came, two ravens suddenly appeared. They brought a most curious gift — a human hand with a gold ring on it.

The birds dropped the hand in the mother's lap, and as she sat there looking at it she called to Boshko's widow:

"Tell me, daughter-in-law, whose hand is this?"

"Oh, I recognise it . . . surely that was our wedding ring."

Mother Yugovich clasped Boshko's hand in her arms and spoke to it: "Oh, my dear hand, my dear green apple, where did you grow, from what tree did you spring? Alas, did you grow up on my lap, only to be plucked at faraway Kosovo?"

At this Mother Yugovich burst into tears, weeping until her heart burst with sorrow, for her nine sons, the nine Yugoviches, and for old Yug-Bogdan, her husband.

WHEN MARKO WENT TO PLOUGH

Marko was sitting with his mother in one of the chambers of Prilep Castle, passing the time by sipping wine. All of a sudden old Yevrosima put aside her goblet and, fixing her eyes on the prince, said to him: "You are brave, my son, but when I look at your hands, my heart bleeds for you. How many times have I had to wash your bloodstained tunic? How many sleepless nights have I passed fearfully waiting to know whether you would return? What use are all these heroic deeds of yours, these skirmishes and battles?"

Marko bowed his head and stroked his damascene sabre thoughtfully.
"We no longer have heroes as we used to in the past, Mother," he replied.
"Turkish janissaries have occupied our villages, which have gone to
rack and ruin. Who do you think will drive them out?"

"Can you drive them out by yourself? How long has this been going on
now! And all the time the soldiers wander about the countryside, pillaging, burning and plundering. No one sows corn; no one harvests it.
You are strong, my son. Why don't you yoke the oxen to the plough?
Go and make furrows, scatter the wheat so that our people do not suffer
from hunger. Then they will gladly help you when battle comes."

Marko obeyed his mother and yoked the strongest pair of oxen to his
plough. He ploughed flat fields, he ploughed on the hillsides and in the
valleys, and when the furrows spread as far as the eye could see, he
made for the Sultan's great highway. Bit by bit he ploughed it up, and
whenever he came to another road or path he put that to the plough.

Before long three waggons full of janissaries came rattling towards him.

"What's that you're doing, Marko?" cried the Turks. "Stop ploughing
up our roads!"

"Out of my way!" exclaimed Marko, and the Turks barely had time to
jump aside as he drove along their path.

"Stop ploughing the sultan's highways!" cried the Turks once more,
angrily drawing their sabres.

But Marko also lost his temper. Raising his plough in the air, oxen and
all, he slew every single one of the janissaries where they stood, knocking
them down like so many ripe poppy-heads. Then he drove their horses
and waggons to his castle.

When Yevrosima saw them she could scarcely believe her eyes.

"So you have been fighting again," she called. "You have broken your
promise."

"No, I have not, Mother," replied Prince Marko. "As far as the eye can
see there are straight furrows made by my plough. And these horses and
waggons are a gift I have brought for you in the bargain."

FATHER NOVAK

The green mantle of spring had covered Mount Romanya many times since Father Novak and his brigands had made their home there. And many laden wagons stolen from the rich Turks had been driven up the mountain after the brigands had defeated the Turks in fierce combat. But one day as they sat on the mountain drinking wine — Father Novak, his brother Radivoy, his two sons Gruyitsa and Tatomir, and thirty brigands — his brother Radivoy said to Novak:

"It seems to me, brother, that you have grown old. You no longer ride out to unburden the merchants, nor will you let us harass them. I'll stay here with you no more!"

Not waiting for a reply, Radivoy got up, took his sabre, and left. All the brigands followed, going out into the forest behind him and leaving Novak there alone, with only his sons Gruyitsa and Tatomir for company.

Radivoy meant to set out in search of booty, and as soon as he and his men came out of the undergrowth and reached the road, it seemed that luck was on his side. Three Turkish wagons were coming their way, each laden with gold and the finest of cloth.

It was a tempting prize, only this time Radivoy had met his match. Before the brigands realised what was happening, thirty Turks came charging at them, all seasoned veterans, with Mehmed Pasha at their head.

It was all over in a flash. Like thirty serpents the Turkish sabres hissed in the air, each finding its target. Radivoy was the only one Mehmed Pasha left alive; the Turks bound his hands behind his back and drove him along the road in front of them.

Radivoy knew that he could expect no mercy. But while he still had breath and could look up at green Mount Romanya, he sang about it.

Gruyitsa heard the song and went running back to his father.

"Out there in the distance someone is singing about Mount Romanya," he told him. "I believe it is Uncle Radivoy. Either he has taken rich booty or he has met with some misfortune. Let's go and help him!"

All three were soon lying well hidden by the roadside: Father Novak, Gruyitsa and Tatomir. They were just in time, for the bound Radivoy appeared, dragging three wagons behind him, followed by Mehmed Pasha and his soldiers.

Novak called out to his sons, as he attacked Mehmed Pasha with his sabre. He felled the pasha with a terrible blow, and he quickly cut the ropes which bound Radivoy. Handing his brother the Turk's sabre, they made short shrift of the enemy: those who escaped Radivoy had Tatomir to contend with, those who got past Tatomir were tackled by young Gruyitsa, and any Turk who still lived after that found Father Novak barring his way.

They killed all the Turks, and were left with the rich booty. Sitting down to rest and drink wine, Novak asked his brother:

"Tell me, my dear Radivoy, what is better: your old brother or thirty brigands?"

To which Radivoy truthfully replied:

"They were thirty stalwart lads, but they had neither your luck nor your experience. Woe to him who fails to listen to the advice of his elders!"

MARKO FINDS HIS FATHER'S SABRE

The dew on the grass had hardly started to glisten in the pale glow of dawn when a beautiful Turkish girl hurried down to the river Maritsa to bleach cloth.

The water flowed quickly, forming white ripples as it splashed against the stones. Suddenly it became dark and muddy. But it was not the sun rising over the crest of the hill that coloured the water. No, it was blood, the blood of the Serbian heroes massacred by the Turks at Chrmen. And dead horses and the bodies of the Serbian warriors came floating down the river.

The horrified girl stopped her task; she dearly wanted to run away but she could not tear her eyes from the surface of the water. Suddenly a white arm rose up in the middle of the stream. Then a feeble voice could be heard in the murmur of the rapids:

"Help me, sister, throw me a piece of cloth so I may reach the bank!"

The Turkish girl quickly unwound the longest piece of cloth and threw it to the drowning man. The current was very strong and the Maritsa fought hard to keep her captive. But at last, spent and exhausted, the hero managed to climb out on to the river bank.

The girl looked at him in amazement — he was no longer young, a grey beard adorning his face, but his clothing showed that he was a noble-man. His sabre was fit for a king, its hilt made of three gold pieces set with precious stones.

"Where do you live, my dear?" he asked the girl, trying to get to his feet. The seventeen wounds he had received made him so weak, how-ever, that he fell back and remained lying on the ground.

"I live in a white house not far from here," the girl replied.

"And who else lives there with you?"

"Only my aged mother and my brother Mustaph-aga."

"Go then, my dear, to your house and tell your brother, Mustaph-aga, to come and carry me in. I have on me three pouches with three hundred ducats in each. The first I wish to give you, the second will be your brother's for his help, and I shall only keep the third to pay for my cure."

The girl ran home and told Mustaph-aga what had happened on the banks of the Maritsa, and she asked him to go and carry the wounded hero to their house.

Her brother agreed and hurried to the river.

As he stood there, looking down at the wounded man, he noticed the splendid sabre. The Turk began to covet the wonderful weapon so much that he became quite bereft of reason and compassion. Pulling the sabre from its scabbard, Mustaph-aga cut the hero's head off, and then he stripped the corpse of its fine clothing and he took the ducats before

returning home. His sister was watching out for him and, seeing him return alone, she guessed what he had done. Lamenting, she fled before him.

"Why, in God's name, did you do this, brother?

Simply to possess this gold sabre?

Beware — for some day your own head may be cut off by it!"

Sometime later the sultan himself sent a note to the white house ordering Mustaph-aga to join the army. Mustaph-aga therefore buckled on the sabre and left for the sultan's camp.

No one failed to notice that sabre — it was passed from hand to hand, but nobody could pull it out of its scabbard. Only when Prince Marko tried did the sabre slide out as if of its own accord. Marko gazed astonished at the blade, where three names had been engraved: those of Novak the blacksmith, of King Vukashin, and his own.

"Where did you get this weapon, Turk?" Prince Marko cried. "Did you buy it or gain it on the battlefield? Or was it perhaps part of your bride's dowry?"

Mustaph-aga was loath to tell the truth, but in the end he had no choice but to reveal exactly how he came to own the sabre.

"Do you know whose head you struck off? My father's head — it was none other than King Vukashin!" exclaimed Prince Marko in despair. "Instead of the kingly reward you would have had if you'd dressed his wounds, I'll reward you differently now!" And Marko struck out so violently that the Turk's head flew from his shoulders. He then picked up his mace and stormed into the sultan's tent, sitting down on the carpet without first taking off his shoes.

The sultan looked at him and, seeing the angry tears in his bloodshot eyes, drew away from the enraged prince.

"What has made you so angry, my friend?" he asked, keeping his eyes on Marko's mace.

"I've recognised my father's sabre," replied Marko. "And it was lucky for you that you did not have it in your hand, sultan, for you would have fared no better than the man I've just despatched."

THE DEATH OF PRINCE MARKO

Marko got up exceptionally early one Sunday morning, before the rays of the sun had had time to flood the earth with light. He rode a long way along the sea shore, to Mount Urvina, and as he started to ascend its steep slopes, his horse Sharats stumbled. And he stumbled a second time, and a third, shedding large tears.

"Now then, what's the matter, my old friend?" Marko asked him. "We have known each other a hundred and sixty years, and in all that time your legs have been swift and nimble."

This was a bad omen, thought the prince. Who knew but that perhaps one of them — Sharats or himself — would find a last resting place there on the mountain.

And, as if to confirm his fears, he heard a well-known voice from the forest — the voice of his friend, the fairy.

"Why do you think your old horse has stumbled,
why are his eyes shedding bitter tears?
He weeps for you, my prince, your life he mourns."

But Marko replied: "This time I do not believe you, fairy. Is there a better and braver hero in all this world than I? And no better horse will you find anywhere than my Sharats. We have ridden together countless miles, to the East and to the West; we know many lands and many towns. No, while my head sits on these shoulders, no one can part my horse and me!"

There was a brief silence, and then the boughs above Marko's head whispered again:

"Indeed, there is no one in all this world
who in truth can call himself your equal.
Nor would you find a better horse than yours.
But it is God's will that your life should end."

"I don't believe it!" cried Marko defiantly.

"Go to the mountain top where two slim pines
reach up towards the sky. Between their trunks
a stream you'll find — the stream of truth.
There read your fate, and then you may believe ."

The fairy spoke once more, but then her voice faded forever in the dim forest. Receiving no reply to his calls, Marko continued humbly on his way to the top of Mount Urvina.

There, as foretold, he found two slim pine-trees and in their shade a small stream. The prince tied Sharats to one of the pines, knelt down by the stream, and looked down. And mirrored in the water he saw his own, old and wrinkled face — but this was no longer his face, it was a death's-head that stared at him from the glittering surface.

Now Marko knew the truth about his fate, which he could neither cheat nor escape. Though there was no one to hear him, he complained:

"No sooner have I enjoyed myself a little in this world than I am supposed to leave it." Having said this, he drew his sabre and with a single mighty blow he struck off his faithful horse's head. He could not allow Sharats to fall into anyone else's hands, particularly not into those of the Turks.

He buried the horse, and then broke his damascene sabre into four pieces. He also broke his lance, throwing the seven parts that were left up into the branches of the pine tree for the birds to carry away. Taking his mace, he flung it with all his strength down from the mountain-top into the sea, with the words:

"When you rise to the surface again, let another hero, such as me, come into the world."

Then Marko took out his pen and a clean white sheet of paper, and started to write his last message:

"Whoever finds my cold body,
let him bury me in a Christian grave.
Three belts full of ducats will he find here.
Let him keep one for my interment,
use another to endow a chapel,
and the third as alms for the blind and crippled,
who carry their violins round the Balkans
to sing my praises in their famous songs,
to sing my praises in their songs and legends
about the brave exploits of Prince Marko."

Having finished, Marko threw the golden ink-pot and the pen into the water, attached his message to a branch so that it could be seen easily from the path, took off his green coat, and spread it underneath the pine tree.

As he lay on the coat, looking up into the crown of the tree above him, his eyes growing dim, he saw not only the green branches; he en-

countered once again all the heroes of old whom he had helped and by whose side he had fought in many battles; he saw and heard his mother Yevrosima, and perhaps also the various girls he had known on his travels about the world. No one can tell what passed through the prince's mind in his last hour . . .

Prince Marko had been in his eternal sleep for a whole day, then a second, and a third, and still those who happened to pass by and see him avoided him carefully, thinking that he was resting and knowing that he was not a man to be trifled with.

A week had gone by when abbot Vaso with one of his novices, Isaiah, came that way, on their way home to the Holy Mountain. Their attention was caught by the white sheet of paper among the branches; the old man dismounted and, taking great care not to wake the sleeping Marko, approached closer and read the message.

He could not believe his eyes, and he spent a long time weeping over the prince's body, hoping that Marko would awaken. But then he took the three belts full of ducats and, helped by his young friend, put the dead Marko on a horse and slowly rode down from the top of Mount Urvina to the seashore, where a ship was already waiting to take them to their home below the Holy Mountain, at the church of Hilandar.

In the middle of the church they secretly buried Prince Marko, the abbot giving all the honours due to a hero such as he. They buried the prince in secret to prevent his enemies from disturbing his rest.

And that is how it came about that instead of a tombstone it is the songs of the anonymous blind musicians, known as *guslari,* which keep the memory of Prince Marko alive to this day.

RUSSIAN LEGENDS

In the famous town of Kiev,
at the court of Prince Vladimir,
many a merry feast was held
for many boyars and princes,
for many brave Russian heroes,
and many brave Russian warriors.

How Ilya Became a Hero

Far away in the heart of Holy Russia, in the village of Karacharov near the town of Murom, there lived, with his parents, a young man by the name of Ilya, who led a very dull life because, for thirty years, he could only sit or lie on top of the oven, looking out of the window at the back yard.

Ilya's legs were quite useless, like a pair of stone pillars — he could not walk a single step. And his hands too, though white and smooth, hung helpless by his side.

One morning, after his mother and father had gone to work in the fields,
leaving Ilya alone in the cottage, he suddenly heard voices outside.
Turning round to gaze out of the window, he saw two old pilgrims
peeping in at him.

"Get up, Ilya," said one of the wandering friars, "and run down to the
cellar for a jug of beer. We're thirsty."

Ilya smiled sadly.

"For thirty years my legs have refused to obey me. Why, I can't even
climb down from the oven. I'm sorry, I can't help you . . ."

"Try it and see," the old man urged him.

Ilya propped himself up on his white hands, and they did not give way
under him. Then he jumped down on the much-trodden floor, and his
legs did not buckle under him. And when he went down the stairs to
the cellar, he found that he could move his legs quite naturally, as if
they had been healthy all his life.

He brought the pilgrims a jug filled to the brim with beer and, when
they had emptied it and wiped their white chins, the old man said to
him:

"And now you drink as well, Ilya."

Ilya had still not recovered from his astonishment, but he did as the
old man told him. With the very first sip he felt a new strength enter
his body. And it grew and grew until he could no longer restrain it.
He stamped his foot on the ground and in consequence the cottage
almost fell apart.

The two old pilgrims looked at one another.

"Go down to the cellar once more, Ilya," they ordered him.

He did not have to be told twice. He fetched another jugful of the magic
beverage and, seeing the old men nod in agreement, he drank it all.
This time, however, his strength grew less — he no longer felt that the
earth could not carry him, but he knew that he could take on anyone
in combat.

"I've given you a hero's strength," explained the first pilgrim, "so that
you might help people and not frighten them. Now you can defeat

any adversary. Only beware of the giant Svatohor, and be sure not to fight against any of the other heroes you may chance to meet."

"And before you set out to see the world," added the second pilgrim, "get yourself a horse, no matter how decrepit. But don't forget to give him white wheat to eat and cold water to drink, and bathe him in the dew. You'll see what a fine horse he'll then become."

Ilya made as if to speak, but the pilgrims would stay no longer. All they said as they left was:

"You are destined to become a great warrior, Ilya. Neither death in battle nor on this earth will be your lot."

Alone again, Ilya at once went to look for his parents in the fields.

From afar he could see his father and mother chasing cattle out of a field, stumbling over roots and becoming entangled in the bushes. Ilya therefore went to their assistance, driving the animals away with one hand while with the other he tore up the roots, as he built a fence round the field with the oaklings he had removed.

His parents could hardly believe their eyes — here was Ilya Ivanovich, no longer a cripple but healthy and miraculously strong. They quickly called all their neighbours to come and see for themselves. Then Ilya took his father by the arm and said to him:

"I'd like to go to the city of Kiev, to meet the good Prince Vladimir. To do this, I need a horse . . . even the most hopeless hack would do . . ."

His old father, Ivan Muromets, went and bought him a horse at once. It was a cheap horse and not much to look at, but after Ilya had fed it on white wheat for three months, given it cold water to drink, and bathed it in dew every night, there was not a horse in all of Russia more handsome, fleet-footed and untiring than his own.

And then one fine day Ilya saddled his grey mount and equipped himself in a way fitting for a hero — a bow over his shoulder, a quiver full of arrows at his side, a steel mace in one hand and his horse's reins in the other. Taking leave of his parents, he started his long journey to meet Vladimir, the Prince of Kiev.

ILYA MUROMETS AND THE GIANT SVATOHOR

Ilya was on his way to meet Prince Vladimir. He had attended morning Mass at Murom, and decided that he wanted to hear the church bells of Kiev by noon. That was why his horse flew like a bird across the countryside, the reins loose, the earth trembling under its hooves.

Ilya soon reached the Holy Mountains. Suddenly the rocks shook and split apart, but not under the hooves of Ilya's grey horse. They shook under the hooves of a huge horse in whose saddle sat the giant Svatohor, who was so tall that his head disappeared in the clouds.

Amazed at the sight, Ilya Muromets called out to the unknown hero. But the latter did not deign to turn his head — it seemed as if he were asleep in the saddle.

"What, do you mean to mock me?" cried Ilya, charging at Svatohor with his mace held high. He struck the giant fiercely, so hard that his arm was almost wrenched out of its socket, but still Svatohor sat unmoved. Ilya rode off a little way and galloped up once more, the blow he struck this time producing a shower of sparks from his mace. Again Svatohor did not seem to notice anything unusual happening, and he continued on his way. Only when Ilya attacked him a third time, breaking his iron mace into a thousand pieces, did the giant turn round and say:

"How tiresome these Russian flies are!" And, grasping Ilya by his yellow curls, he put him and the grey horse into his pocket.

He might have forgotten all about Ilya, had his horse not stumbled after a while and then, stopping, said in a human voice:

"I can't go on, dear master. While I only had you to carry, I cleared all the Holy Mountains, one after the other. But now I'm supposed to carry two Russian heroes, and a horse besides . . ."

Reminded of Ilya Muromets, Svatohor reached into his pocket and put Ilya and his horse down on the ground. Then he said:

"Do you know with whom you wanted to fight, young man? I am Svatohor, and my strength is such that soft earth cannot bear me up. That is why I live here among the rocks. Now do you feel like pitting your strength against mine?"

"Why should we fight," replied Ilya, "and shed the blood of heroes? Let us rather exchange crosses and become brothers."

And they both got down from their horses and exchanged the golden crosses they wore round their necks, embracing and kissing each other three times like true brothers. Then they travelled on together over the mountains, sharing all their food and drink, as well as the tent in which they slept at night.

One day a strange thing happened to them: it was as if someone had dug a ditch for their horses to fall into. Coming nearer they discovered it was not a ditch but a coffin — a stone coffin lying in the ground, with an oak lid next to it.

"Who do you think is supposed to lie in it?" Svatohor asked his younger brother. "Try it, Ilya, and see if it fits you . . ."

Ilya obligingly lay down in the coffin. But it was much too big for him; big enough for three such as he. Then Svatohor tried it for size — and he fitted the coffin perfectly, with not an inch to spare. He could not make the slightest move, it was such a tight fit.

"Now cover me with the lid," he told Ilya. Ilya hesitated, as he had a bad premonition, but when the other repeated his request he placed the oak lid on top of the coffin. No sooner had he done so than the lid fell into place with a crash.

Ilya tried lifting it, but to no avail; he tried to smash it with his iron mace, but the lid would not budge.

Svatohor called to him from inside the coffin:

"Use my hero's sword, brother. That'll do the trick!"

Ilya unbuckled the sword from the saddle, but he found he was unable to lift it as the sword was too heavy.

"Come closer," Svatohor called again, "and I'll breathe a hero's strength into you."

Ilya leaned over the coffin. Through a chink in the lid he felt the breath of his brother Svatohor, and every vein in his body pulsed with blood as Svatohor's strength poured into him.

He picked up the huge sword, making a fiery figure of eight in the air. But, as he struck the coffin, an iron loop appeared on it. He struck again, so mightily that he almost split the earth in two, and another loop clamped itself round the coffin like an iron snake. He was about to strike a third time when Svatohor's voice made him hold back.

"Lean down once more, so I can breathe all my strength into you!"

"I don't need it," replied Ilya. "It would not help you out of the coffin and, what is more, Mother Earth could not carry me afterwards . . ."

"Right you are," said Svatohor after a moment's thought. "It is obviously my fate to stay here forever, and you would only be destroyed by my breath. One thing I must ask you before you go, however: do not leave my hero's horse to roam without his master. Tie him to the nearby oak, so that the dank earth may swallow us up together."

Ilya willingly carried out Svatohor's last wish. Catching the brown horse by the rein, he tied him to a spreading oak tree.

Then he said farewell to his brother and, with the memory of Svatohor in his heart forever and the hero's strength in his body, he set out for the city of Kiev, to meet the good Prince Vladimir.

NIGHTINGALE THE ROBBER

Ilya continued his journey to meet the good Prince Vladimir. He presented a fine sight: his Circassian saddle covered with gold, his harness set with precious stones, his reins made of pure silk. He himself was clad in shining armour, brightly coloured leather boots on his feet and a sable cap on his head. His weapons were even more splendid — a steel sabre at his side and a ninety-pound iron mace in his hand. Over his shoulder he carried a strong bow with a silken string; in his quiver he had arrows of tempered steel.

Before he saw the domes of Kiev, however, he made a halt outside the town of Chernigov, for he came upon a group of Tartars, encamped there like so many black crows in a field. As he watched them, the Tartars were getting ready to attack the town and its inhabitants. Without a second thought the hero swept down upon the heathen. He swung his sabre in the air and cut a path through their ranks; he released an arrow from his bow and a whole row of Tartar soldiers fell lifeless to the ground; he whirled his ninety-pound mace, and it was as if a storm had uprooted a forest. Ilya Muromets rode this way and that among the Tartars and any that were not killed by him were trampled to death by his steed.

Ilya, having destroyed the Tartars, set off for the city and the muzhiks of Chernigov opened the city gates for him, bowing low and saying:

"Stay with us, famous hero, stay and be our duke."

But the Cossack replied:

"I cannot stay. I am late as it is. Just tell me which direction to take for Kiev, the capital."

At this the muzhiks all looked at one another, as if badly frightened. Finally one of them plucked up his courage and said:

"For thirty years now the road has been unused; it has become grown over with weeds. You won't see man or beast there, not even a solitary bird. No one dares to go there because Nightingale the robber sits by the river Smorodinka, there by the Levanidov cross in the black marshes. And when he whistles like a bird, or roars like a wild beast, or hisses like a snake, the tall grass is flattened, the flowers wilt, and every living creature in sight drops dead in its tracks."

Ilya nevertheless turned his horse in that direction and, taking the unused road, got as far as the river Smorodinka. In the black marshland his horse's hooves sank into the boggy ground, but the hero tore up some saplings and threw them under his horse's legs, and so they reached the Levanidov cross without mishap.

Just then Nightingale the robber, in his perch in the oak tree, caught sight of Ilya. He took a deep breath and the tall grass was flattened by his nightingale's whistle. The flowers wilted when he roared like a wild beast, and Ilya's horse stumbled when he hissed like a snake.

"Don't you want to go any farther?" cried Ilya angrily. "You have never yet been whipped by a hero." And taking his silken whip he lashed his horse mercilessly so that the good animal quite forgot about the robber.

Ilya then reached for his bow, put a tempered arrow on the silken string and released it straight at Nightingale.

The arrow hit the robber exactly where Ilya had meant to hit him — on his right temple just above the eye. The pain made Nightingale lose his footing in the tree and he fell into the grass.

Ilya at once seized his white hands and tied them together; then he seized his strong legs and roped the robber's ankles. And then he chained the robber to his stirrup and travelled on towards Kiev.

They first came to Nightingale's lair, where he lived with his three charming daughters and their husbands. The eldest daughter was leaning out of the window, and she called out to her sisters:

"Father is coming home, bringing with him a yokel chained to his left stirrup!"

The middle daughter said:

"No, he has the yokel chained to his right stirrup!"

The third sister also looked out of the window; she looked long and carefully and then she cried:

"Are you blind, both of you? Can't you see that the peasant is riding a good horse and it is our father who is chained to the stirrup like a sheaf of corn! Quickly," she called to Nightingale's three sons-in-law, "take your spears and kill the terrible fellow!"

The husbands of the robber's three daughters took up their spears and ran out to face Ilya Muromets, intending to kill him. But they were stopped by Nightingale himself, who called out to them:

"Throw down your arms, dear sons-in-law, and lead this hero from Murom inside our house. Treat him to sweet foods and honeyed drinks, give him rich gifts, or he will not let me go!"

His sons-in-law would have done as he said, but before they had time
to reach Ilya, his grey horse had covered thirty-five miles in one jump,
seventy in the next, and with a third leap stood in the middle of the
courtyard of Prince Vladimir's palace in Kiev.

Ilya left his horse and the robber there and went inside the white stone
palace. There he saw many strange faces, and met all the famous heroes,
as well as the good Prince Vladimir himself. As was the custom he
bowed in all four directions and then once more to the prince.

Vladimir looked him up and down, and then asked:

"Where have you come from, young man, from what land? What is
your name, so I know what to call you, and who is your father, so I
know what rank you merit?"

The hero replied in a clear voice:

"I come from the village of Karacharov near the famous town of
Murom and I am a peasant's son, Ivan's Ilya Ivanovich. I wish to serve
you with all my strength and loyalty, to protect you and the Christian
faith."

Prince Vladimir thought about this, and then put another question:

"And tell me, Ilya of Murom, have you come to Kiev by the direct
route or did you make a detour?"

"I came by the direct route," replied Ilya truthfully.

"Surely you know that road is grown over with weeds," the prince
interrupted him. "Surely you know that the terrible robber Nightingale sits in an oak tree by the river Smorodinka, there by the Levanidov
cross in the black marshes. Are you trying to mock us with this lie?"

"Yes, I know," replied Ilya, nothing daunted. "Nightingale the robber
whistles, roars and hisses, destroying every living thing that comes
near him. I've brought him in chains to your courtyard."

The prince quickly put on his marten-fur cloak and, followed by his
courtiers, ran out to take a look at the notorious robber.

When they had all had a good look, Prince Vladimir gave an order:

"Whistle for us, Nightingale, roar like a wild beast, hiss like a snake!"

But the robber replied:

"I haven't eaten anything at your court, Vladimir, nor have I had a drink, and therefore I shall not obey you. That Cossack Ilya is the only one from whom I'll take orders."

Hearing this, the prince had a cup of green wine poured for Nightingale and when the robber had emptied it, Ilya said to him:

"Now whistle, Nightingale, but only half strength; roar and hiss, but only by halves!"

Yet the robber, Nightingale, suddenly felt not only the wine he had drunk, he was also conscious of his approaching death; and so he whistled as loud as he could, making the grass lie flat; he roared with all his might so that people fell dead all around him, and he hissed so furiously that the glass window panes were shattered. The good Prince Vladimir was so alarmed that he started running round in circles, trying to hide his face in his fur cloak.

"Why did you do that?" Ilya asked the robber. "Why did you disobey me?"

"It was for the last time," replied Nightingale. "I feel in my bones that I am about to die . . ."

At that Ilya untied the robber's hands and legs, and unchained him from the stirrup. Leading him out of the palace courtyard to Kulik's Field, he cut off Nightingale's head on an oaken block. He then threw half of the robber's body to the grey wolves, the other half to the black ravens.

Vladimir's Wedding
AND THE DEATH OF DANUBE IVANOVICH

When Ilya Muromets arrived in Kiev, with the robber Nightingale chained to his stirrup, he did not know that Prince Vladimir was holding a large feast for all his heroes, princes, boyars and merchants. He did not know then, but he soon discovered the fact, for he was led into the banqueting hall and given a prominent seat among the heroes. Ilya looked round and watched the guests as they talked to each other. The stupid man praised his young wife, the clever man his mother. One man was boasting of his strength, another of his good fortune in war. Noon came and went, the afternoon passed, and it was evening when Prince Vladimir himself entered the conversation:

"My dear heroes, boyars and merchants. You're all married and living here in Kiev. You all have families . . . Only I am alone, having no one with whom to pass the time. Will no one tell me where to find a bride with cheeks like freshly fallen snow, lashes black as sable and eyes as bright as a falcon's? Which of you will tell me where to find such a bride, whom I might cherish and all of you honour as your prince's consort?"

All of a sudden the gay talk ceased. Wherever the prince turned to look, the tall were hiding behind the medium-sized, the medium-sized behind the small. No one knew what to say. But then, rising from the heroes' bench where he sat next to Ilya, Danube Ivanovich stood up, he who had travelled all round Holy Russia in his time, and he said:

"I know, Vladimir of Kiev, of a country called Lithuania, where a brave king and his two daughters live. You will rarely find the elder daughter, Nastasya, at home — she prefers to ride abroad on horseback — but the younger, Apraksya, is the bride you seek. Her cheeks are like freshly fallen snow, her lashes black as sable, her eyes bright as a falcon's. She likes to stay at home. With her, dear prince, time will pass very quickly for you and we'll all honour and cherish her."

Hearing these tempting words, the prince replied:

"Do me a service then, my dear hero. Bring the Lithuanian princess Apraksya to me. Take as much gold as you wish, as well as three hundred men to help you."

"I don't need your gold," said Danube. "And as for company, I only want the hero Dobrynya Nikitich and two spare horses."

Danube hastily prepared to carry out his mission. Together with Dobrynya he saddled the two spare horses, and they left before Vladimir and his guests had had time to notice their absence.

Theirs was a long journey. They made first for the mother of cities, stone-built Moscow, and from there they travelled on to Lithuania.

Arriving at the royal palace, they stopped their horses in the middle of
the large courtyard. Danube jumped down from his horse and said to
Dobrynya:

"Stay here, brother. Keep good watch, so that we can be off at once if
danger threatens."

Then Danube knocked on the door of the castle before entering. He
bowed low before the King of Lithuania, who said in friendly tones:

"Welcome, hero of Kiev. Have you come for a visit, or do you wish to
serve us?"

"I have something far more important on my mind. I have been sent by
our Prince Vladimir to ask for the hand of your daughter Apraksya,
whom he wishes to marry."

The Lithuanian king grew red in the face with rage.

"Then you have chosen a bad cause, Danube Ivanovich! I shall certainly
not give my daughter to that shrimp of a prince, and I'll put you in
a deep dungeon to make you see sense!"

It was Danube's turn to be angry. He stepped forward to the table and
struck it with his bare fist so that the heavy oak top broke in two and
the ground trembled underfoot. All he said was:

"I have with me another fellow from Kiev — Dobrynya Nikitich."

Just then some frightened servants came running in, and they confirmed
what Danube had said:

"King of Lithuania, our father! While you sit here talking a fellow is
running about your royal courtyard, leading two horses in one hand
and waving a Saracen scimitar in the other, threatening to kill every
single one of us!"

The king now became much humbler, seeing that there was nothing he
could do against these two heroes.

"All right," he said, "take Apraksya, if Fate intends her to be Vladimir's
wife. But first speak to your comrade and tell him not to create havoc
in my palace."

Danube called out in a clear voice:

"Stop it, Dobrynya Nikitich! With God's help we got what we wanted."

296 ✦ The king ordered the nurses to make everything ready for his beloved Apraksya's journey to Kiev and her marriage to Prince Vladimir. When everything was ready, Danube bowed before the King of Lithuania, making the sign of the cross in farewell. He put Apraksya upon a horse and with Dobrynya Nikitich they set out on the journey home.

They could not reach Kiev that day. When they were only half way there, night fell and they had no choice but to put up a white tent and try to sleep. They lay down, but sleep they could not. Out in the darkness a Tartar was riding on horseback, round and round, whistling, shouting, singing; but he left before daybreak.

As soon as he came out of the tent next morning Danube carefully examined the path along which the Tartar had ridden. He saw deep tracks and stones scattered three arrow-flights away by a horse's hooves. He was so fascinated by all this that he told Apraksya and Dobrynya to go on by themselves, while he set out with one of the spare horses in pursuit of the unknown horseman.

He did not have far to go — he soon caught up with the Tartar out in the fields.

"Where are you off to?" he called out to him, but the rider went on his way regardless. When Danube knocked him from the saddle with the blunt end of his lance and reined up to take a closer look, his eyes widened with surprise. It was no Tartar but a beautiful maiden with cheeks like freshly fallen snow, lashes like those of a black sable, and eyes as bright as a falcon's: it was none other than Nastasya.

"Kill me if you must," the girl told him. "I have followed Apraksya, either to bring her back or to lay down my life for her . . ."

Danube Ivanovich did not kill her. Instead, he put her on his spare horse and took her straight to Kiev, to the church in which the good Prince Vladimir was just being married to the beautiful Apraksya. And there were two weddings instead of one, for Danube married Nastasya.

After the double wedding there had to be a double feast. They ate and drank, feasted and boasted. Even the good Danube began to brag when the green wine had gone to his head.

"There is no other shot in all of Mother Russia as good as Danube Ivan-ovich!" he cried.

The other heroes were about to make reply — Ilya Muromets was on the point of teaching him a lesson — when Nastasya herself intervened:

"I haven't been in Kiev long, but in our country we consider a man a good shot when he can shoot a tempered arrow through a gold ring at fifty paces."

They all fell silent after these thoughtless words, but Danube got up at once and measured off fifty paces. Then, putting a ring on top of his unruly head, he waited for Nastasya to shoot.

Not once but three times in succession did his skilful wife shoot a tempered arrow through the ring; three times in succession the wedding guests cried out in wonder and admiration.

But when Danube made ready to shoot, they tried to stop him.

"You had better wait, Danube. Wait until tomorrow, when your hand will be steadier."

However, they protested in vain. Danube stood on wavering legs, pulled his silk bowstring taut, and released the arrow. It did not fly far enough.

"Don't shoot now, Danube, wait at least an hour!" his brother heroes warned him, but to no avail.

His arrow did not hurt anyone once again, but flew high up to the oak ceiling.

When he prepared to shoot a third time, Nastasya herself begged him:

"Don't shoot, don't kill me, or you'll kill the two heroic sons whom I'll give you!"

But it was too late. Danube did not control his aim, he did not give his head time to cool — and shot Nastasya in her white breast. Only then did he start shedding hot tears, his sorrow being so great that he fell upon a steel dagger and ended his own life.

Yet they both live on to this day, for where they were buried in their separate graves, there flow two rivers carrying their names — the Danube and the Nastasya.

THE EARLY DAYS OF DOBRYNYA NIKITICH

It was a sad feast that took place at Prince Vladimir's court after the death of Danube Ivanovich; no one felt like singing, none wanted to dance. And so the Cossack Ilya Muromets quietly asked the man sitting next to him on the bench what kind of a hero this Dobrynya Nikitich was, the man who had given such valuable help to Danube at the court of the Lithuanian king. And equally quietly his neighbour told him:

Dobrynya came from a rich Ryazan family. He was the son of old Nikita and his good wife Amelfa Timofeyevna. Just before he was born a very strange thing happened.

There was no thunderstorm that day, nor whistling wind to drive the clouds over Ryazan, but a whole flock of dragons and wild beasts came pounding across the countryside, shaking the earth. In front ran the lion monster Skimen, who did not stop until he reached the river Dnieper. There he sat down on his haunches and emitted a frightful roar, so loud that it made the river leave its banks. This was because he knew that Dobrynya was about to be born, and that he would bring destruction to the entire dragon and monster races.

Soon after this Dobrynya came into the world. He grew quickly, and when he was only six he could already write, and was able to read wise books. When he was twelve he rode out into the field with his followers, fearing nothing and no one.

One day the young Dobrynya wanted to cool himself in the river Puchay. He told Amelfa Timofeyevna, but his good mother was loath to let him go.

"Puchay is a wild, evil river. It will destroy you. If you must go, at least don't swim past the first rapids, and you must also beware of the second rapids!"

Her son did not heed her advice. Reaching the river bank, he took his clothes off and jumped in. He negotiated the first rapids with ease. Coming to the second rapids, he succeeded in getting through them as well, but the third were the strongest of all, and however much he struggled, he could not prevent them from carrying him to a cave of

300 white stone, which proved to be the lair of the ugly and terrible dragon Gorynich.

Dobrynya did not have so much as a pebble with which to defend himself, and so the dragon felt he could do as he liked with the boy. He spouted fire and smoke from all his twelve mouths, singeing Dobrynya's body and driving him down to the sandy river bank.

This saved Dobrynya's life. Just as the monster prepared to kill him, Dobrynya saw a *kalpak* lying on the ground. He quickly filled it with sand, and when the dragon attacked, Dobrynya threw the triangular hat at him with such force that it severed two of his talons and toppled the monster into the water. And then, before Gorynich could scramble out again, the boy tore up an oak tree and beat the dragon to death with it.

Finally Dobrynya destroyed the dragon's lair, and trod on the baby dragons that were inside. Tying the dead Gorynich to the oak tree, he threw him over his shoulder and hurried home.

He could not find his mother in Ryazan, though. The poor woman had gone to Kiev, in despair, to see Prince Vladimir. She told him, with tears in her eyes how Dobrynya had failed to obey her and how he had been killed by the dragon Gorynich.

Prince Vladimir nodded his good head; Amelfa Timofeyevna wept and lamented. And then the door was thrown open, and in came Dobrynya Nikitich himself, alive and well.

There was a splendid reunion. They all rejoiced, and Dobrynya won undying glory by his deed. Since that day he has lived with the rest of the heroes at the court of Prince Vladimir, the Sun of Kiev, and he has added many more valiant deeds to his record.

Ilya Muromets wanted to enquire about Dobrynya's other exploits, but then his attention was caught by another hero, Alyosha Popovich, sitting on top of the oven a little apart from the rest of the company.

ALYOSHA POPOVICH AND TUGARIN

Alyosha Popovich was not sitting on the oven apart from the company because he was considered less of a hero than the rest. Quite the contrary. When he, a priest's son from the famous city of Rostov, had arrived in Kiev, his great renown had travelled before him. He met Prince Vladimir, and he was able to choose his own place at every feast — either next to the illustrious prince or facing him — he could sit wherever he pleased. And since he preferred to sit on the oven, sit there he did.

He was sitting there on this occasion, and he had a great deal to look at during the feast.

After a time the young monster Tugarin was brought in. And what a monster he was! Three times six feet tall, six feet broad across his shoulders, and a space the length of a tempered arrow between his two eyes. Whenever he opened his huge jaws, the flames came shooting out, while a column of black smoke bellowed from either ear.

The young monster Tugarin gave no Christian greeting when he came in but went straight to Princess Apraksya, squatting down between her and Prince Vladimir, pushing and squeezing so that he almost sat on top of them. And he grasped Apraksya's hands, nearly wrenching them off.

This was too much for Alyosha, who said:

"Are you and the princess at loggerheads, Vladimir of Kiev, that you suffer this heathen monster to sit between you?"

At that moment the clever cooks brought sumptuous foods to the table, a golden-roast swan among them. Tugarin took his steel dagger and speared the swan before swallowing it whole.

"What kind of an uncouth creature have we here among us?" asked Alyosha again. "My father in Rostov also had an impudent cur like

this, which didn't know its place and was always stuffing itself. In the
end it choked on a swan bone . . ."

Hearing him speak, Tugarin scowled, and his countenance grew as black
as night; Alyosha on the other hand laughed like a full moon.

Then the cooks brought in a bowl full of delicious *pirozhki*. No sooner
had they set it down on the table than the monster seized it and gulped
down every single morsel of the pastry.

Watching him as he did so, Alyosha said:

"What loutish glutton have we at our table today? My father, the priest in Rostov, had a voracious cow in his yard — one day she walked into the kitchen, drank some malmsey, and burst. The same thing will happen to this fiend . . ."

This enraged the monster Tugarin so much that he went berserk. Seizing a twelve-pound knife he threw it at Alyosha, but the faithful servant Yekim caught it before it could do any damage.

"Come and fight!" cried the enraged Tugarin. "Come out into the open and fight!"

Alyosha accepted his challenge, and they agreed to fight on the following day. Everyone immediately began to place bets on Tugarin's victory — the princes bet a hundred roubles each, the boyars fifty, every peasant five. There were even some rich merchants who bet three ships laden with foreign merchandise. Only the thane of Chernigov bet on Alyosha.

Before they left the banqueting hall, Princess Apraksya said to the hero:

"You fool! Why don't you leave our guest in peace?"

But Alyosha either did not hear or disdained to reply — he mounted his splendid horse and left with the others, to spend the night on the banks of the Safat river. There they pitched their white tents and spread their blankets. They all slept while Alyosha stayed awake all night, praying to God:

"Please, Lord, make it cloudy tomorrow; let it rain on the monster Tugarin. Make hailstones fall on him."

God was not deaf to the hero's prayer. In the morning, when Alyosha rode out on his horse and Tugarin soared up into the sky, it began to pour with rain. The rain soaked the monster's paper wings, and made him fall to the ground like an ordinary dog.

Alyosha saw this, grasped his sharp sabre, and spurred his horse.

Tugarin greeted him at a distance, roaring:

"Do you want me to scorch you with my flame? Would you rather I trampled you on the spot, or am I to tear you with my claws?"

And Alyosha replied:

❦ "Listen to me, Tugarin Dragonovich! We're fighting to decide a big wager, but you're supposed to be fighting me alone. Why have you brought a whole army against me, since I am single-handed?"

Tugarin turned round to see what army Alyosha was talking about. Alyosha jumped forward, waved his sharp sabre in the air, and struck off the monster's head.

The head fell to the ground with a thump. The hero tied it to his saddle as a trophy in proof of his victory, and rode back with it to Prince Vladimir's court.

As soon as Vladimir saw that Alyosha was alive, he ordered a splendid banquet in the hero's honour, to celebrate his valiant deed.

STAVRO GODINOVICH AND HIS CLEVER WIFE

The prince's guests were almost sated and their thirst nearly quenched when they began to sing their own praises. Most of the time they flattered the Sun of Kiev, Prince Vladimir, himself. One extolled the Kiev palace, another its treasures. A third acclaimed the beauty of Princess Apraksya, while a fourth enthused about the horses in Vladimir's stables.

Only the boyar Stavro Godinovich whispered to his friend:

"As if I didn't know better than this palace. Why, my own farmstead is no worse than the best in Kiev. My rooms are panelled in light oak, and there are beaver skins on the walls. On the floors I have sable furs. And as to treasure — all the door handles and chains and bolts gleam with pure gold. If only they knew my wife Vasilisa, such a beautiful and clever woman, I don't think they'd talk like this about the princess . . ."

Stavro's bold words soon carried to the ears of Prince Vladimir. The Sun of Kiev grew overcast and he had the disrespectful boyar put behind iron doors and steel locks, in the deepest dungeon. Then he sent a messenger to Stavro's house with orders to seal it up and to bring his wife Vasilisa to Kiev.

However, Vasilisa heard the bad news about her husband before the messenger even arrived, and instead of waiting meekly at home, she set off for Kiev, dressed like a hero:

She cut her long hair, put on a pair of coloured leather boots and male apparel of the finest materials. For her weapon she picked a firm bow with strong arrows, for her retinue a company of thirty-nine youths, every one of them an excellent warrior.

They were half way to Kiev when they met Vladimir's messenger. Vasilisa introduced herself to him thus:

"We travel a great distance, sent by the great Tsar of the Golden Horde to collect dues and taxes from Prince Vladimir. He has not paid up for twelve years, and it comes to three thousand ducats each year."

The Kiev messenger was taken aback, and all he could do was to stammer:

"I have been sent from Kiev to close up the house of the boyar Stavro and to bring his young wife to the prince."

And Vasilisa replied:

"We rode past a beautiful house, but there was nobody in it; I believe Stavro's wife has gone away for a visit."

Hearing this, Vladimir's messenger turned his horse round and hurried back to Kiev, to warn his master whom to expect.

The news disturbed and frightened Vladimir so much that he did not know where to turn. While he dithered, the messengers from the Golden Horde arrived in the city, and they tramped inside the palace, with Vasilisa at their head.

Princess Apraksya was the first to scrutinise her. And as she looked, she quickly whispered to her husband:

"This is no messenger from the Golden Horde — it's Stavro's wife, Vasilisa. She waddled across the courtyard like a duck, she crept up the stairs like a mouse, and now she sits here pressing her knees together."

Prince Vladimir thought this over, and, while he treated his honoured visitor to wine, he had an idea. He would match the messenger against his heroes in combat; then he would see whether this was indeed a man or not.

Seven stalwart wrestlers were called in, and they competed with Vasilisa in the courtyard. She dislocated the first one's arm, broke the second one's leg, threw the third down on the ground like a sack of barley; the others waited no longer but took to their heels.

Prince Vladimir spat disdainfully and said to his wife:

"You are long of hair but short of wit — imagine calling a hero a woman! I've never seen a messenger such as this one in my life."

But Apraksya still insisted, saying: "And yet it is Stavro's wife!"

"We shall see, then. Let her compete with my heroes in shooting arrows," Vladimir decided.

Twelve Kiev heroes took their places two miles away from a mighty oak. They stretched their silken bowstrings, bent their firm bows. Their strong arrows swished through the air and hit the target; the huge tree swayed but did not fall. And then the messenger from the Golden Horde took up his bow, put a steel arrow to the bowstring, and shot it. The arrow cut the oak into two equal pieces, as if it had been split by a knife.

"I'm not sorry for that ancient tree," said Vasilisa, "but I do regret losing my arrow. Who is going to search for it in the fields?"

Again Prince Vladimir spat when no one was looking at him, but his wife's words gnawed at his brain like a worm. He decided to put the messenger to the test himself, and so he brought a chess set with golden pieces.

But the prince lost the first game, and in the second the young stranger beat him again. When the third game ended with a check-mate for the Prince of Kiev, his opponent swept the pieces from the board and said:

"Now it is your turn, my dear Vladimir! Hand over the taxes you have been owing my tsar for the past twelve years. They come to three thousand a year."

Prince Vladimir tried to evade the issue in every conceivable way. He sought to put off the day of payment, but when this did not work, he confessed:

"I have nothing with which to pay that debt, except my own head and that of my wife Apraksya."

The messenger did not seem to be listening to him, but started on another tack:

"Tell me, Vladimir, what do you do to amuse yourself? Do you ever have any entertainment at your palace?"

The prince immediately gave orders for a great feast to be held, to which he invited all the clowns in Kiev. They all made merry and told jokes; only the messenger did not smile once, and he asked Vladimir:

"Isn't there anyone in the place who knows how to play the violin?"

And now Prince Vladimir was put in mind of that fine violinist, Stavro Godinovich. He went to the dungeon and personally released the boyar, bringing him to the banqueting hall and handing him a violin.

Stavro sat down opposite Vasilisa, and as he played songs about Stamboul and Jerusalem, as well as plaintive Hebrew melodies, the messenger felt sleepy, and so he said:

"I'll tell you what we'll do, Prince Vladimir — you can keep those dues and taxes if only you'll give me this fine violinist of yours, Stavro Godinovich."

Vladimir was delighted. He agreed readily, and with Princess Apraksya at his side he accompanied the honoured guest and Stavro Godinovich as far as the river Dnieper.

SUKHMAN

The feast in the palace of Prince Vladimir, the Sun of Kiev, was in full swing again. All the guests were chatting and bragging loudly to each other. The prince walked about, exchanging a word here, drinking a toast there. Suddenly he noticed that one of the heroes, Sukhman by name, was sitting in silence, neither eating his food nor drinking his wine. He went up to him and said:

"Why are you looking like thunder, Sukhman Odikhmantyevich? You have touched neither food nor wine. Have they failed to toast you; haven't you been given the place that belongs to you by right?"

"No, everything is as it should be, dear Vladimir," replied Sukhman. "But rather than waste time here, I'll go and find a live swan for you." And Sukhman galloped out of the courtyard on his horse.

He rode a long way, a very long way, right to the edge of the blue sea. He scanned the first calm bay, but saw neither a goose nor a swan, not even a single grey duck there. He rode on to the second bay, but fared no better than before. And when he left the third bay, still empty-handed, he said to himself: I had better go to old Mother Dnieper and ask her to help me.

He spurred his good horse on, and did not stop riding until he came to the river Dnieper. But he was disappointed to see that the stream was not as clear as usual but muddied and thick with sand.

He asked the river what was happening, and the Dnieper replied:

"Why shouldn't my waters grow muddy, when they cannot flow as freely as they used to. Nearby on the other bank a large Tartar host has made its camp, forty thousand head of heathen, and day after day they build new bridges across me, and day after day I wreck them to prevent the heathen from reaching our glorious city of Kiev. But now my strength is gone, I can do no more . . ."

Sukhman's heart hammered in his chest with anger, and he urged his horse across the river in a single leap, straight into the Tartar camp. There he drew his oak cudgel and smote the enemy, showing no mercy, until he remained alone on the battlefield.

But he had not killed all the Tartars — three had succeeded in hiding themselves like treacherous snakes in the rushes by the banks of the river. Then they aimed their arrows and pierced Sukhman's white body.

The hero felt an excruciating pain, but he plucked out the arrows, and covered his wounds with poppy leaves, before beheading the three Tartars with his sabre. Then he mounted his horse and raced like the wind back to Kiev.

In the courtyard of the palace he hastily tied his brown steed to a golden ring on a carved pillar. Vladimir, the Sun of Kiev, welcomed him with the words: "Have you kept your promise, Sukhman Odikhmantyevich, and brought me a live swan as you said you would?"

"How could I bring it to you, good prince," replied the hero, and he started telling Vladimir about his adventure by the river Dnieper.

Vladimir, however, did not believe him, and had him put in irons like a common liar. But on Ilya's advice he sent Dobrynya to look at the field by the river Dnieper and find out the truth of the matter.

Dobrynya did not take long in getting there, and one look was enough to tell him that Sukhman had spoken the truth. The battlefield was strewn with dead Tartars and a bloodstained oak cudgel lay among them.

Dobrynya picked the cudgel up and took it back to Kiev with him.

The good Vladimir at last believed his hero. And just as before he had accused Sukhman of being an atrocious liar, he now praised him and showered him with golden treasures.

But the hero no longer cared for the prince's gratitude. He prepared to leave the palace and, by way of farewell, he took the poppy leaves off his wounds. When the blood started to flow, he said:

"Let my hot blood continue to flow. It was shed in vain, but perhaps one day it will form a river, to commemorate my name."

And with those words he rode away, never to be seen by anyone again.

HOW PRINCE VLADIMIR OFFENDED ILYA AND WHAT FOLLOWED

The Cossack Ilya Muromets was also to find out how fickle the favour
 of the mighty was, and especially that of princes.
On every other Saturday Vladimir, the Sun of Kiev, held a great feast.
 He sent letters of invitation to all those he wanted to treat, forgetting
 only Ilya, his best warrior.
And so, while the guests were tying their horses in the courtyard of
 Vladimir's palace, an angry Ilya went out with his bow into the streets
 of Kiev.

Coming to a square he stood and took aim with an arrow, and shot off the golden cross on the spire of the nearest church. Then he shattered the golden ball on another tower, and he strode on, shooting arrows as he went, until there wasn't a gold or silver ornament left on any roof — they all lay at Ilya's feet.

"Come and take what you want!" he shouted. "Let's have a spree!"

The first to answer his call were all the riff-raff from the taverns, followed by the peasants, the muzhiks, and then even the respectable townsmen strutted up.

They sold the golden crosses, weighed the glittering orbs, and in return received countless full barrels. Everyone could drink whatever he chose: green wine, heady beer, sweet mead. And all the time Ilya kept egging them on:

"Go on, help yourselves, don't hold back! I'll give you a better time than the good Prince Vladimir ever could."

Before long the city rocked with noise as the rabble led by Ilya Muromets caroused and shouted merrily. Prince Vladimir was slowly but surely becoming alarmed by the unbridled revelry, and he asked the good Dobrynya Nikitich:

"Go, talk to that Cossack Ilya Muromets. Tell him to stop blashpheming against his prince and against God. Tell him that I want to invite him to my feast at the palace . . ."

Dobrynya found the exhilarated Ilya just when the revelry was at its highest. Tapping him on his broad shoulder, Dobrynya said:

"Greetings, dear brother!"

Ilya turned to him, saying: "Welcome, Dobrynyushka, what brings you here?"

"I have come as your brother, Ilya. And though it is written down as a Christian commandment, and proved by many deeds that the young should obey their elders, please listen now to young Dobrynya who asks you to go to the palace with him, you old Cossack. The good Prince Vladimir invites you to his Saturday feast."

"Ah, the prince knew whom to send for me," replied Ilya. "He knew

that I shouldn't listen to anyone else. However, there's no hurry — why
don't you have a drink here with me first, with me and all these good
people at this plain table."

Dobrynya therefore tasted the beer, the green wine and the mead, drinking two and a half pails of each.

Then the two of them got up from that plain table, leaving those good
people, and went to the prince's palace.

Prince Vladimir was already waiting for them. But he did not lead Ilya
to the table, as he had promised; he did not give him the seat of honour
by his side. Instead, on the advice of wicked schemers, he had him
thrown into the deepest dungeon.

He was soon to regret his rash deed, for the twelve famous heroes who
together with Ilya had defended Holy Russia against all her enemies,
became very angry with Prince Vladimir and left him to journey
abroad .

ILYA MUROMETS AND TSAR KALIN

It seemed that everyone had forgotten about the famous heroes, and they had even forgotten Ilya Muromets, who was waiting for death to release him from the dungeon. Prince Vladimir went on feasting with the double-tongued boyars as if nothing had happened.

But the prince's kind daughter, the beautiful Zabava Putyatichna, did not let the old Cossack perish in prison. She secretly obtained the keys of his dungeon and kept sending him everything he needed: soft blankets, a hero's clothing, and every day some good food and drink.

Prince Vladimir was not able to feast for very long. Russia was invaded by the heathen host of Tsar Kalin.

One day they got within sixteen miles of Kiev, and the terrible Tsar sent Prince Vladimir the following message:

"Empty all your cellars and have barrels of rich mead placed in rows in all the streets and alleyways, so that when I and my soldiers come, we can take our pleasure . . ."

Vladimir read the letter from beginning to end, and again from the end to the beginning, and he cleverly saw how he could gain a little time. He therefore wrote back to Tsar Kalin:

"What you ask, my dear tsar, is no trifle. Kindly give me three years' grace, three years and three months, which I need if I am to welcome you as you deserve and as you have ordered."

And Kalin promised to wait.

But a day goes by like a raindrop falling, week follows week like water in a mountain stream. The three years and three months Vladimir had asked for were over, and Tsar Kalin with his heathen army stood outside the walls of Kiev.

Prince Vladimir paced up and down the palace chambers, in tears, complaining: "There's no one here to defend Kiev and my own head against the enemy. All my heroes have left me because I destroyed the strongest of them all, Ilya Muromets."

"No, you didn't destroy him, Father," said his daughter, Zabava Putyatichna. "He is still alive in his prison, and lacks nothing of his former strength."

Vladimir he ran straightaway to release Ilya. With his own hands he changed his clothes, kissed him like a brother, and led him to the table. Then he told him about Tsar Kalin, explaining that only he, Ilyushka, could save Kiev and the prince from humiliation.

The old Cossack only replied:

"It is not for you, Vladimir, that I'm going to fight today. I am concerned for our Christian faith, our glorious city of Kiev, and your good daughter Putyatichna!"

And with these words Ilya went to the stable to prepare for the fray.

His grey horse had not seen his master for a long time but Ilya had his faithful servant to thank that his steed was as fit and sturdy as when he had last rode him, and Ilya embraced and kissed the man.

He hastened to the city walls, and as soon as he passed through the gate he saw the Tartar host. Whichever way he looked he could see nothing but heathen warriors; he climbed two mountains, and still the Tartars darkened the horizon. Only when he reached the top of the third mountain did another sight present itself to his eyes:

Away in the distance twelve tents showed white, and by the tents twelve heroes' horses were munching wheat.

"I'm in luck!" said Ilya to himself, galloping in that direction. And leaving his horse outside, he entered the largest of the tents.

Inside sat the twelve Russian heroes, eating their midday meal of bread and salt. Ilya bowed to the eldest among them, Samson Samoylovich, and when they had all recovered from their surprise, he said:

"I come to you, my brothers, with a plea for help. Tsar Kalin stands outside the gates of our glorious Kiev, his soldiers thick as flies. We must go at once and fight him!"

But Samson Samoylovich replied, voicing the opinion of all twelve:

"We'll not go and fight for Prince Vladimir and Princess Apraksya. He treated us, as well as you, very badly — now let him seek help from the two-faced boyars whose counsel he heeds."

In vain Ilya tried to convince Samson that he was not preparing to fight on behalf of Prince Vladimir but for Kiev and the Christian faith. The twelve heroes remained in the tent, and the old Cossack was left alone to fight an uneven battle with the Tartar hordes.

At first everything went well for him. He stormed into Kalin's camp, clouting the enemy warriors with his cudgel and running them through with his lance, slaying them with his sabre and bringing them down with his strong arrows.

Perhaps he would have routed the whole army all by himself if the cunning chieftains had not dug three treacherous pits.

Ilya's grey mount fell into the first one, but managed to scramble out again with difficulty. Ilya had to help him out of the second, and when they fell in the third, he succeeded in throwing his horse out, while remaining trapped himself.

The enemy encircled Ilya, and the circle grew narrower and narrower. At last the hero had only a single arrow left, and before he fired it, he prayed:

"Fly, my arrow, fly into the white tent of the twelve heroes and fall on the white chest of Samson Samoylovich, so he will see what desperate straits I am in. Let him come to my aid!"

And the arrow fell exactly where Ilya had intended — on Samson Samoylovich's white chest.

"Away we go, my brothers!" exclaimed Samson. "Let us hurry to aid that old Cossack, Ilya Muromets!"

And the twelve heroes galloped into the battle, leaving no one alive. They hacked their way right to Tsar Kalin's tent. There, too, they found Ilya, fighting for his life. He had climbed out of the pit at last, and catching one Tartar by the arms was clubbing the others to death with the body, making them fall like ripe corn stalks all around him.

Now the twelve heroes fought with Tsar Kalin but Ilya stopped them:

"Do not kill the tsar — just bind him in chains and bring him to Kiev. Let Prince Vladimir decide what's to be done with him."

And so they did. They took Tsar Kalin to Kiev a captive, and Prince Vladimir signed an agreement with him, the tsar promising to pay an annual war tax and never to invade Holy Russia again.

After the battle Prince Vladimir prepared a feast in honour of the heroes, but they refused to sit down at the oak table, nor would they become reconciled with him. All thirteen rode from one end of Russia to the other, helping the righteous and punishing evil-doers.

No one knows where and when the thirteen heroes ended their pilgrimage. And since they were not destined to die either in battle or on this earth, they continued their adventures, which were remembered and retold by people in tales known as *byliny*.

THE FINNISH KALEVALA

The frost whispered songs in my
ear, the rain sang runes for me to hear,
the breeze brought them within my ken,
the waves sent them I know not when,
the birds helped me compose them.

There is a land far to the North where the following adventure happened, in a place called Kalevala:

The old and wise Väinämöinen sat listening to his brother Ilmarinen, as he spoke of the country called Pohjola:

"The most precious possession they have there, my dear Väinö, is the mill Sampo which I once made for them in exchange for my bride. I have no bride, but the mill works to this day, grinding flour for all . . ."

"Let's go and bring Sampo home with us, then," suggested the old Väinämöinen, but the blacksmith shook his head:

"No one can carry Sampo away. It has become lodged sixty feet down in a copper mountain, and is secured with nine locks. One of its roots is held fast by Mother Earth, the second has grown into the copper mountain, and the third has become embedded in the sea."

"Be that as it may, let us go to Pohjola!" cried Väinämöinen. "We'll build a stout ship, big enough to carry the mill."

"It is better to go by land," said Ilmarinen. "A ship can strike a rock, a storm may capsize it, the waves may swallow it."

"Go by land, if you wish. But while you plod along the roads, the ship speeds swiftly to its destination. However, let us not argue," decided Väinämöinen. "Make me a sword, blacksmith, for the dark Sariola, for those glowering Pohjolians, so that we may wrest Sampo from them."

The blacksmith set to work. His apprentices fanned the fire, and soon the iron was molten, and the steel was molten, as well as the silver and the gold. And then Ilmarinen hammered away at his anvil, and when he handed his brother the finished weapon, his face glowed with pleasure. It was a sword fit for a hero: its point glittered like moonlight, the sun shone from the blade, the stars twinkled on the hilt. With such a sword it was possible to split a rock in two.

Before long the two brothers were ready to start their journey. In the grove they selected a colt with a golden mane and, jumping into its saddle, they prodded it and made it trot.

As they rode along the seashore they suddenly heard piteous weeping, as if a maiden were crying for her lost lover. But it was not a girl's lament; when they came round the corner of the bay they found an abandoned pinewood boat wailing on the shore.

"Tell us, boat, why do you weep so bitterly?" old Väinämöinen asked.

"Why shouldn't I complain? So many ugly ships plough through the sea, yet the snakes are crawling beneath my keel. So many ragged sails are billowing in the wind, yet my masts are disfigured by the nests of birds."

"Can you carry people as well as your looks would imply?" wise Väinämöinen asked.

"Certainly I can. I could carry a hundred strong oarsmen. No, a thousand, if they were to line up on the lower deck."

At this Väinämöinen sang a magic song, and with its aid he provided a crew: stalwart youths lined one side of the boat, beautiful maidens lined the other, and old men stood in the middle.

Väinämöinen took the helm, and he ordered the strong men to row. Yet the boat remained where it was, and even when the girls helped, and the old men bent to the oars, they did not make any progress. Only the blacksmith Ilmarinen succeeded in launching the boat, and then the wind whistled in the rigging, the timber creaked, and the waves splashed merrily against the bows.

They had not been sailing long, however, when on the northern horizon they saw a promontory with some crumbling cottages on its shore. And by the poorest cottage, the hero Ahti was just making himself a boat.

He saw the strange ship sailing by, and as it was about to pass the headland, he shouted at the sailors:

"Who are you, and where are you making for?"

"And who might you be, that you do not recognise the hero at the helm, nor the one at the oars?" replied the men and women on board.

Ahti recognised Väinämöinen and Ilmarinen. "Of course I do. I know who they are," cried Ahti. "But what is your destination?"

"We're sailing to the North," replied old Väinämöinen, turning round as he stood at the helm. "We're going to the copper mountain, to win back Sampo for Kalevala."

"Take me with you for a third," called Ahti. "I'll prove my worth."

And when the wise Väinämöinen agreed, Ahti joined them on the boat in an instant, bringing with him a rough piece of wood.

"This is just in case the bottom or the bows give way in a storm," he explained.

"To safeguard against that, this warship has its sides covered with iron," said Väinämöinen.

They continued their voyage, the old man steering and singing, Ahti cast spells to ward off the water-nymphs and Kivi Kimm, Lord of the Rocks. Ilmarinen was rowing.

And yet all of a sudden the boat stopped, and though the blacksmith exerted all his great strength, they could not move from the spot.

"We've become stuck on the back of a gigantic pike!" exclaimed Ahti, drawing his sword and slashing at the water so vigorously that he fell overboard. Ilmarinen just managed to grab him by the hair and pull him up again. He then tried to strike the fish himself but his weapon was smashed to pieces.

It was left to Väinämöinen to cut the fish in two and haul it up on board with his sword.

He made for the shore, where he carefully cut the fish, and gave the pieces to ten virgins to make breakfast for the ship's company.

All ate happily, and enjoyed their meat in harmony together. And when they had finished, the old man noticed the white pike's bones.

"A pity to leave them here," he said. "I wonder what purpose they might serve?"

"No purpose," replied Ilmarinen. "What use are a pike's bones and teeth to anybody?"

But Väinämöinen had a good idea: he decided to make himself a new

kantele, the stringed instrument of the Kalevala minstrels. He made it with the fish's jaw-bones, the teeth serving as pins, and the hair from the horse of the god Hiiri as strings.

No one knew how to play the instrument, however, but the old man, who placed it on his knees and set it singing beautiful songs with his sensitive fingers.

At that moment it seemed as though all living things became aware of the music. The squirrel came hurrying out of the wood, the bear rose up out of the heather, even the eagle descended from the clouds. And that is not to say how it moved all men and women, the forest fairies, and the rulers of the elements .

The old man played for a whole day, then a second, and a third. He produced such moving tones that the tears fell from his eyes like showers of rain, drenching his clothes and running into the sea in rivulets.

At last the *kantele* grew silent. Väinämöinen looked round and asked:

"Who'll bring back my tears?"

The raven tried to, but returned with an empty beak. The blue duck tried next, and she put gleaming pearls in the old man's lap, saying:

"This is what the tears have become, to give joy and pleasure to all."

The boat's keel continued to cut through the blue surface of the sea, the prow aimed towards dark Pohjola, towards dark Sariola. And when they at last arrived, they quickly pulled the boat up on the shore and hurried to the nearest houses.

"What have you brought us, heroes from Kalevala?" asked Louhi, the beautiful lady who ruled Pohjola.

"They say that Sampo keeps grinding away, giving so much flour that you have nowhere to put it," replied the wise Väinämöinen. "And since it was Ilmarinen here who made the mill, we've come to share it with you."

"Who would want to share a succulent partridge? Why should I share my Sampo?" asked the Lady of Pohjola.

"If you won't see reason, we'll take the whole mill," said the old man.

But Louhi would not be intimidated. She beckoned to her subjects, and at once armed Pohjolians came running to her, clustering menacingly round the small Finnish group.

Väinämöinen took his *kantele* and started to play. The hostile expressions disappeared from the faces of the foes, they all began to smile, and before long dreams had closed their eyelids. Louhi, too, fell asleep.

The Finns wasted no time but went straight to the copper mountain. Ilmarinen opened the nine locks, and young Ahti seized Sampo, to wrest it from its roots.

But he could not move the mill an inch. He had to yoke a sturdy bull to plough up the roots, and then all three heroes had to push hard against Sampo before they could free it from its captivity.

They loaded it quickly into their boat, and in a short while they were once more skimming across the azure waters, sailing home to Kalevala. The boat, driven by a favourable wind and by the efforts of the oars-men, flew forward like an arrow.

Their swift progress lulled Ahti into a sense of security, so that he began to insist:

"It is a custom among experienced seafarers not to keep their mouths shut tight after a successful hunt, but to sing. Take your *kantele*, Väinö, and play for us."

"We're not out of danger yet," the old man said to damp Ahti's ardour. "There will be time enough to sing when we land in Kalevala."

When he saw that he could not persuade Väinämöinen to change his mind, Ahti still wished to have his own way, and he began to whoop and shout, screech and bellow until he could be heard beyond seven hills, and whoever did hear him, quickly blocked their ears.

Even a crane, who had been resting in a meadow, soared up in alarm, making straight for Pohjola. There he alighted near the houses and cursed the unskilful singer so loudly that all the Pohjolians woke up.

Louhi jumped to her feet at once, wanting to find out if their unin-vited guests from Kalevala had taken advantage of her followers' sleep.

The herds were all intact, nor had anyone tampered with the granaries, but when the Lady of Pohjola came to the copper mountain, the blood froze in her veins. The nine locks had been burst open, the nine doors stood agape, and there was no sign of Sampo anywhere!

"How can I stop the boat from Kalevala?" Louhi asked herself. And then she thought of a way. "Yes, that's it. Uutar, the Queen of Fogs, will help me. And if the fogs are not enough, then Iku-Turso, Spirit of the Sea, must aid me and drown them in the depths, leaving only Sampo afloat to be brought back to me by the waves."

Finally she entreated the highest deity of all:

"Should neither the fogs nor the maelstroms suffice, hear me, Ukko, Lord of the Clouds, and send such a storm down on the boat that not one member of its crew is left alive!"

Uutar granted Louhi's wish, and she covered the sea with a fog so thick that for three days and three nights Väinämöinen could not find his bearings. The boat wandered like a lost soul over the waters.

But then he lost his patience and he struck the surface of the water with his sword, so that the thick greyness disappeared as suddenly as it had come.

Väinö was about to grip the helm firmly in his hands again when huge waves began to beat against their bow. Ilmarinen covered his eyes so that he should not witness their dreadful end.

The old man in the stern, however, was keeping a good look-out, and he saw Iku-Turso in the sea. He had the spirit by the ears before he could escape.

"What are you doing here, Iku-Turso?" Väinämöinen asked. "Why are you trying to capsize us?"

"I wanted to bring Sampo back to Pohjola," admitted the spirit after a while. "But if you spare me now, I swear no human being will ever see me again."

Wise Väinämöinen trusted his word, and he released Iku-Turso. Soon afterwards the waves died down, and the boat resumed its voyage.

That was the moment the mighty Ukko had been waiting for. He gave a roar and a howl, and at once a great storm stripped the trees of their leaves, blew roofs from houses, and swept the murky waters over the boat.

The hurricane came with such suddenness that it caught them completely unawares, and the first thing it took and swallowed in the depths was the pike-bone *kantele*.

Väinämöinen did not waste time mourning his loss. Instead, he cast spells to ward off the storm, while Ahti repaired the boat with the wood he had brought on board with him.

And while the men of Kalevala were fighting the storm, Louhi prepared for battle. She called together all her warriors, distributing bows, arrows, and swords. She raised a slim mast on her war ship, spread the sails on the yard-arms, and set out in pursuit of the fugitives.

Väinämöinen sensed the coming danger, and he said to Ahti: "Climb up to the top of the mast and take a look round."

"The way is clear up ahead," Ahti called out from his perch among the sails. "And behind us there is only a small cloud trailing . . . no, it is no cloud — it's an island with birch-trees and aspens on it."

"Look again!" cried Väinämöinen. "Isn't it rather a ship under sail with warriors on board?"

"Yes, it must be. Now I can see a hundred men at the oars — the ship is coming closer, she's making great speed . . ."

"Row harder, all of you!" cried the wise old man at the helm, and the pinewood boat leapt forward, with waves hissing under it. Yet still the Pohjolian ship drew closer and closer.

Väinö wondered how to thwart the enemy. He quickly reached for his tinder-box. Throwing the flint into the water behind, he whispered:

"May you turn into a hidden reef on which the Pohjolian ship will come to grief!"

No sooner had he uttered those words than a submerged rock grew up on the spot, and the enemy ship ran straight on to it.

The ship was smashed to pieces, but Louhi's desire for revenge drove her on. Picking up some scythes from the hold, she attached them to her fingers like dreadful talons. Half the wreck she tied to her waist.

The ship's sides served her as wings, while she used the helm for a tail.

She placed a hundred warriors on her wings, a thousand bowmen on her trunk, and, like some monstrous eagle, swooped down on Väinämöinen.

She alighted on the mast and reached out to grab Sampo. The Finnish boat heeled. The gay Ahti was closest to Louhi, and he drew his sword and hacked away at her talons.

"Oh, you perfidious wretch!" cried the terrible hag. "To deceive your own mother like this! Didn't you promise her that you wouldn't fight for sixty years, not even if you were offered silver or gold?"

The time came for Väinämöinen to take a hand. He picked up the helm and swung it at the old woman, severing her talons and her fingers, so that only her little finger was left. The Pohjolians all fell into the sea, and Louhi dropped from the mast.

Desperately trying to find something to cling to, she caught Sampo in her arms and dragged it down into the depths with her.

Väinämöinen saw the magic mill sink to the bottom of the sea, saw the waves break it into pieces, and he knew that the world's greatest treasure was lying on the ocean bed, never to be retrieved.

As he watched the sparkling waves he noticed little pieces of Sampo floating on the surface. The wind was taking them with the incoming tide to the nearby shores of Kalevala. As soon as he landed, Väinämöinen walked along the beach, painstakingly collecting the fragments, which would bring the Finns good crops and prosperity.

Louhi managed to get back to her native Pohjola, the land of the Lapps. All she had for her pains was one tiny piece of the mill, which had lodged under the nail of her little finger. Her country has suffered with much hunger and little prosperity ever since.

In vain Louhi threatened that she would destroy the crops of Kalevala with frost and hail; that she would snatch the sun and the moon from the sky and hide them in a dark cave; that she would send the plague and other diseases down on the Finns, as well as a ferocious bear to devour their herds. But the wise Väinämöinen knew that Ukko, Lord of the Clouds, would not allow her threats to be fulfilled.

Väinämöinen rejoiced at the rich harvests, fat cattle, and the beautiful houses which the Finns built for themselves. Only one thing made him sad: there was no song in the land; no strings were plucked to vibrate with melody.

Therefore, the wise old man asked Ilmarinen to make him a long rake. The blacksmith promised to do so, and he made a rake the like of which the world had never seen before. Its prongs were a hundred fathoms long and the handle five times as long again.

With this rake Väinämöinen then set out to sea, hoping to lift the pike-bone *kantele* from the ocean bed. But he sent his little boat skimming across the waters in vain. He raked the grasses and the rocks under the sea, but he did not succeed in finding his instrument.

He beached his boat and, with his head hung in sorrow, started for home. As he passed through a small wood he heard someone weeping bitterly. He listened a while, and then noticed a lonely birch that stood in the middle of a clearing, shedding tears.

"Why are you crying like this?" asked Väinö, going closer, and the birch tree replied:

"It may seem to you that I have no cause for tears, that the birdsong I hear all day ought to make me happy. But I stand here all alone, and whoever comes by manages to hurt me. In the spring the lads strip the bark from my body, in summer the girls sit in my shade and then they snap my branches to make brooms. And as for the men — they're the worst of all, cutting me up into logs."

The birch tree lamented, adding how sorely it suffered in winter, and how the autumn deprived it of its leaves.

"You'll never weep again," promised the wise old man, "or if you do, then it will be with joy and in song."

330

And he took the forlorn birch tree and from its white trunk he made
the body of his new *kantele*. Only the pins and strings were missing,
and he knew where to look for those.

Outside in his back yard stood an ever-young, ever-merry oak. It was
merry because each of its twigs was weighted with an acorn, and on
each acorn sat a cuckoo. From one of these twigs Väinämöinen made
the pins for his new instrument, and then he sought something that
might serve for the strings.

He wandered about the woods and the meadows, until he reached a
stream where he met a beautiful fair-haired maiden.

"Give me a strand of your golden hair," Väinö asked her. "I'll use it
to make strings for my new *kantele*."

The maiden readily agreed and gave the wise old minstrel a strand of
her golden hair.

Väinö stretched the hair on the pins and on the bridge, and, having tuned
his kantele, he ran his sensitive fingers over the strings.

As he played, the music became louder and louder, rivers left their banks,
trees bent down their boughs, animals came out of the forests, and birds
flocked to the old man from the whole countryside. Väinämöinen
travelled all round Kalevala. Men surrounded him in respectful admiration, women were so moved by his beautiful music that they left
whatever they were doing, and the children all joined in .